Apples from the Desert

THE HELEN ROSE SCHEUER JEWISH WOMEN'S SERIES

Apples from the Desert

SELECTED STORIES

BY SAVYON LIEBRECHT

Translated from the Hebrew
by Marganit Weinberger-Rotman,
Jeffrey M. Green, Barbara Harshav, Gilead Morahg,
and Riva Rubin under the direction of
The Institute for Translation of Hebrew Literature

FOREWORD BY GRACE PALEY
INTRODUCTION BY LILY RATTOK

THE HELEN ROSE SCHEUER JEWISH WOMEN'S SERIES

THE FEMINIST PRESS
AT THE CITY UNIVERSITY OF NEW YORK
NEW YORK

Published in the United States and Canada by
The Feminist Press at The City University of New York
Wingate Hall, City College
Convent Avenue at 138th Street
New York, NY 10031

Published simultaneously in Great Britain by Loki Books Ltd.
38 Chalcot Crescent, London NW1 8YD

First English-language edition, 1998

Library of Congress Cataloging-in-Publication Data

Liebrecht, Savyon, 1948-
        [Short stories. English. Selections.]
Apples from the desert : selected stories / by Savyon Liebrecht ; translated from the Hebrew by
Marganit Weinberger-Rotman ... [et al.] under the director of The Institute for the Translation
of Hebrew Literature ; foreword by Grace Paley ; introduction by Lily Rattok.
        p. cm. — (The Helen Rose Scheuer Jewish women's series)
        Includes bibliographical references.
        ISBN 1-55861-190-8 (hardcover : alk. paper)
    1. Liebrecht, Savyon, 1948-   —Translations into English. I. Weinberger-Rotman, Marganit.
II. Makhon le-tirgum sifrut 'Ivrit (Israel). III. Title. IV. Series.
        PJ5054.L444T3613   1998   892.4'36—dc21
                                                                                       CIP

Steven H. Scheuer, in memory of his mother and in celebration of her life and the 100th anniversary of her birth (1995), has been pleased to endow the Helen Rose Scheuer Jewish Women's
Series. *Apples from the Desert* is the fourth named book in the series.

Text design by Dayna Navaro
Printed on acid-free paper by R.R. Donnelley and Sons
Manufactured in the United States of America

Contents

Foreword

SEVERAL YEARS AGO I was one of about fifteen Jewish writers who met in Switzerland. Some were from Israel; others were from the diaspora—the United States, Britain, Canada, France, Germany, Brazil, Argentina. Our parents, grandparents, a few of us as babies, had probably spoken Russian, Yiddish, Polish, German.

We had those languages in our ears—those tones, inflections, accents—as we wrote in English, Portuguese, Spanish, Hebrew.

It was a wonderful meeting. But when I looked at the six Israeli participants—including Yehuda Amichai and Aharon Appelfield, whose work I loved and knew well—I couldn't help asking, "But where are my Israeli sisters?"

The men, suddenly looking like my Russian-Jewish uncles caught in a not-so-terrible but embarrassing mistake, looked at one another, startled, and said, "Yes, yes, of course, we should . . . Yes, What about Celia? Dahlia?"

I am writing this perhaps ten years later. I am in Vietnam at a meeting with Vietnamese writers, editors, and publishers discussing a new copyright law. I know three or four of the poets here and their fine work. Among the thirty of them, just two are women. And again I have to ask, "Where are our Vietnamese sisters?"

In both cases, the women literary workers existed and could be found. But is there no end to the aggressive need to ask that question,

"Where are the women writers?"

I am particularly happy to welcome *Apples from the Desert* by Savyon Liebrecht. These are wonderful stories. They are told by a woman who knows she is living in a country occupied by two nations. She knows she is a citizen, a speaker, in a country, Israel, where one nation, the Israeli, looks down on or looks coldly upon the other nation, the Palestinian, and the other language, Arabic. And then she tells everyday stories about what those cultural and political facts are doing to the characters and ordinary lives of both groups of people—the way in which both are deformed: one by pride, one by despair.

She understands, as well, the damage rendered by the chasm of misapprehension and mistrust between Ashkenazic and Sephardic Jews, between men and women, and between people of different generations—especially the older generation that lived through the Holocaust and the younger generation that would like to forget it.

She tells her stories with domestic irony—but it's all straightforward history. The stories are elegantly understated and movingly personal—but they are also fierce pleas for understanding and justice. I compliment Savyon Liebrecht on her achievement. And I thank The Feminist Press again for bringing us women's words in our own language and in translation from the rich other languages of the world.

Grace Paley
Hanoi, Vietnam
January 1998

Introduction:
The Healing Power of
Storytelling

SAVYON LIEBRECHT IS considered one of the most impressive voices in contemporary Hebrew literature, and is among the most prominent women writers of fiction in Israel. She gained immediate public recognition with the publication of her first collection of short stories, *Apples from the Desert,* in 1986. Her maturity as a writer and her mastery of the art of short story writing were amply demonstrated in that first volume, which garnered her the Alterman Prize. Liebrecht continued to develop the short story form in her next three books, *Horses on the Highway* (1988), *What Am I Speaking, Chinese? She Said to Him* (1992), and *On Love Stories and Other Endings* (1995).[1] (It is from her first three collections that this volume of her selected stories—the first book by Liebrecht available in English—is drawn.) Her books were favorably received by the critics, and they also became bestsellers—an unusual phenomenon for a collection of short stories.

Liebrecht's success, in literary as well as in commercial terms, stems from the fact that she knows how to spin an intriguing story. She excels in weaving gripping plots without sacrificing psychological insight and rich symbolic meaning. The dramatic element in her stories involves a clear conflict between characters—a conflict whose significance and implications are gradually revealed and whose solution is always surprising and interesting.

The social involvement that characterizes Liebrecht's stories undoubtedly also figures in their warm reception. Her work deals with topics on the public agenda in Israel and have contributed a measure of profundity to the current debates. Liebrecht's eloquent and fluent linguistic style has captured the unique qualities of various social and ethnic groups, and her stories reflect the diversity of the reality evolving in present-day Israel.

Liebrecht's stories focus on issues that are specific to Israel but at the same time, because of her great sensitivity to human suffering and distress, they also address universal themes. Nearly all of her stories demonstrate a special compassion for characters who are oppressed or disempowered in society—members of the Arab minority, Sephardic Jews (the weaker ethnic group among Israeli Jews), women, children, and aging Holocaust survivors. In fact, this ability to empathize with the victim draws in part upon the experience of the Holocaust, which is at the center of Liebrecht's writing—and her life.

Biographical Background

Savyon Liebrecht was born in Munich, Germany, in 1948, to parents who were both Holocaust survivors from Poland. She was their eldest daughter, born shortly after her parents' liberation from concentration camps. When she was a year old, her parents brought her to Israel, where she was raised and educated.

During her military service, required of all young Israeli men and women, Liebrecht requested to serve on a kibbutz. After her discharge she went to London to study journalism. Disappointed with the level of instruction at her London school, Liebrecht returned to Israel and obtained a B.A. in philosophy and English literature. She married at the age of twenty-six and six years later had a daughter, then a son. She has raised her family in a suburb of Tel Aviv.

Liebrecht admits that she guards her privacy jealously. This fact may be connected to the silence that reigned in the house of her parents, the Holocaust survivors. This silence was born of the parents' inability to talk about their past experiences, and of the children's fear that their questions might open up old wounds. In a 1992 interview with the poet Amalia Argaman-Barnea, Liebrecht spoke about the "silent home"; she cited as an example of the conspiracy of silence her own reluctance to question her father about the family he had before the war. The existence of that family was revealed to her only through an old photograph in a family album, in which her father is seen smiling happily in the company of a woman and a little girl.

The wall of silence did not crumble when the writer took a trip to Poland with her parents. Even though her father made an attempt to tell her about his past life, during a train ride to Treblinka concentration camp, he did so in Polish, a language that he had never spoken to her before and that she did not understand. One can feel the anguish in her realization that "he was finally telling me his story, but to this day I have not heard it."

In an article Liebrecht wrote about the impact of the Holocaust on her writing (125), she again emphasizes the fact that she knows practically nothing about her parents' past: how many brothers and sisters they had, what these siblings' names were, and what happened to them during the war. She knows that her father was incarcerated in several concentration camps, but she does not know which ones. The silence her parents maintained regarding their experiences during the Holocaust was total. Liebrecht contends that this historical lacuna resulted in children of survivors developing problems of identity.

Her family background had a significant impact on one of the major developments in Savyon Liebrecht's professional career: the delay in the publication of her first collection of short stories. She began writing fiction at eighteen, but her first novel was rejected by a publisher and she shelved it; later, she wrote another novel, but it was also rejected by the same publisher. When she got married, she stopped writing and channeled her creativity in other directions. She studied art and sculpture at an art institute, but soon sensed that this was not the right art form for her.

When she was thirty-five, she joined a creative writing workshop under the guidance of Amalia Kahana-Carmon,[2] who immediately noticed her talent and encouraged her. Kahana-Carmon submitted Liebrecht's story "Apples from the Desert" to a literary magazine, *Iton* 77. Following its publication, one publishing house offered to issue a collection of her short stories. Liebrecht wrote half the stories in her first book while it was in the process of publication.

This turning point in the acceptance of Liebrecht's work can be attributed to several factors. One is the maturation of her artistic craft in the years between the rejection of her earlier works and the enthusiastic reception of her later ones. Another is the receptiveness to the female voice that has developed in Israel only in the 1980s and 1990s, according to Rochelle Furstenberg (5). In addition, Israel's more open attitude and its acceptance of the Holocaust, a subject that Liebrecht sees as "the biggest riddle, not only regarding my own life, but regarding the entire human existence,"[3] opened before her an avenue of expression that had perhaps been blocked, both for internal and external reasons.

One must not forget, however, that a major reason for the delay in publication was Liebrecht's deliberate decision to repress her writing impulse to satisfy the need to have a family. In many families of Holocaust survivors, this is a supreme imperative, and perhaps Liebrecht needed a new family as a power-base of security and normality. Her assertion, in the interview with Argaman-Barnea, that "I am a normal woman, living a normal life" emphasizes how much she needed this kind of solid foundation in order to obtain the freedom to soar on the wings of her imagination.

Liebrecht chose to bear children before she could dedicate herself to her art because she believes that "for a woman writer, each new book is one less baby." She sees this as a major difference between male and female writers. Liebrecht also sees a difference between women's wider emotional range and men's narrower, more power-oriented range. But despite this observation, she rejects any differentiation between the writing of men and women, since, as she put it, "the hand that writes is genderless," and she denies the existence of a discrete women's literature.

Liebrecht's objection to such categorization is interesting precisely because her literature belongs, in my opinion, to the domain of women's literature. In most of her stories, the woman's point of view is dominant, and relationships within the intimate feminine circle occupy a central position. Relationships between mothers and daughters, sisters and friends, are rendered with great depth and sensitivity, whereas relationships with men—lovers, husbands, or fathers—while also treated perceptively, are most often relegated to second place. In her stories, Liebrecht also criticizes patriarchal society for having victimized women and exploited them by denying them any position of power. The female protagonists in her stories often reveal great strength, but they are also characterized by vulnerability and compassion, and Liebrecht's work as a whole successfully embodies the female moral code defined by Carol Gilligan as an ethics of help in distress, caring, and nurturing.

Liebrecht's stories reflect her deep yearning for reconciliation between people placed on opposing sides of conflicts. The starting point is often a rift, an intense confrontation, that resolves itself at the conclusion with the opponents reaching a moment of grace, of *rapprochement*. Even though not all of Liebrecht's stories end on a note of reconciliation, as Esther Fuchs has argued (47), they all manifest a strong, inherent need for harmony. The emotional intensity in Liebrecht's work stems, on the one hand, from animosity and hatred often expressed in terms of warfare, and on the other hand, from a longing for unity and for a sense of belonging that overcomes the divisive forces.[4] This yearning for reconciliation can be traced to several elements in the author's biography: her exposure to the trauma of the Holocaust, her awareness of the continuous conflict in the Middle East, and—for me, of paramount importance—the fact that she is a woman, and therefore acutely sensitive to situations of distress, weakness, and vulnerability.[5]

BREAKING SILENCES

Liebrecht's stories do not describe the horrors of the concentration camps; instead, they touch upon the memories of the survivors, which surface in their minds years after the liberation, tearing the veil of normality that they have striven so hard to maintain. The story "Excision," for example, depicts the compulsive behavior of a Holocaust survivor, who chops off her grandchild's beautiful hair just because she finds out that the child may have head lice, a fact that brings back a horrifying memory of the camps. The story's ambiguous title (meaning both "removal" and "cutting") indicates that the theme is not just the cutting of hair, but the cutting off, the destruction, of life in the Holocaust.

Liebrecht criticizes Israeli society, especially the relatives of survivors, for their reluctance to open their hearts to the sufferers, to listen and to empathize with the tormented souls. The conspiracy of silence that surrounds the atrocities they have endured only adds to the survivors' anguish. In the story "Hayuta's Engagement Party," the grand-daughter represents contemporary Israeli society, which is alienated from and impervious to the survivors' pain. Hayuta tries to keep her loving grandfather, Grandpa Mendel, from attending a family gathering for fear that he might spoil the party with his horror stories about the concentration camps. These memories tend to resurface in his mind particularly on festive occasions, since the family gathered around set tables reminds him of those lost relatives who cannot be present at the feast. Grandpa Mendel's daughter Bella, who understands his need to remind others of those who have perished, shudders at the thought that the old man will be excluded from the party by his own grand-daughter: "We are raising monsters . . . hearts of stone!" (84). The story ends tragically, with Grandpa Mendel dying in the middle of the party after he is prevented from expressing himself on the subject of the Holocaust. The last sentence in the story encapsulates how Israeli society tries to cover up the tremendous anguish with the "sweet frosting" of the new reality: "Then [Bella] took another tissue and very gently, as if she could still inflict pain, wiped the anguished face which knew no final relief, and the handsome moustache, and the closed eyes, and the lips that were tightly pursed under a layer of sweet frosting, firmly treasuring the words that would now never bring salvation, nor conciliation, not even a momentary relief" (91–92).

Israeli society, where many Holocaust survivors found a new home, had considerable difficulty in opening up and accepting the descriptions of what the Jews of Europe had endured under the Nazis.[6] This difficulty was primarily due to the unimaginable and unbearable nature of the atrocities inflicted by the Nazi exterminating machine on a defenseless, innocent population, a reality so terrible that it could hardly be conveyed in words. But apart from the depth of the atrocities themselves, there were specific components in the makeup of the young Israeli state, established in 1948 after a bloody war of independence, that contributed to the difficulty in accepting and empathizing with the survivors. The sharp contrast between the self-image of the Israeli as a fierce freedom fighter and the abject image of the Jew as a helpless victim, led to annihilation almost without resistance, gave rise to an ambivalent attitude toward the survivors.

A difficulty of another sort resulted from guilt feelings produced by the inability of those who had settled in Israel before the Holocaust to rescue their relatives left in the European communities that were later liquidated. These difficulties, compounded by a conscious decision by many survivors after liberation not to open their wounds and not to dwell on their experiences, also contributed to a repression of the Holocaust.

Further contributing to this national repression was the state's decree of one general day of mourning to commemorate the six million Jews who had perished in the Holocaust, officially named "Day of Holocaust and Heroism." This ritualization of the remembrance of the Holocaust was not conducive to personal expressions of sorrow and mourning, but rather helped to block them.[7] While the memory of the Holocaust became a crucial element in forging a new Jewish identity, the emphasis was placed on heroism, to which only a few could lay claim, rather than on passive suffering, which reflected the personal experience of the majority of survivors. The slogan "From Holocaust to Recovery" was coined for the dual purpose of giving meaning to the victims' suffering and providing a justification for the establishment of a new national home for them. This slogan, as well as the date set for Holocaust and Heroism Day—a week before Memorial Day and Independence Day—created, according to Handelman and Katz (83), the desired connection between the victims of the Holocaust and the victims of the struggle for the establishment of the state, thus producing an inverted process: a terrible national catastrophe leading to national redemption.

As long as the existence of the national home was threatened by neighboring countries, Israeli society was not free to deal with the issue of the Holocaust. Only in the late seventies, with the continued existence of the State of Israel relatively more secure, did the repression begin to abate, and Israeli society become ready to put the Holocaust at the center of its public agenda. Contributing to this trend of raising the legacy of the Holocaust to the center of Israeli consciousness were native Israeli writers, some of whom, like Savyon Liebrecht, were second-generation Holocaust survivors, whose personal experiences were at last receiving validation and legitimacy.[8]

THE SECOND GENERATION OF THE HOLOCAUST

A strong urge to belong, first to a family, then to the nascent state, is discernible throughout Liebrecht's work, and it probably played a part in her own life as well. This need has to do with the emotional state of Holocaust survivors and their children. The traumatic separation from family and friends and the inability of the victims to protect the lives of their loved ones left deep scars on their psyches. Following the liberation from the camps, when they found out that their relatives had perished, their congregations had been annihilated, and the world they had known no longer existed, survivors were overcome by unbearable feelings of guilt, extreme loneliness, and total emptiness.

Consequently, the need to start a new family became the most compelling drive in their lives. However, the expectations the survivors had of the new family were partially thwarted, since the conditions of its creation were greatly inadequate; for the most part, couples got married in a hurry, while still in a state of shock and suffering from confusion and disintegration. Due to these circumstances, in addition to the scars left from having lived in the shadow of death, many of these new unions failed to provide the yearned-for solace and intimacy, and the wish for warmth and loving kindness went unanswered. The story "A Married Woman" presents the relationship between a husband and wife, who met by chance while looking for their lost relatives, as based on pity and desperation more than on love: "Tremendous compassion and loving kindness impelled her to touch his back gently, to quell in him the overpowering sense of despair. Then he suddenly turned back and his laughing mouth asked, 'Shall we get married?'" (75). The couple's daughter suffers from this compromised relationship, since neither of her parents can nourish her emotionally. "She was only eighteen, but her face was the face of a weary, miserable person" (74).

Children of survivors, born into these conditions, were particularly vulnerable. In her essay on the impact of the Holocaust on her work (128), Savyon Liebrecht claims that, in some respects, children of survivors had an even harder time than their parents. She herself was born to devastated parents who had lost everything, including their language and their culture. The inability to rebel against such parents, so as not to hurt those who had already known so much suffering, created an additional burden with which the children of survivors had to contend. Dina Wardi describes the role of children in these families: they were perceived as replacements and compensation for the relatives who had perished, and they became the central preoccupation of the parents' lives—a state of affairs that made it difficult for the children to develop discrete, individual personalities.[9]

Despite the parents' attempts to provide their children with everything and to shield them from pain, all children of the second generation knew pain and suffering. Most of the victims' families lived in an atmosphere of dejection, anxiety, and worry, viewing their immediate environment with fear and suspicion (easily understood, in view of their past). Concern for the continued existence of the family was of the highest priority for survivors, many of whom were almost obsessively preoccupied with physical survival.[10] Self-preservation and personal security were the only meaningful causes in those families. Personal happiness and creative expressions of individuality were, by and large, discounted and ignored.

This kind of troubled psychological existence pervades most of Savyon Liebrecht's stories, not only those that directly or indirectly deal with the Holocaust.[11] Her focus on the family cannot be explained simply by the central position the family occupies in Jewish tradition and Israeli society, as Atmon and Izraeli demonstrated (2); its centrality in her work must be accounted for by the experience of the second generation of the Holocaust. Liebrecht has written very little about childhood, youth, and love, and her characters are hardly ever presented as solitary figures or as couples. The family, on the other hand, is the typical arena where events take place in her stories, and it is always minutely detailed and highly charged. In "The Homesick Scientist," for instance, the story of the relationship between the elderly uncle who has lost his son and the nephew who fills the void in the uncle's life overshadows the intricate love story and relegates it to a secondary position. The love of the uncle and his nephew for the same girl, whom neither of them gets in the end, becomes ancillary to the unique father-son relationship that develops between the older man and the boy.

When characters in Liebrecht's stories find themselves in a conflict, torn between family and another concern, they always prefer the family connection. This is particularly evident in the story "A Married

Woman," which explores the concealed reasons behind the powerful familial connection; not even the legal procedure of divorce can destroy the family ties.[12] The woman in the story continues to care for the man she divorced under pressure from their daughter, even though he has cheated on her with other women countless times and has spent her money on drinking and gambling. The fatal connection between them, which nothing can undo or annul, is the result of their common loss of everything they had before the Holocaust. The wife is aware of this terrible truth; there is an affinity between them that cannot be repudiated, and so the relationship is maintained even though it inflicts pain on her, because her husband is all she has left that connects her to her previous life.[13]

In the story "Mother's Photo Album," the father does leave his wife and son, but it is in order to be reunited with his first wife who, unbeknownst to him, had survived the war. This is an exception that proves the rule: only previous familial ties—not love or passion, as in an affair—can supplant later familial ties. The mental illness that consequently afflicts the abandoned woman in "Mother's Photo Album" testifies to the fact that the family served the survivors as an essential existential anchor, even when it did not satisfy many of their emotional needs.

Liebrecht's stories underline the inability of a mother to bestow love on her children because she herself has been emotionally deprived by her equally damaged husband. Yearnings for a mother's love, which the characters never received as children, are quite common in Liebrecht stories. In "What Am I Speaking, Chinese? She Said to Him," the protagonist bears her mother a grudge for "the gratuitous bitterness she has injected into her life, for the poison she had accumulated in her heart over all those years, letting it fester and bubble like molten lava, locking her heart even against rare moments of sweetness" (163). Although the daughter is aware of the atrocities her mother lived through during the war, she does not understand how that trauma affected her mother's sexuality.[14]

The protagonist, who never dared rebel against her mother when the latter was alive for fear that she would add to her pain and suffering, now, after the mother's death, tries to divest herself of the depressing heritage that was bequeathed to her. She has sex with a total stranger—

the real estate agent who, at her request, takes her to her parents' old apartment, which is now for sale—in order to take revenge on her mother. In an act symbolizing her separate individuality, she makes love to the man in the exact spot where she used to hear her mother rebuff her father's advances. This hasty, meaningless sexual encounter marks the differentiation between the daughter, who enjoys her sensuality, and the mother, who denied her physical urges. The daughter wants to prove to herself that she is capable of enjoying sex even without emotional ties, and so she seduces a stranger and makes love to him in the empty apartment, on an expensive fur coat given to her by her husband on their anniversary.[15]

Only after this act of rebellion can the woman begin to think about her mother with some understanding and ponder the reasons why her mother could not enjoy her own body and what lingering effects this hostility toward physical pleasure had on her. The daughter's plea to her mother is a combination of sorrow and helpless rage: "I wonder why you never accepted the consolation of the body, why you never taught me this great conciliatory gift, this immeasurable pleasure, and I had to learn all this by myself, as if I were a pioneer" (167). Only in this extreme situation is the daughter capable of separating from her mother and father to become an individual person—although it is doubtful that this symbolic rebellion is sufficient to relieve her of the heavy burden left by her family.[16]

Through Loving Eyes

Psychological studies examining the impact of the Holocaust on survivors' children have demonstrated that many of them are marked by unusual sensitivity to other people's suffering. The explanation, according to Wardi (106), is the high level of empathy these children have for their parents' anguish. Their sense of justice regarding civil rights and the rights of minorities, disadvantaged, and deviant individuals in society is remarkably strong. Liebrecht's identification with the victim is demonstrated in various social situations throughout her work. Her protagonists often identify with the "Other": Arabs, Sephardic Jews, the elderly, women, children.

Particularly noteworthy is her protagonists' ability to identify with members of the Arab minority in Israel, who suffer discrimination as a corollary of the continuous conflict between Jews and Arabs in the Middle East. The Other in this instance is a former enemy, a compatriot of the present adversary.[17]

Liebrecht tries to play the role of a healer, presenting possibilities for mending the rifts that threaten the existence of Israeli society. Her work describes the healing of breaches between Jews and Arabs, the building of amicable relationships, and the disappearance, at least on a small scale, of the gaps that separate Ashkenazic Jews, who constitute the elite of Israeli society, and Sephardic Jews, the disadvantaged ethnic group. Her stories offer moments of grace that span the gulfs between secular and observant Jews, between old and young. In such moments of grace, the Other is revealed as a complete human being, and a new social integration is created.

The literary paradigm by which Liebrecht constructs this vision of integration is the observation of the Other through the eyes of a representative of the ruling group. This pattern relies on strongly accentuating the motif of the observing eye, and on using the observer's point of view as a means of effecting a change of attitude toward the object of scrutiny. The pattern comprises two stages that stand in contrast to each other: in the first stage the protagonist sees the Other in the conventional way, that is, as a different, offensive, threatening figure. In the second stage, however, the protagonist comes to realize and appreciate the Other's unique qualities and thus regards him or her with more compassion. Readers who identify with the protagonist may thus change their own attitudes toward the Other, by seeing the Other through her loving eyes.

This literary pattern recalls Kaja Silverman's analysis in her book *The Threshold of The Visible World,* in which she claims that the art form of the cinema can play an important political role in changing spectators' attitudes toward people whom they have learned to fear or despise. Her argument is that this change may take place when the undesirable people are presented through the loving eyes of the main character in the movie. Silverman's argument pertains mainly to changes in attitude toward people whose skin color or sexual orientation are different from the spectators'. She maintains that the success of this process depends on repeated presentations in different movies.

A similar pattern emerges in Savyon Liebrecht's stories, since they emphasize visual elements and are based on intensive mutual observation of characters. Liebrecht's technique favors a telling of the plot through nonverbal means, a fact that also explains her predilection for screenwriting. Liebrecht herself commented on her nonverbal sensitivity in her interview with Amalia Argaman-Barnea, connecting it to the fact that she is a daughter of Holocaust survivors: "Our home was a silent home. In a home of this type, a child learns very early on to observe and absorb clues from nonverbal sources."

The events in Liebrecht's story "A Room on the Roof" are conveyed largely through silences and exchanges of looks, since the characters do not really have a common language. The heroine is a young Jewish woman who is asserting her independence by having a room built on the roof of her house, using three Arab construction workers. She does not speak Arabic, and the workers' Hebrew is broken and limited in vocabulary. The room is built against the wishes of her husband and during his absence, which results in uncommon closeness between the woman and the strange workers who find themselves inside her house.

This unexpected closeness enables the woman to get to know the most threatening Other figure in Israeli Jewish reality, under unusual circumstances. Unlike most Israeli women, who have no contact with Arabs from the occupied territories, the protagonist in this story maintains personal contact, on a daily basis, with the Arab workers in her employ. It is a very complex relationship, conducted against the background of the protracted conflict between the two peoples. Hence the woman's fear that the Arabs may harm her, and her momentary anxiety about a possible connection between them and some acts of terrorism carried out against the civilian population in her area: "Could these hands, serving coffee, be the ones that planted the booby-trapped doll at the gate of the religious school at the end of the street? Her heart, which had been on guard all the time, began to see something, but it still didn't know; this was just the beginning, appearing like a figure leaping out of the fog" (49).

Under these conditions, the woman's decision to hire the Arabs to work inside her house without any male supervision evinces considerable courage. This decision can also be interpreted as a political-feminist protest against the state of affairs between the two nations, for which men are by and large responsible. Thus, the feminist project of building "a room of one's own" is contingent on cooperation between a woman and Arabs—members of two groups of Others in Israeli society.

An element that contributes to this protest is the love that evolves between this Jewish woman and one of the Arabs, Hassan. It is a hesitant, fragile, and hopeless love, but even in its incipient, germinal existence, it points to another kind of relationship that could exist between the two peoples. The turning point in the relationship between the two main characters in the story is marked by this emergent love and by a change in the balance of power between them. While in the beginning of the story the relationship is that of conqueror and conquered, the turning point enables the characters, now finding themselves on the same level, to experience a measure of reciprocity and a true egalitarian rapport. This turning point comes with the baby's fall from his cradle and the woman's subsequent panic; Hassan, who has studied medicine for a couple of years, succeeds in calming down both mother and child, and thereby changes the nature of the relationship.

For the first time, Hassan speaks to the woman "without the forced humility she was familiar with" (54); for the first time he speaks to her in English, not in broken Hebrew. Even his Arabic—the language he uses when he pacifies the baby—sounds different to the woman, lyrical and fascinating. "She heard Hassan talking softly to the baby in Arabic, like a loving father talking to his child in a caressing voice, the words running together in a pleasant flow, containing a supreme beauty, like the words of a poem in an ancient language, which you don't understand, but which well up inside you" (53–54).

At this point, it becomes apparent that Hassan is an educated, sensitive, and charming man, and he awakens in the woman warm feelings. When she compares Hassan's gentle treatment of the baby to the cold, distant attitude of the baby's father, she clearly prefers the stranger to her husband. Liebrecht does not invest Hassan with stereotypical qualities; he does not represent some charicature of Arab virility, but rather full, rounded humanity. The Jewish male, on the other hand, is presented as someone who has paid a heavy price for occupation and domination; he has lost the ability to maintain a viable, flowing relationship with his wife and baby.

Criticism of Israeli male aggressiveness, which supplanted the sensibility and tenderness that marked Jewish men in the past, features also in "The Road to Cedar City," another story depicting relations between Jews and Arabs. Due to unforeseen circumstances, two families—one Jewish, one Palestinian—find themselves sharing a ride in a van while vacationing in the United States. The Jewish family consists of an older couple and their son, who is about to be drafted into the army. The Arab family consists of a young couple with their baby boy. At the end of the story, the Jewish woman, Hassida, who identifies with the Arab couple and is fascinated by their baby, decides to separate from her alienating husband and son and continue the trip in the company of her new friends.

The friendship between the two women, the Jewish and the Arab, forms almost without words; it is an affinity born out of their shared concern for the baby's needs and well-being. The two women collaborate in caring for the baby, while the men squabble and bicker about political and military issues. During the ride, the Arab-Israeli conflict is the main topic of conversation, but the women take no part in it. They cannot tolerate the animosity between the two families and want to put a stop to it. Both women see themselves as entrusted with the task of preserving life, and they derive pleasure from taking care of the helpless baby.

Hassida's decision to leave her husband and son results from their cruel and derisive treatment of her. The two men make fun of her sentimentality, mock her poor sense of direction, and scoff at her depressions, induced by menopause and by being cut off from her familiar surroundings. The two humiliate her in front of strangers, making her feel like a burden they would gladly be rid of at the first opportunity. In her profound distress, isolated and shunned, she suspects that "they are conspiring to drive her out of her mind, to have her locked up in prison in this strange country so they can be rid of her and go home without her" (125).

The unspoken pact between the husband and the son has changed the relationships in the family. Their newly forged male camaraderie, which replaces the tension that existed between the two when the son was young, turns the mother into an outsider and a victim. The men join forces against her, tormenting her in every possible way. Their callousness leaves her with an overwhelming sense of helplessness, which in turn gives rise to a profound empathy with the Arab minority that feels equally helpless and weak in relation to the Israeli occupier.

It is against this background that the alliance is formed between Hassida and the Arab family, which she now prefers to her own. Though it begins as a pact between the two women, it later expands to include the Palestinian man, because of his warmth and compassion toward his baby. Hassida is touched by the warm aura that envelops the Arab couple when they look at their baby. As she watches them, she feels "a radiance permeating her, as if she had witnessed a rare vision. 'Of all the sights I have seen in America—cities, waterfalls, wide highways—this is the most beautiful'" (147). Through her loving eyes, the Others are revealed in all their splendor, utterly human and inviting.

THE POWER OF SISTERHOOD

The maternal element is a principal component in the female comradeship that Liebrecht captures so marvelously in her stories. This sisterhood has the power to overcome hostility between Jews and Arabs. It is also capable of bridging the gap that exists in Israeli society between the ruling elite, the Ashkenazic Jews, and the weaker ethnic group, the Sephardic Jews. Nurturing babies and caring for the well-being of children bring together women of different generations, disparate world views, and diametrically opposed religious beliefs. In Liebrecht's work, women have a special and very important task: they are the guardians of life.

The story "Written in Stone" describes how the power of this kind of sisterhood overcomes differences in age, education, and mentality, and brings together women belonging to different worlds to cooperate for the sake of preserving and perpetuating life. The story centers around the relationship between an older Sephardi woman and her Ashkenazi daughter-in-law, Erella. The death of the son/husband, Shlomi, during reserve duty causes excruciating pain to both women. Erella, whose beloved husband was killed less than three months after their marriage, has difficulty coming to grips with her loss. She refuses to relinquish his place in her life and clings to Shlomi's mother, hoping that she will acknowledge and accept her. But the bereaved mother demonstrably ignores her daughter-in-law, never granting her a word or a look.

The mother's thundering silence is explained by the loud accusations hurled at the young widow by the older female members of the family. According to them, Erella is to blame for Shlomi's death. This unreasonable accusation stems from an identification of Erella with the ruling establishment. It was the establishment that tore the boy away from his village and from his family, sending him to study in town in a program for gifted students. It was the promise of higher education and social advancement, the women believe, that cost the young man his life. While studying at the university, Shlomi met the Ashkenazi girl, and by marrying her, only deepened his estrangement from his family and ethnic group. Sharing his life with Erella, Shlomi no longer observed the religious commandments, and that was the reason why he was killed.[19]

The hostility the family shows toward Erella does not lessen over the years. There is nothing the young woman can do to change their attitude. They are not even placated by her loyalty to Shlomi's memory, symbolized by the fact that she never removes the wedding ring he gave her. Even the fact that she faithfully shows up at his mother's house every year on the anniversary of his death does not soften the hearts of the women of the family. When she remarries and becomes pregnant, the mother asks her to stop coming to her house, but the young woman does not accede to her demand and continues to come, hoping that her suffering will alleviate her guilt and sorrow.[20]

The turning point in the story comes only years later, when Erella herself has joined the circle of bereaved mothers after the death of her own daughter from her second marriage, who was named Shlomit after the dead Shlomi. The old woman breaks her silence and talks to her daughter-in-law only now, when Erella is married for the third time and pregnant again. This time the old woman is determined to remove the young woman from the circle of death, so that the fetus in her womb may have a chance to live. In order to persuade her, she shows her a love letter that Shlomi wrote to Erella, returned to her by the army authorities with his belongings after he was killed. The reason she gives for never forwarding the letter explains the motive behind her cold attitude toward her daughter-in-law. "A mother, her son dies—she dies. A wife, her husband dies—she lives" (115).

Erella is shocked by this explanation, which sheds new light on the troubled relations between them. She is astounded by a new realization: "All these years you wanted to protect me" (117). The old woman's attempts to keep her away from the family, from the house of mourning, suddenly assume a new significance. To her amazement, she learns that her mother-in-law, too, was a young widow, and that her first husband's name was also Shlomo. Now Erella comprehends the old woman's guilt for having named her son Shlomi, after her first husband—a name that, according to her belief, brought him death.

Erella now understands the old woman's admonition not to name her new baby after Shlomi, because this is a "name written in stone," on a grave (117). Erella realizes the profound logic of putting a boundary line between the living and the dead. The wisdom of generations and a bitter personal experience have prompted the old woman to try and keep her away from the forbidden territory. One cannot build a new life in the shadow of a life that was cut off; one has to find the spiritual strength to tear oneself away and begin anew.

The story concludes with a description of the profound change that has taken place within Erella: "Today she had been set free! This woman had the power to release her from the vow that neither of them had ever understood. And she had done it. The old woman had let her go" (117). Her pregnancy, so burdensome to her before, now fills her whole being with unfamiliar happiness. She feels wondrously weightless, "as if her body were made of light" (118). Liebrecht breaks away from the stereotypical pattern of a mother-in-law envious of her young daughter-in-law, and instead describes the pact between the two as a bond between mothers. In "Written in Stone," this bond overcomes the gap between the Sephardic culture and the Ashkenazic, and focuses on an Israeli common denominator—fostering the next generation.[21]

FEMINIST PROTEST

A more extreme protest against the disfranchisement of women by the patriarchal religious establishment is found in the most feminist of Liebrecht's stories, "Compassion." The ironic title refers to the misfortunes of the female protagonist, Clarissa, a Holocaust survivor who was hidden in a convent during the war years and afterward came to Israel. The transition from an orthodox Jewish home to a Christian convent and then to a secular kibbutz in Israel totally undermined her sense of belonging, so when she later fell in love with an Arab, she went to live with him in his village. After she had borne him children, the husband demanded that she marry an old uncle of his, so that he could marry a younger wife. Her refusal to comply did not stop him from marrying the woman anyway, since as a Moslem he was allowed to have four wives. Still, the husband punished her by locking her up in a shack and keeping her totally isolated.[22]

Clarissa's predicament does not break her spirit, but when she finds out that her husband and her son are about to murder her daughter because she refused to marry an old man, preferring her young beloved, Clarissa is gripped by a powerless rage. From her place of confinement, she sees her husband and son setting out on their murderous expedition, and she is prepared to kill them in order to prevent them from carrying out their scheme. "Had she been free and light-footed, had she had a knife in her hand, she would have sped after them on the mountain slope to stick the knife in their backs, withdrawing it and plunging it in again and again until they sank dead at her feet" (193).

The isolated, abused, and humiliated woman knows that nobody will come to her aid. In the village she is considered a "witch" and is ostracized for her rebelliousness. The women in the Arab village are resigned to the absolute sway their men have on their lives, as dictated by Islamic law; they will not come to the rescue of this woman or her rebellious daughter. The villagers mock her, saying, "She used to be a Jew, she used to be a Christian, and she used to be a Moslem—not one God wanted her" (196).

Clarissa resolves to kill her cruel son's two-month-old daughter, entrusted to her care because the baby's mother is ill. The grandmother's decision to drown her little grandchild in a well is a horrendous deed that combines both revenge on her son and compassion for his daughter. Death is preferable to a woman's existence in this kind of reality, Clarissa thinks. She sees herself as performing an act of charity—a mercy killing. She cleans the baby, feeds her, and hugs her, making her last moments as pleasant as possible, then gently puts her in the water.

The murder, which to some extent is also a symbolic suicide, is an act of desperation, meant to spare the little girl the suffering that is every woman's lot in the Arab village: "the homelessness, the helplessness, her father and her brothers and her uncles, her husband and her husband's brothers and her sisters' husbands, who would close in around her, the household chores from one night to the next, the loneliness, the heart fluttering, encased in the body, the man in her bed, rolling her over as he wished, coming into her as into a wound, and the fear for her daughters and their spilled blood" (200).

This description attests to Liebrecht's unique ability to explore a foreign reality and to grasp, with great sensitivity, what takes place there. She gives expression to the suffering of women in the Arab village, but without purporting to fully understand it. By making the protagonist a Jew who married a Moslem of her own free will, Liebrecht deliberately eschews "speaking for the 'Other.'"[23] Against this alien background, she is able to depict a woman in distress so extreme that it produces a horrendous reaction, and to make an emphatic protest against the kind of conditions in which infanticide might be understood as an act of loving kindness.

FEMINIST REVISION

In her first published story, "Apples from the Desert," Savyon Liebrecht has pointed to a possible way out of the impasse that faces every woman in patriarchal society. Rivka, the young heroine of the story, recognizes the need to free herself from economic dependence on men in order to achieve equality with them. She joins a kibbutz, where she works for a living and is independent in every respect.[24] Her decision to live with the man she loves without marriage is meant to ensure her absolute emotional freedom as well. For Rivka, her move is a revolutionary one, since the secular, basically Ashkenazic kibbutz is so different from the traditional, Sephardic community in which she grew up. Her decision is an expression of her rebellion against her father, who has ignored her all her life, thought she was an inferior specimen of womanhood, and tried to find a match for her without even consulting her.

In fact, Rivka's departure from home is a concealed rebellion, since she never confronts her father. The confrontation takes place via her mother, Victoria, who comes to the kibbutz in order to bring her rebellious daughter home. But Victoria betrays the mother's traditional role, dictated by the patriarchal system, of making daughters conform and accept male domination. Victoria not only fails to quell her daughter's rebellion; she actually colludes with Rivka in keeping the father in the dark about what is going on. This surprising development has several causes. The first is Victoria's rediscovery of her daughter through the eyes of the young man with whom Rivka lives. Victoria is moved by the way her daughter has blossomed and is amazed at the changes in her. Another reason is her identification with the young couple's love, viewed against her own missed opportunity in her youth, an episode she recalls upon witnessing her daughter's loving relationship.

Victoria decides to help her daughter realize her dream of a love-filled life, and not let Rivka languish, as she herself has, in a cold, loveless marriage. The bond between the women allows Rivka to help her mother gain a measure of freedom and independence, and at the same time allows Victoria to protect her daughter and offer her emotional support. Victoria's decision to become her daughter's ally is motivated by a symbolic dream she has in which the image of the lost beloved of her youth is merged with the image of the young man who wishes to marry Rivka. In the dream, this composite figure appears in the Garden of Eden, hinting at the wondrous nature of love. The apple held in the figure's hand turns out to be "precious stones," indicating the riches that love harbors (71).

But "Apples from the Desert" is a subversive story not only by virtue of its plot. It also employs "emancipatory strategies," as defined by Patricia Yaeger. The suggestive title of the story highlights the motif of the apple, linking it through the dream to the Genesis story of the Garden of Eden. But Liebrecht's Garden of Eden is an inversion of the biblical one; sexuality is not a sin here, and the woman is not viewed as responsible for the expulsion from paradise for having tempting the man to eat the apple. This is a sensual paradise, where the sin punishable by expulsion is the refusal to heed the call of love. Here it is the man who offers an apple to the woman, and she who must recognize its power.

The power that grows apples in the desert is the power of devoted love. The story creates an analogy between growing apples in the desert and making it bloom and the blossoming of Rivka, whose life was a wasteland as long as she lived in Jerusalem among family members who did not appreciate her virtues. Only when she found love did she become handsome—"milk and honey," as her mother says. This expression, used in the Bible to describe the land of Israel as "the land of milk and honey," creates an analogy between the love of the land and the love of a man for a woman. Liebrecht depicts an ideal reality, where love and fertility coexist in the image of a kibbutz named "Neve Midbar" (oasis). The heroine's name, Rivka, also has symbolic overtones, since it recalls the independent spirit of the Biblical Rebecca, as discussed by Nehama Ashkenazi (12); the mother's name, Victoria, underlines the triumph of sisterhood over patriarchy.

THE HEALING POWER OF STORYTELLING

This first publication in English of Savyon Liebrecht's selected stories is indeed an important event. For readers outside of her native land, Liebrecht's stories provide essential insights into contemporary Israeli society. But as really fine literature does, they also reach toward deeper truths that know no national boundaries. Liebrecht's protagonists, in their own ways, commit quiet acts of courage or achieve small epiphanies of understanding, which change and often enlarge them as human beings—and through her fiction, she offers her readers the opportunity to do the same.

Liebrecht's skill as a writer, combined with her perceptiveness, her compassion, and her deep humanity, create a body of work that is testament to the healing power of storytelling. It is a power that can help to close old wounds, to inspire new levels of empathy and understanding, to build bridges across the chasms that divide people—to make apples grow even in the desert.

Lily Rattok
Tel Aviv
March 1998

NOTES

1. In her youth, Liebrecht wrote two novels that were rejected by the publisher she approached, but her mature output in fiction consists entirely of short stories. Liebrecht has also written prize-winning film scripts, and one of her short stories has been made into a play.

2. Amalia Kahana-Carmon is one of the central figures in modern Hebrew lit-

erature, and, in my opinion, one of the two founding mothers of Israeli women's literature (see Rattok, xx–xxv). A strong friendship formed between the well-known author and the fledgling writer, although it should be noted that Kahana-Carmon's artistic influence on Liebrecht has gradually diminished over the years.

3. Quotations in this and the subsequent two paragraphs come from Liebrecht's 1992 interview with Amalia Argaman-Barnea.

4. In two stories, "Written in Stone" and "Dreams Lie," the dynamics are of hostility giving way to reconciliation. "Dreams Lie" (from the collection *Apples from the Desert*), contains descriptions of an astonishing physical struggle between an old woman and her granddaughter. "Like two blind women, their fingers clutched at each other's throats, grabbing hold of it with hatred, with a true intention to hurt, to beat unconscious, to cleanse the body from the malice that seeps through the hands and thrashes frantically." In "Written in Stone," the violence is mental: Erella prepares to meet her dead husband's relatives, "whose eyes flashed daggers at her"; she imagines that they wait for her "with eyes like hidden traps" (99).

5. In the interview with Amalia Argaman-Barnea, Liebrecht said that women cope much better than men in situations that are beyond their control, and that a sense of helplessness may lead directly to insanity. Consequently, one expects women to feel compassion—the most important element in the feminist ethos, according to Lugones and Spelman (1987: 235).

6. This difficulty is presented in the stories "Excision" and "Hayuta's Engagement Party" through the figures of the daughters-in-law. Savyon Liebrecht, in her essay on the Holocaust's influence on her writing (128), justified her use of these figures as the vehicles for venting aggression toward the survivors; according to her, the children of the victims would never dare utter the words said by the daughters-in-law in the stories. Only those family members who did not grow in the shadow of the Holocaust could do so.

7. An example of the problematic function of Holocaust and Heroism Day in Israeli reality can be found in "Hayuta's Engagement Party," in the words of the survivor's daughter-in-law when she tries to shut him up. "Don't we have Memorial Day and Holocaust Day and commemorative assemblies and what have you? They never let you forget for a minute. So why do I need to be reminded of it at every meal?" (88)

8. In the article "The Holocaust in Hebrew literature: Trends in Israeli Fiction in the Eighties," Avner Holtzman writes that he considers Savyon Liebrecht one of the most important writers in this respect (24).

9. Wardi calls children of Holocaust survivors "memorial candles," underlying their role in preserving the memory of relatives who perished in the war. It is this role that makes the natural separation during adolescence so painful for the parents, resulting in difficulty in individuation for the children. Savyon Liebrecht overcame this difficulty by requesting to work on a kibbutz during her miliary service and, particularly, by going to London to study immediately after her discharge. Her father was angry at her and would not talk to her for a year after she left, even though she was almost twenty at the time.

10. The main characters in "Dreams Lie" and "General Montgomery's Victory" (published in the collection *On Love Stories and Other Endings*) are both grandmothers who channel all their efforts and energy to preparing food and nourishing their grandchildren in order to ensure their health and well-being.

11. The most direct descriptions of the Holocaust are found in Liebrecht's third collection of short Stories, *What Am I Speaking, Chinese? She Said to Him* (1992), particularly in the stories "Morning in the Park with the Nannies" and "The Strawberry Girl." The majority of her stories, however, present echoes that the trauma of the Holocaust left in the survivors' souls, either through memories or as an ideological position. For example, in the story "Pigeons," which appeared in *Apples from the Desert,* the protagonist loses her faith in God as a result of the atrocities she has lived through, and becomes active in a movement fighting religious coercion, claiming that "God went up in smoke in the chimneys of Auschwitz."

12. In "A Married Woman," there is a sharp juxtaposition between the story's title and the opening sentence, which presents the main character as a divorced woman. "Only when the divorce bill lay in her hand did Hannah Rabinsky remove her wedding picture from the wall next to her bed" (73). That photograph is the symbolic expression of a survivor's yearning to have a family and to live a normal life, and it is more powerful than the legal document, the letter of divorce. It is clear from the events in the story that the title conveys a profound truth; Hannah remains a married woman even though she has divorced her husband. One can see "A Married Woman" as a negative image of S. Y. Agnon's story "Metamorphosis." Both stories open with a description of a divorce proceeding, and both allude to a reversal at the end. However, in Liebrecht's story, "the marriage wasn't really a marriage and the divorce won't really be a divorce" (78).

13. A somewhat similar pattern of relationships is portrayed in the story "A Love Story Needs an Ending" (from the collection *Love Stories and Other Endings*),

in which the protagonist, a Holocaust survivor, cheats on his devoted wife. The wife is resigned to her lot, but agonizes over what she regards as the betrayal of her daughter. After the father's death, the daughter decides to take revenge on one of the women he has loved, whose love affair with her father she witnessed as a child. That affair was a source of anxiety for her, since she feared that her father might be enticed by the bewitching power of love to step outside the family circle, and so she tried to prevent him from leaving by using childish ruses. In this story, the Oedipal elements in the father-daughter relation are prominent, discernible when the mother tells her daughter, "Sometimes I thought that it was not normal, the way you loved him. Perhaps this should not be between father and child, such love." (Similar elements can be found in subtler form stories such as "What Am I Speaking, Chinese? She Said to Him.") Dina Wardi points out that such relationships are not uncommon in families of survivors; the father often turns to the daughter for the fulfillment of emotional needs because of the mother's precarious mental state, steeped in chronic mourning and depression.

14. Wardi cites research showing that women who suffered during the Holocaust had difficulties functioning emotionally and sexually with their husbands.

15. Unlike Leon Yudkin, who interprets the incident as a failed attempt on the daughter's part to reconcile her parents to each other (178), I see it as the daughter taking a position with her sensuous father against the mother who denied her sexuality. Moreover, it is a failed attempt to wipe out the stains of the past, symbolically represented by the stains on the bedroom ceiling, which the mother implores the father to blot out. The stains of the past, indelibly lodged in the depth of the mother's psyche, have left scars on the daughter as well. This is not a story about "lack of communication," as Yudkin has claimed, but a work describing the insurmountable difficulty of understanding the survivors, who forever feel as if they were speaking Chinese to those around them.

16. Many characters in Liebrecht's stories suffer from an inability to forge for themselves a unique individual identity, because they bear the brunt of their parents' past on their shoulders. According to Wardi (40), this difficulty is characteristic of the second generation of survivors, due to the parents' expectations that their children will stand in for family members who have perished, and also that they will fulfill the aspirations that they themselves were unable to realize because of the war. Thus, the second generation is saddled with the dual task of "pulling a hearse" and of carrying out the "youthful wishes" of the survivors. This heavy burden lies on the shoulders of the protagonist of Liebrecht's *ars poetica* story "To Bear the Great Beauty" (published in the

collection *Apples from the Desert*). Even though the mother in the story is not presented as a Holocaust survivor, her severe medical condition and the death of all her immediate relatives in a disaster serve as a "camouflage" in this respect. The mother who suffers from depression, untreated chronic mourning, and an inability to relate even to the people closest to her, is in fact characterized by "survivor's syndrome," defined by psychologists as the emotional condition of concentration-camp survivors. (See, for example, W. G. Niderland.) Her son, the protagonist, feels that he has to carry, for her sake, the memory of her dead relatives and, at the same time, write the poems that she herself was unable to produce because of the traumas she has suffered.

17. The protagonist of the story "Reserve Duty," from the collection *Apples from the Desert,* is not content with merely wishing for peace and with working diligently and clandestinely to bring it about; he is willing to cross the line that separate the two peoples, to come and live in the Arab village as one of its native sons. This urge to "desert his nation," to immerse himself in the world of the Other, comes over him at the least expected or appropriate moment: when he enters the village as the commander of an army detail searching for indigenous persons suspected of hostile activity.

It is important to note that Liebrecht is not the first nor the only writer in Hebrew literature to express guilt feelings vis-à-vis the Arab minority in Israel. According to Benjamin Tammuz and Leon Yudkin (16), Hebrew literature has been dealing with these feelings for many years now. The best known stories in this respect are S. Yizhar's "The Prisoner" and "Hirbet Hiz'ee."

A. B. Yehoshua, in the story "Facing the Forests," describes the dissolution of the Zionist enterprise by an Arab and a Jew who collaborate in the act of destruction. The Jewish forest ranger whose mission is to watch over the symbolic forest sets fire to it, in collaboration with an old Arab who has found refuge in the forest. Thus, the old Arab avenges the destruction of his village during the war of independence and the obliteration of its site by the planting a forest on its ruins. The young Israeli joins him out of a desire to rebel against his parents, who have subjugated his life to a cause sacred to their heart—the guarding of the forest (the State) that they have created. (For a detailed analysis of Yehoshua's story, see Gila Ramraz-Rauch, 128–40).

Yehoshua's story is more extreme than any of Liebrecht's, both in its violent tone and in its political implications. It not only gives vent to the guilt feelings of the younger generation in Israel, but also warns against a destructive eruption that threatens the entire Zionist enterprise because it has ignored the needs of the Arab minority. Liebrecht, on the other hand, is interested mostly in expressing the malaise of conscientious Jews, escaping to an unrealizable, momentary fantasy about resuming a harmonious relationship between Jews and Arabs. The dream of forming an alliance, of creating a brotherhood between Jews and Arabs, expresses the profound need to overcome the power struggle and the animosity that exist between the two peoples.

18. This is in contrast to the presentation of the Arab as the epitome of sexual attraction in Amos Oz's "My Michael," where he remains voiceless. Liebrecht grants the Arab in her story a more humane and complex presence.

19. The fierce tension between the Sephardic culture and the dominant Ashkenazic culture in Israel is described in Ella Shohat's *Israeli Cinema: East/West and the Politics of Representation* (115–78).

20. The mourning customs of the various ethnic groups in Israel are described in Phyllis Palgi's book *Death, Mourning, and Bereavement in Israel.*

21. Sisterly bonding that transcends the deep chasms between orthodox and secular Jews in Israeli society is the theme of Liebrecht's story "Purple Meadows" (published in the collection *"What Am I Speaking, Chinese?" She Said to Him*). The friendship that develops between two women whose lifestyles and world views are so different is motivated by a wish to rehabilitate the shattered life of a little girl. The girl's life fell apart when her mother was raped and consequently became pregnant. The rabbis instructed her to abort the fetus, divorce her husband, and sever all ties with her daughter. This woman is, in fact, a victim of a double rape: the physical rape perpetrated on her body by a strange man, and the more horrendous spiritual rape perpetrated by members of her congregation under the instructions of the patriarchal religious establishment. Here, the affinity between the women is based on another element—on the bond created by female vulnerability. (The traits and practices of the ultra-Orthodox Haredi community are described by Menachem [130–33].)

22. Risa Domb discusses the patriarchal structure of Arab society in *The Arab in Hebrew Prose, 1911–1948* (29).

23. This is how Gunew and Spivak define the (in their opinion) reprehensible attempt to represent marginal groups through "token figures" (416).

24. The status of women in the kibbutz is succinctly described by Calvin Goldscheider (162–63) and by Judith Buber-Agassi (395–421).

WORKS CITED

Agnon, S.Y. "Metamorphosis." In *Twenty-One Stories.* New York: Schocken, 1970.

Ashkenazi, Nehama. *Eve's Journey: Feminine Images in Hebraic Literary Tradition.* Detroit: Wayne State University Press, 1986.

Azmon, Yael and Dafna N. Izraeli., eds. *Women in Israel: Studies of Israeli Society.* New Brunswick, N.J., and London: Transaction Publishers, 1995.

Buber-Agassi. Judith. "Theories of Gender Equality: Lessons from the Israeli Kibbutz." In Azmon, Yael and Dafna N. Izraeli., eds. *Women in Israel: Studies of Israeli Society.* New Brunswick, N.J., and London: Transaction Publishers, 1995, 395–421.

Domb, Risa. *The Arab in Hebrew Prose, 1911–1948.* London: Valentine, Mitchell, 1982.

Friedman, Menachem. "Life Tradition and the Book: Tradition in the Development of Ultra-Orthodox Judaism." In *Israeli Judaism,* edited by Shlomo Deshen, Charles S. Liebman, and Moshe Shokied. New Bruswick, N.J. and London: Transaction Publishers, 1995, 127–44.

Fuchs, Esther. "Apples from the Desert." In *Modern Hebrew Literature* 3–4 (Spring 1988): 46–47.

Furstenberg, Rochelle. "Dreaming of Flying: Women's Prose of the Last Decade." In *Modern Hebrew Literature* 6 (Spring/Summer 1991): 5–7.

Gilligan, Carol. *In a Different Voice: Psychological Theory and Women's Development.* Cambridge, Mass., and London: Harvard University Press, 1982.

Goldscheider, Calvin. *Israel's Changing Society: Population, Ethnicity, and Development.* Boulder, Co.: Western Press, 1996.

Gunew, Sneja and Gayatri Chakravorty Spivak. "Questions of Multiculturalism." In *Women's Writing in Exile,* edited by Mary Lynn Broe and Angela Ingram. Chapel Hill and London: University of North Carolina Press, 1989, 412–20.

Handelman, Dov and Elihu Katz. "State Ceremonies of Israel: Remembrance Day and Independence Day." In *Israeli Judaism,* edited by Shlomo Deshen, Charles S. Liebman, and Moshe Shokied. New Brunswick, N.J., and London: 1995, 75–85.

Holtzman, Avner. "The Holocaust in Hebrew Literature: Trends in Israeli Fiction in the 1980s." *Modern Hebrew Literature* 8–9 (Spring/Fall 1992): 23–27.

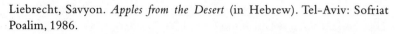

Liebrecht, Savyon. *Apples from the Desert* (in Hebrew). Tel-Aviv: Sofriat Poalim, 1986.

———. "The Influence of the Holocaust on My Work." In *Hebrew Literature in the Wake of the Holocaust,* edited by Leon Yudkin. Rutherford, Madison, and Teaneck, N.J.: Fairleigh Dickinson University Press; London and Toronto: Associated University Presses, 1993, 125–30.

———. Interview with Argaman-Barnea, Amalia (in Hebrew). *Yediot Ah'ronot,* 6 May 1992.

———. *Horses on the Highway* (in Hebrew). Tel-Aviv: Shifrat Poalim, 1988.

———. *On Love Stories and Other Endings* (in Hebrew). Jerusalem: Keter, 1995.

———. *What Am I Speaking, Chinese? She Said to Him* (in Hebrew). Jerusalem: Keter, 1992.

Lugones, Marcia and Elizabeth V. Spelman. "Competition, Compassion, and Community: A Model for a Feminist Ethos." *In Competition: A Feminist Taboo?* edited by Valerie Miner and Helen E. Longino. New York: The Feminist Press at CUNY, 1987, 234–47.

Niderland, W. G. "Clinical Observation on the 'Survivor Syndrome': Symposium on Psychic Traumatization Through Social Catastrophe." *International Journal of Psychoanalysis* 49 (1968): 313–31.

Oz, Amos. *My Michael.* London: Chatto and Windus, 1975.

Palgi, Phyllis. *Death, Mourning, and Bereavement in Israel.* Jerusalem: Jerusalem Academic Press, 1973.

Ramraz-Rauch, Gila. *The Arab in Israeli Literature.* Bloomington and Indianapolis: Indiana University Press; London: I. B. Tauris, 1989.

Rattok, Lily and Carol Diamant, eds. *Ribcage: Israeli Women's Fiction.* New York: Hadassah, 1994.

Shohat, Ella. *Israeli Cinema: East/West and the Politics of Representation.* Austin: University of Texas Press, 1989.

Silverman, Kaja. *The Threshold of the Visible World.* New York and London: Routledge, 1996.

Tammuz, Benjamin and Leon Yudkin, eds. *Meetings with the Angel.* London: Andre Deutch, 1974.

Wardi, Dina. *Memorial Candles: Children of the Holocaust.* New York and London: Routledge, 1992.

Yaeger, Patricia. *Honey-Mad Women: Emancipatory Strategies in Women's Writing*. New York: Columbia University Press, 1988.

Yehoshua, A. B. "Facing the Forests." In *Three Days and a Child*. New York: Doubleday, 1970.

Yizhar, S. "The Prisoner" and "Hirbet Hiz'ee." In *Modern Hebrew Literature*, edited by Robert Alter. New York: Behrman House, 1975.

Yudkin, Leon. *A Home Within: Varieties of Jewish Expressions in Modern Fiction*. Northwood, Middlesex: Spence Reviews, 1996.

Translated from the Hebrew by Marganit Weinberger-Rotman

A Room on the Roof

THAT SUMMER SHE sat on the patio under the rounded awning of the Italian swing, as the straw fringes intertwined with the edges of the cloth dome rustled softly, sounding like forest noises, her eyes on the red glow flowing from the western horizon at sunset, her baby already standing on his own two widespread legs, his chubby fingers grasping the bars of the square playpen made of interlocked wooden bars. The lilylike hibiscus waved its circlet of toothed leaves bound in an envelope of buds, only their heads peeping out of long, laden calyxes, pouting like the lips of a coquettish girl, the abundant tranquillity all about deluding only the part of her already dormant, not the part that was driven, tensed toward something beyond the apparent silence, knowing the restlessness of someone under eyes constantly prying but always unseen.

That early winter—the mud, the puddles of cement, and the rusty fragments of iron—already seemed distant and impossible, with the three Arab men giving off the stench of wood smoke and unwashed flesh. The men with their bad teeth, with high-heeled shoes that were once fashionable, now looking oversized, with the leather crushed under the heels.

In her dreams they still visited her sometimes, coming too close to her, which, perhaps, where they live too, could be interpreted as what they might have meant to hint, though perhaps it was done inadvertently. For a long time she wondered about it: did Ahmad draw close to her unintentionally, touching her legs with his rear as he dragged a sack of cement, with his back to her? And later, was it by chance that his elbow touched her breast when he passed by her, balancing a bag of lime on his shoulder, while she raised her arms to the lintel of the door to check the concrete rim as it dried? And did Hassan really believe that she would invite him in on that black night when he came back for his coat?

That summer, for a long time after they went off without ever reappearing, she avoided the roof when it was dark, fearing that they might pop up from behind the high potted plants. Sometimes, when she happened to pass the back corner, which was imprisoned within three walls and served, for the moment, as a storage area, and she saw the tools they had left behind and never came back to collect, a chill would climb up her back like a crawling creature with many legs, stirring a column of water in the depths of her belly like the pitching that afflicts you when you're seasick.

But there was no one else to accuse. She had brought the whole thing down on her own head. And if her baby wasn't slaughtered, and her jewels weren't stolen, and nothing bad happened to her—she should bless her good fortune and erase those two winter months from her memory as if they had never been.

Yoel, her husband, had been opposed to the idea from the moment she had brought it up, still just an idle notion in her mouth and still lacking that fervor, that stubbornness, and that unyielding feeling of necessity that were later to possess her.

"A room on the roof?" He twisted his face and took off his glasses as he did when he was angry. "Do you know how filthy construction is? Do you have a notion how many tons of soil and rocks will fall on your head when they break through the ceiling for the stairs? And I don't see why we need another room. There are already two unused rooms in the house. And if you want sunlight—you have half a dunam of private lawn." Against her rebelliously pursed lips, which for a long time, until his initial patience broke down, were to convey a defiant silence, he added, "What gave you this sudden notion of building? What do you need that for, with a four-month-old baby?"

"So why did we take the trouble to run to the engineer and the municipality to get a building license?" she countered his argument. "And didn't we pay all the fees and the property improvement tax and all that?"

"So we'd have it in hand," he replied, "so that if we want to sell the house one day—it will be more valuable, with the license already in hand."

But the idea had already taken root, twisting up inside her with its own force, like an ovum that had embraced the sperm and was now germinating, and the fetus was already stretching the skin of the belly, and there was no way of putting that growth to sleep.

All that time she was wrapped up in her firstborn son, Udi, who summoned her from her dreams at night. She would come to him with her eyes almost closed, as though moonstruck, and her hands turning the tiny baby clothes of their own volition. On her walks, pushing the baby carriage across broken paving stones, past piles of sand, she found herself lingering around houses under construction, raising her head to see the men walking with assurance on the rim of high walls, amazed, learning how stories grow, how windows are squared into dark frames, shutters raised panel after panel by an enormous yellow machine with the look of arm-bones scraped free of flesh.

From one of the yawning holes that would be a window, some-one shouted at her with an Arabic accent, "You looking for someone to service you, lady?" She blushed as though caught in wrongdoing and pushed her baby away in a panic. Near a building that she often passed, a contractor told her while looking into the carriage, "Excuse me for saying this, but this is no place to wander around with a baby. Dirt and cinder blocks or iron rods sometimes fall around here, and it's very dangerous."

After she started leaving Udi with a baby-sitter in the mornings, a woman who looked after a few infants in her home, she would go to those places in her old trousers worn at the knees, climb up the diag-onal concrete slabs, supporting herself on the rough rafters, and grope in the darkness of stairwells still floored with sand. Here, she would later say to herself, she saw them face to face for the first time, in the chill damp peculiar to houses under construction. They came toward her from corners that stank of urine, all of them with the same face: dark, scalding eyes, sunk in caves of black shadows, hair cut in the old-fashioned way, shoes spotted with lime and cement, and dusty clothes.

Here, too, their peculiar odor came to her nostrils: sweat mingled with cigarette smoke and soot. While she exchanged words with the Jewish foreman, oblique glances would be cast at her by the Arab workers, down on all fours laying floor tiles; panting as they transported sacks of cement or stacks of tiles; running to ease the effort; ripping out hunks of food with their teeth, half a loaf of bread in one hand, an unpeeled cucumber in the other.

Some foremen were irritable, refusing to answer her questions, dismissing her with a contemptuous wave of the hand and continuing to give directions to their workers, ignoring her as she stood behind them, ashamed, sensing how the Arabs were laughing at her inside, in collusion with their Jewish foreman. But sometimes the foremen answered her willingly, watching as she took down what they said in her notebook like a diligent pupil. As she turned to leave, they would say with amusement, "So we have to watch out for you, huh? You're the competition!"

In her notebook the pages were already densely packed with details about reinforced concrete, the thickness of inner and outer walls, various gauges of iron rods, a sketch of the way the rods were fastened for casting concrete pillars, the ceiling, plaster, flooring, conduits for electricity and water, tar, addresses of building materials manufacturers. She hid her notebook from Yoel in a carton with her university notebooks. Once, when he asked, "What's going on? Zvika said that twice he saw you coming out of the building they're putting up on Herzl Street," she looked him straight in the eye and said in her usual tone of voice, "Probably someone who looks like me." And he responded, "It's about time you changed your hairstyle. Last week I saw someone from behind, and I was sure it was you. She even had the same walk and the same handbag."

Afterward, when everything was ripe, like a girl coming of age, Yoel came back from work one day, his eyes troubled. He said, "They want me to attend a training course in Texas for two months. We're getting a new computer. I said I couldn't leave you alone with the baby. Let them find someone else." She answered firmly, alarmed at the swift feeling that leapt up in her like the shock wave of an explosion, "I'll be quite all right—you should go." And when the tempest had died down within her she thought: a sign has been sent from heaven.

The day after she saw Yoel to his plane, David, the Jewish foreman, came accompanied by three Arab workers, members of the same family, looking amazingly alike. They all wore old woolen hats. They sat on the edges of the chairs, careful not to ruin the upholstery, with their eyes cast down most of the time. Only occasionally would they raise their eyelids and cast a quick glance at her and the apartment, squinting at the baby on her lap. David wrote down some kind of agreement on a piece of paper, explaining some sentences in Arabic, and they nodded their heads in consent. David copied their names from a form he'd brought with him and their identity numbers from the creased documents they took out of their pockets. He wrote out a description of the dimensions of the room they were to build, detailing the thickness of the walls, the number of electric sockets and their location in the room, the break through the opening for the stairs, the type and color of the plaster. Beside the description he wrote the amounts to be paid as the work progressed. Before signing, she insisted that a final deadline be clearly written, obligating them to finish the work within two months, before Yoel's return.

Then the three of them stood up at the same time and headed for the door. There, on the threshold, after she thanked him for his assistance, David replied, "Think nothing of it, dear lady. It's because I can see you're a fine girl, with an adventurous character. Not many women would do something like this. So here's to you! And if you need something—ask for David in the Hershkovitz building any time. Good luck! They're good workers, up on scaffolds from the age of fifteen," and in her ear softly, "Better than ours, believe me."

Sitting on the open roof that summer, opposite the sky spread above her with rows of painted white clouds, hearing her baby babble, his voice rising and falling as he tried out his vocal cords, she thought: how did things go so far that those men, whose gaze avoided her eyes, who shrank in her presence with shoulders bowed as though narrowing their bodies, answering her questions with a soft voice as though forever guilty, how did it happen that on that first evening in November they sat on the edge of the chairs, and by December they were already marching through her house like lords of the manor, turning on Yoel's radio, opening the refrigerator to look for fresh vegetables, rummaging through the cabinet for fragrant shaving cream, and patting her baby on the head?

AT FIRST THEY still seemed to her like a single person, before she learned that Hassan had elongated eyes whose bright color was like the band of wet sand at the water's edge. Ahmad had a broad nose, sitting in the middle of his flattened face, between his narrow eyes, his lips thick like an African's. Salah's ears were pointed and his cheeks were sunken. Only the pimples on his face gave it some thickness, making it look like the pocked, thick skin of an orange.

On the first day, they arrived in an old pickup truck that had once been orange, but now on its dented face there were only islands of peeling paint and its windows were missing. They got out and unloaded gray cinder blocks near the parking lot. Then the truck pulled away with a grinding noise, returning in a short while with a long wooden beam on top. After a short consultation among themselves, the truck was parked in the parking lot and the beam laid on an angle, the lower part leaning on the back of the truck and the top rising above the edge of the roof. Until the baby started crying inside the house, she stood at a little distance, her hands in the pockets of her slacks, and watched how one of them drew out a tangle of ropes with a saddle-shaped yoke at the end. He stood on the roof and harnessed himself with knots, looking like a coolie in a historical film. One of the others loaded block after block into the basket on the rope, and the worker on the roof pulled them up along the apartment beam, while the third worker, standing on the edge of the roof, leaned over and gathered the bricks one by one. Examining them from below, she saw how their faces grew sweaty with the effort, and their hands became dusty and scratched by the rough blocks. By the time she had put the baby to bed and come out again, she saw that they had unloaded the rest of the blocks on the lawn and disappeared with the truck, though she hadn't heard the sound of the motor. The next day, after turning the matter over in her mind for sleepless hours, she decided she must demonstrate her authority over them, and was ready and waiting for them in her window, cradling the baby in her rounded arms, anger lending force to her movements. From the window she shouted at them as they approached, "Why did you leave in the middle of work yesterday? And today . . ." She looked at her watch with a clumsy movement, stretching her neck over the baby lying at her breast. "Today you come at nine! You said you'd start working at six! This way you won't finish in ten months!"

"Lady," said the one with the golden eyes, insulted, "Today was police roadblocked. Not possible we leave early before four morning, lady."

Something in her recoiled at the sight of the beaten dog's eyes he raised up toward her in her window, at the sound of his broken voice. But she, tensing her strength to suppress the tremor that awoke within her, threatening to soften her anger, shouted, "And yesterday what happened? Was also roadblocked?" Maliciously she imitated his grammatical error. "You went away and left half the blocks down there on the grass."

For the first time she saw the movement that was later to become routine: the jaws clamping down on each other as though chewing something very hard, digging a channel along the line of his teeth. Later she was to learn: that's how they suppress anger, hatred. They clench their teeth to suppress the wild rage that surges up, that only rarely breaks out and flashes in their pupils.

"Yesterday my friend Ahmad, he hurted his, the nail his finger."

Behind him his companion raised a bandaged hand, and she looked out of her pretty window, framed with Catalan-style wooden blocks, feeling how the three men in their tattered work clothes were defeating her, looking up at her from their places.

And two hours later, when she had fed and changed the baby and put him to sleep in his crib, her mind was constantly on the uncomfortable feeling that had dwelt in her ever since her conversation with them, when she had spoken to them like a cruel lord of the manor. Now, knowing full well she was doing something she shouldn't, but still letting the spirit of the moment drown out the voice of reason, she went out of the front door carrying a large tray, bearing a china coffeepot decorated with rosebuds, surrounded by cups with matching saucers, spoons with an engraved pattern, and a platter of round honey cakes. She stood there clutching the heavy tray, her head tilted back, debating whether to put the tray down on the marble landing of the stairs, climb up the wooden ladder that leaned against the building, reaching the edge of the roof, and invite them down for coffee; or perhaps it would be better to call them from where she stood. Relentlessly aware of her ridiculous position, she suddenly discovered she didn't remember any of their names. Then a head appeared over the edge of the roof, and she found herself calling to him quickly, before he disappeared, "Hello, hello, I have some coffee for you." Ashamed of the shout that had burst from her, she set down the tray and escaped before one of them came down and brought her offering up to his companions.

That afternoon, placing her wide-awake baby in his crib, she put on old jeans and Yoel's army jacket and climbed up to the roof to see how they were getting along with the work. The tray with the rose-bud pattern coffeepot and the pretty cups stood in a corner of the roof, cigarette butts crushed in the remainder of the murky liquid in the saucers. She stood and looked for a long while at the sight, which she would recall afterward as a kind of symbol: the fine Rosental china from the rich collection her grandmother had brought from Germany heaped up carelessly, lying next to sacks of cement and heavy hammers.

"We finished the concrete rim," said Hassan, who seemed to have taken upon himself the task of spokesman. "Now we have to put water and it dry."

"Is it twenty centimeter?" she spoke like them.

"It twenty to the meter" He took a metal measuring tape out of his pocket.

"Is it two centimeters over the edge of the floor?"

It seemed to her they exchanged hurried glances, as if they had con-spired together before she came, and she grew tense and suspicious.

"Did you bring it up two centimeters above the floor?" she repeated her question, her voice sharp and higher than at first.

"It twenty to the meter," he told her again.

"But does it come out above the floor or not?"

"Level with the floor," he spread out his hand to emphasize his words, with a satisfied expression, like a merchant praising his wares.

"That means it's no good," she said.

"Why no good, lady?"

"Because the rain will leak in," she said impatiently, her anger grow-ing at the game he was playing with her while the concrete band was drying steadily. "It has to be two centimeters higher. That's what David said to you, and that's what's written in the contract."

"We say David twenty centimeter."

"At least twenty centimeters," she corrected him, her voice rising and turning into a shout. "And of that, two centimeters above the floor."

"There is twenty centimeter, lady," he said again, his voice like a patient merchant standing up to a customer making a nuisance.

She pursed her lips as if to demonstrate the conversation was useless. She swung her legs over the low wall around the roof and placed her feet on the rungs of the ladder.

"I'm going to get David," she said to the three men standing and looking at her, anxious to see how things would develop. "If that's the way you're starting—then it's no good," she added. She went down the ladder with a rush to demonstrate the bellicose spirit that animated her steps, inwardly calculating how long it would take her to get to the building on Herzl Street and locate David, and whether it would be better to take Udi with her, or leave him in his crib and hope he was asleep. Planting her feet on the ground, she strode vigorously toward her car, determined to call David in before the concrete band dried. Then she heard a thick voice calling to her from the roof: "Lady, you don't need David. We add two centimeters."

She turned her face upward, suppressing the feeling of relief and victory that surged over her anger, seeking the three dark heads bunched together. "Quickly then, before it dries," she said in a loud, hard voice.

That evening, her sister Noa declared, her voice coming through the pay phone from Jerusalem mingled with other voices, "You made a mistake about the coffee. Let them make it themselves, and don't serve them anything anymore. If they enter the house—you'll never get rid of them."

"Don't worry. No one gets into my house without an invitation," she shouted over the strangers' voices.

But the next day, in the doorway, smiling to her with his eyes tinted yellow in the winter sun, Hassan, whose name she had learned, said to her, with gentle bashfulness in his voice, "Yesterday lady make coffee. Today I make coffee like in my house." From a plastic bag he withdrew a container of coffee that gave off a fragrance like the one in cramped spice shops where coffee grinders crush the dark beans into pungent grains.

Taken aback by the friendly gesture, as though they hadn't sparred with each other the day before, as though she hadn't been wracked all night long with worry as to how she would mobilize the police and the courts if they again tried to violate the agreement they had signed, she took a step backward, and before she grasped what was happening, he slipped through the space between her body and the doorjamb, stepped over to the stove, and put the plastic bag on the marble counter. With precise, expert movements, he took out a long-handled blue coffeepot and a spoon, measured a heaped spoonful of coffee, added sugar that he poured out of another bag, and filled the pot with water. Then after fiddling lightly with the lighter and the knobs on the stove, he lit it and placed the coffeepot on the glowing ring. She observed his motions with astonishment, stunned at the liberty he took in her kitchen, her eyes drawn to his graceful, fluent movements, knowing danger was latent in what was happening before her.

He stood on one foot, his other foot to the side, like a dancer at rest, peeking into the coffeepot now and then. A hissing rose from it, heralding the onset of boiling, and the spoon in his hand stirred without stopping, with a fixed circular movement. He said, "We put two more centimeter of cement from yesterday." And she answered, "Fine, I hope there won't be any more problems. David told me you were good workers—so do things right."

Then she combed her hair and washed her face, and before she could change out of her soft mohair shirt (which had once been burned in the front by a cigarette, so she wore it only around the house) she found herself sitting at the table with his two fellow workers, for whom Hassan had opened the door with a hospitable gesture while she was spreading a cloth on the table in the breakfast nook.

"That's coffee like in our house," he said, looking at her, the smile on his lips not reaching his eyes. She sipped the thick, bitter beverage, and smiled involuntarily. "You mean the coffee I made yesterday wasn't good?"

"It was good," he answered quickly, drawing the words out, alarmed at her insult. "Thank you very much. But we like it this way, strong coffee." He clenched his fist and waved it toward her with vigorous motion, to emphasize his last word.

She heard Udi crying in the next room. This was when he usually had his first bottle of cereal. She excused herself and got up, sensing their eyes on her. She took Udi out of his crib, wrapped him in a blanket decorated with ducklings, and carried him into the breakfast nook. Then she placed in his hands the bottle of cereal that had been standing on the windowsill; it was already lukewarm. Ahmad looked as though hypnotized at the sapphire ring Yoel's parents had given her for their engagement, and the others looked at the baby curled up at her breast in his bright blanket, drinking the cereal with his eyes shut. Hassan smiled suddenly, and his eyes brightened. He enjoyed the sight of the tranquil baby, and he brought his face close to Udi and said fondly, "You eat everything—you be strong like Hassan."

Months afterward she would remember that morning with dismay, when she had sat with them for the first time, as though they were at home there: drinking from cups like welcome guests, eating off the violet lace tablecloth her mother-in-law had brought from Spain, looking at her baby over their cups. She sipped the bitter liquid and only part of her, the part that didn't laugh with them, thought: Could these hands, serving coffee, be the ones that planted the booby-trapped doll at the gate of the religious school at the end of the street? Her heart, which had been on guard all the time, began to foresee something, but it still didn't know: this was just the beginning, appearing like a figure leaping out of the fog. From now on everything would grow clear and roll down like boulders falling into an abyss. The future would clearly be a fall—and no one could stop it.

IN THE AFTERNOON, as she gathered up the toys Udi had scattered on the carpet, there was a knock on the door. Hassan appeared with a sooty aluminum pot in one hand and a plastic bag imprinted with the name of the supermarket on the main street in the other, a friendly smile of familiarity on his lips, and he said, "Excuse. Can put soup on fire, lady?"

She stood in the doorway, guarding her boundary, with her hand stretched toward the door frame as if halting all entry. But the warm smile on his face and the way he had asked the question left no room for refusal. The blocking arm slipped down, and with cordial hospitality, as though to mask her initial hesitation, she moved her hand in an arc and said, "Please, please." Anger at herself welled up inside her for treating him, despite herself, as a welcome guest.

She went back to gathering up the toys, stealing a look at the way he put the pot under the faucet with steady movements, like an expert, boiling water in the blue coffeepot that he pulled out of the bag, finding the barrel-shaped salt cellar in the right-hand drawer, knowingly manipulating the knobs of the gas stove. While she arranged the toys in Udi's room, as he slept between the duckling blanket and the Winnie-the-Pooh sheet, there stole up in her—still faint, still resembling discomfort—the fear born of having people trespass, pushing her boundary back and pretending they were unaware.

When she returned, the other two were already with him in the kitchen. One was cutting vegetables into her new china bowl. The other was standing at the open refrigerator, his hand in the lower vegetable drawer. By the look on his face she could tell he'd been caught in the act. His hand, rummaging among the vegetables, stopped where it was.

"Need cucumber, lady," he said, stepping back.

She went to the refrigerator, slammed the drawer shut, and took a cucumber out of a sealed bag in the back of the top shelf.

"Take it," she said.

"Thank you very much, lady." He took the cucumber from her hand.

"Lady drink coffee?" asked Hassan from the stove, stirring his coffeepot and smiling at her in profile.

Confused, fighting to control the muscles of her face, she said, "No thanks."

"Is good coffee," Salah, who spoke only seldom, tried to persuade her.

"Thanks, I don't drink coffee in the afternoon."

"Afternoon, morning—is good coffee." He wouldn't let up. She, already feeling the teeth of the trap closing on her, said, almost shouting, "No!" She saw Hassan open the china cabinet and take out three plates.

A moment before she abandoned her house and her baby, fleeing to the bedroom and locking the door behind her, breaking out in silent, suppressed, helpless weeping, into which dread was already creeping, she told Hassan in a soft, commanding voice, "I'll thank you not to make any noise—my baby is asleep." A few minutes afterward, when she left her room, her eyes already dry and her voice tranquil though her heart pounded within her, she said, "Maybe you could cook your soup up there. I'll give you a small camping stove. It's inconvenient for me here." Salah threw her a malevolent glance over his steaming bowl of soup. And Hassan said politely, "If you please, lady, thank you very much."

For five days she heard them arriving, but by the time she had fed Udi and put him to sleep in his crib, her workers were no longer on the roof. Angrily she calculated that in the past two days they hadn't raised more than a single row of blocks above the stone rim on top of the window. Suspicion stole into her heart that they had taken on another job and, so it wouldn't slip through their fingers before they finished the construction in her house, they had accepted and bound themselves to another boss. That was the way they did things, as the bank teller who knew about her project had taken the trouble to warn her. But in the afternoon, shaken at the familiar sound of the pickup truck and all the while composing harsh sentences to reproach them with, she saw that the truck was laden with iron rods, thin and thick. The three of them got out of the cab and set about unloading the truck and passing the iron rods from hand to hand up to the roof. Relieved at her window, she watched them at their work. She decided to rest until Udi awoke from his afternoon nap.

For a while she heard them walking around the roof, dragging loads, their voices reaching her through the closed blinds of her room. Later, there was a lot of insistent knocking, which she first took to be part of a dream, and then she heard them at the door. When she opened it, the three of them were standing close to each other, with Hassan half a footstep in front. He said, "Hello, lady, how are you?"

Inwardly bridling at the familiarity he allowed himself in asking that polite question for the first time, and keeping her face frozen, she ignored his question and asked, "Yes?" She was guessing that they would ask permission to heat up their meal.

"Lady, we need some money."

Her sister had warned her about that in their last conversation: You mustn't pay them before they've done the work as agreed. She tensed. Her voice rasped more than she intended: "Did you finish putting the iron in place for pouring the concrete?"

"We put band around roof."

"You did the band, but I'm asking about the iron. Did you get the iron ready for pouring the concrete?"

"That's tomorrow, lady."

"You'll get your money tomorrow."

"We need some. Maybe you'll give us, lady . . ."

"Tomorrow," she said firmly. "Anyway, I don't have that much now. I have to go to the bank."

"Really, lady," Hassan said, looking straight in her eyes and pounding his chest with his fist. "Lady, believe. We coming tomorrow, money or no money."

"No money," she said, knowing how Yoel would smile when she told him about this occasion. Hassan turned to his friends, and they put their heads together and whispered. From where she was standing she saw the back of his neck, his dusty hair, looking gray under the woolen hat with the tattered edges, frayed yarn twisting down. His companions' brows darkened. They put their heads close to each other, taking counsel. One of them pulled a creased wallet from his pocket and seemed to be counting the bank notes in it, his face worried. Inside, she was already prepared to withdraw her position and say, "Look, if it's something pressing, I'm prepared to give you what I have in my purse now . . ." He suddenly turned to her and asked, "Can wash hands in water?" He surprised her so much with the question that, like the morning when he had stood before her with a cooking pot in his hands, she said, "Certainly, certainly," pushing the door wide open, while her only wish was to slam the door in their faces.

They entered hesitantly. Now she saw that Salah was holding a large army knapsack, the kind that Yoel used to extricate from the storeroom when his unit was called up for maneuvers. Hassan led the way to the bathroom, looking at her as though asking permission, and the three men made their way in and locked the door. For a long while she heard the sound of running water and the men's boisterous voices. She, pacing back and forth in the living room, looking out at the large garden with no other house visible, was gripped by sudden fear, thinking of what might be in that big knapsack. Perhaps they were assembling weapons there, spreading the steel parts out on the carpet, as Yoel had once done, kneeling on the floor and joining the shining parts one to another. Maybe they would come out in a little while with their weapons drawn and threaten her and her son. Perhaps they would take them as hostages in their pickup truck. And what about Udi? She had already run out of his special flour, and she wouldn't be able to feed him when the men kept them there in their broken-down shacks in Gaza, among the muddy paths. They had shown those shacks on an American television documentary. Maybe, the thought flashed through her like lightning, she should snatch Udi out of his crib and flee with him, lay him in the back seat of her car and drive immediately to the police station on the main street.

Hassan came out first, and she was startled at his appearance. For a second she imagined a stranger had come out. For the first time she saw him without the woolen cap pulled down over his forehead. His hair, surprisingly light, freshly combed and damp, was brushed back over his temples. He wore a dark, well-pressed jacket over a white shirt and tie. His black dress shoes were highly polished.

He told her, "My friends come out minute, lady."

"Aren't you going home?"

"Have wedding from our aunt in Tulkarem. We today in Tulkarem."

At that moment the baby let out a screech more piercing than any she'd heard since the morning he had burst forth in the maternity ward: high and prolonged, followed by a sudden silence. She herself let out a scream and rushed to the room, pushing his rolling high chair out of the way as she ran. Udi was prostrate on the floor, lying on his stomach, his face on the rug spread at the foot of his crib, with a toy between his fingers. She bent down and picked him up, carrying him in her arms, and he looked at her with cloudy eyes. She clasped him close to her body and started murmuring words without knowing what she was saying, her heart pounding wildly, making her fingers tremble. After a long while he burst out crying, resting his head on her shoulder, sobbing.

"Is okay, lady," Hassan said from the doorway, and she looked around in panic, not realizing he had followed her.

"What?" she asked fearfully.

"Is okay he like so, lady," he traced his finger along his cheek and made a crying expression. "Is nothing. He good that way."

"What's good?" she asked as the baby trembled in her arms.

Hassan approached her and gently lifted Udi from her arms. "Lady, get water," he said softly. "He need drink."

In the kitchen, her hands still trembling, she stood still for a long time, trying to remember where the sugar bowl was. She heard Hassan talking softly to the baby in Arabic, like a loving father talking to his child in a caressing voice, the words running together in a pleasant flow, containing a supreme beauty, like the words of a poem in an ancient language, which you don't understand, but which well up inside you. Udi, resting tranquilly on his chest, reached out toward Hassan's dark face, and Hassan put his head down toward the little fingers and kissed them. She, stunned by the sight, stood where she was and looked at them, as the tremor inspired by fear gradually died down, and another, new kind of trembling arose within her, seeing something that, even as it happens, you already yearn for from a distance, knowing that when it passes nothing like it will happen again. And, as though dividing themselves, her thoughts turned to Yoel, whose eyes examined his son with a certain remoteness. Since the baby's birth he had never clasped him to his body and was careful not to wrinkle his clothes or have them smell of wet diapers.

Hassan looked up at her and said, "Hassan have like this at home in Gaza."

"You have a baby?" She was astonished. "You're married?"

"Also like this. Four years," he said proudly, placing his hand parallel to the floor to measure the height of his son.

"You okay," Hassan said in his soft voice, turning his face to the baby. "You big—you doctor like daddy, yes?"

With the bottle of tea in her hand, she was shaken as though by a distant alarm. Troubled by the suspicion that he knew more than he should, she said, "You can read Hebrew?"

He laughed. "I read one word, another word. I see 'Doctor' on door in English."

"You can read English?" There was some mockery in her voice, like an adult talking to a child about grown-up things.

"I can," he answered in English, for the first time smiling another smile, a hidden one, without the forced humility she was familiar with.

"Where from?" she asked, also in English.

"From the university."

"Which one?"

"The American University of Beirut." She recognized his proper accent from having heard it on television when Arabic-speaking intellectuals were interviewed. She hadn't been able to shake off her Israeli accent in the two years she had lived in Texas, while Yoel finished his degree.

"Really?" She returned to Hebrew.

"Really, lady. I in Beirut two years. Maybe I be doctor that way, of babies."

"Why didn't you complete your studies?"

"Hard. Can't talk." He looked down at this hands, whose nails were free of lime. "Life like that."

Shortly after he left, joining his comrades who were waiting for him and watching him from the door, also scrubbed, she thought: They're nameless and ageless to me, in their faded black sweaters and their dirty elbows and stocking caps. They had a single face and uncouth words came from their mouths. Suddenly they were different: in white collars and jackets, their cheeks shaven, with a wife and baby and a child of four at home.

Even before she heard the bell ring she knew he had returned.

"My jacket, lady," he said, and went to take his jacket, folded carefully on the back of the chair. And at the door, his back to her, he turned around with a carefully planned motion that made itself out to be spontaneous. "If lady want I stay now."

"Where?" she asked in astonishment.

"With lady," he answered seriously. "Mister of lady no here. Maybe need something . . ." And she, stunned at the very words and frightened that he knew of her husband's absence, wondered if he meant what she thought she had heard. She said, "But you're going to a wedding, aren't you?"

"Going to wedding. But if lady want—I can be here . . ."

After she had locked the door behind him, still staggered by his suggestion, she suddenly noticed: Yoel's scent had emanated from them—the delicate odor of the cologne in the right-hand cabinet next to the mirror. They had used her husband's toiletries, dried themselves on her towels. She gingerly set Udi down in the crib and hurried to the bathroom.

With jerky movements, like a madwoman, she gathered up the towels and threw them all, averting her head with a bilious sensation, into the washing machine, throwing the new soap into the garbage pail. She began polishing the faucets and sink and scouring with disinfectant the floor which their bare feet had trod on.

But toward evening a new, tense quiet descended on her. At night, before falling asleep, she remembered how Hassan had held Udi close to his chest and spoken to him in Arabic that sounded like a song; his long fingers, clean for the first time of paint stains; the English he had spoken, sounding like a human language for the first time instead of the broken phrases he knew in Hebrew. Only she preferred to set aside his offer to stay with her and not think about it. She thought back, realizing she had been hard on them. They had gone to a wedding in Tulkarem. Maybe they had asked for money to buy a present for the newlyweds, and she had reacted unfeelingly. The unease that gripped her was assuaged when she promised herself that early the next morning she would take Udi in his carriage and go out to the main street and, in the elegant store that had recently opened, buy clothes for his two children. Then she thought: It would not be right to offer him a gift, as if declaring a special relationship, and not to honor his cousins. Generously she decided she would buy something for them as well. Maybe men's cologne like the kind Yoel kept on his shelf. If the weather was stormy, she'd take Udi in the car. An hour later, she suddenly interrupted herself as she read: if it rained hard, she'd leave Udi at the baby-sitter's.

She waited for them until noon, their gifts in pretty wrapping paper, tied with curling ribbon, lying on the cabinet next to the front door, and the white envelope with their money next to the packages.

AT NOON SHE began to worry: maybe they had drunk too much and had an accident. What if the police came? She panicked. Maybe it wasn't legal for her to employ them. If they were badly injured and couldn't continue the job, the construction would be delayed and maybe not completed by the time Yoel returned. In the afternoon, tired and angry at her helplessness and her concern about the future, she decided to go to the building where David was working. Maybe some members of the same family were working for him, and they too had been invited to the wedding in Tulkarem, and she could find out something from them. For a long time she waited for David, pushing the carriage back and forth on the battered pavement in front of the building site. When he came, he told her that the wedding hadn't been in Tulkarem at all, but in a village near the Lebanese border. Two of his own workers went with them in the orange pickup truck. They would be coming as usual the next day, he reassured her, seeing her worried face. Afterward he scratched the nape of his neck and asked, "So it's okay, the job they're doing?'

"I hope so," she said.

"What are they doing now?"

"They're setting up the iron rods to pour the concrete."

"Are they doing it right?"

"I don't know. I am relying on them."

"Today I'll come and have a look."

THE NEXT DAY, anger making her fingertips tremble, so agitated her breathing was affected, she waited for them on the roof in the morning after leaving Udi with the baby-sitter and arranging to do so again during the coming days. Hassan got out of the cab and smiled brightly at her. With his filthy woolen cap and his shoes down at the heel he was once again what he had been.

"Something happen, lady?" His voice betrayed his surprise at finding her on the roof at that early hour.

"A great deal has happened," she shouted at him, leaning over the wall at the edge of the roof.

"What's the matter, lady?" he asked, climbing the ladder on his way up to her.

"First of all, you lied to me."

"Lied?" The shadow of his smile was erased.

"The wedding was in Tulkarem?" She flung out the words, her hand on her hips, like a mother arguing with a child caught out in a lie.

"No lady. Wedding not in Tulkarem."

"That's what you told me."

"I said my aunt from Tulkarem. The wedding not. There is village near Kibuss."

He turned to face his comrades, as though asking, and Ahmad said, "Kibuss Ga'aton."

"Ga'aton," Hassan repeated the name of the kibbutz, looking at her again.

"But you didn't say you wouldn't come to work yesterday."

"We think sleep in Tulkarem and come work yesterday. No possible."

"That's one thing," she ignored the explanation. "Another thing, David was here yesterday and he said you didn't do anything well.

You didn't raise the concrete band two centimeters the way we said. And you put in number-eight iron rods instead of number twelve, and you made one wall with fifteen-centimeter blocks instead of twenty centimeters . . ."

"That wall has window, lady. Must be little."

"You need a number-three block near the sliding window," she exploded at his effort to fool her. "But it is an outer wall. You were supposed to use twenty-centimeter blocks," she added, berating him, watching how the color ebbed from his face, and how his comrades froze behind him.

"We do everything good. Lady want—David come here. We talk."

"I don't want you to talk!" she screamed. "I want you to work. You've been working for a month. What you've done could have been done in a week. You just drink coffee, disappear, and work somewhere else."

"Somewhere else?" he asked in amazement.

"On Monday. Where were you?"

He wrinkled his forehead in thought. "Monday we bring iron."

"Fine," she said, raising her chin and walking forward with vigor, sitting on the edge of the wall. "I want to see how much you get done today."

For seven hours she sat on the wall, without moving, not going down to turn off the water heater she had lit in the morning, suppressing the hunger that rose within her, the need for a cup of coffee at the hour when her body was used to one, and, in the afternoon, fighting the pain in her back, which cried out for something to lean on, watching as they worked angrily, talking little, boiling water in an empty can on the camping stove she'd lent them, sitting down to eat with their legs crossed, close to each other, whispering to each other. All those hours she watched them as though riveted to the spot, only occasionally looking away from them, allowing her eyes to wander to the tops of the cypress trees and the purple mountains in the distance, the view of which, at a peaceful time, she would usually enjoy. Later, when she recalled that morning, she would tremble as though the event were not irrevocably in the past: How had she had the courage to treat them that way? They could easily have come and pushed her, and she would have fallen and broken her neck. By the time anyone found her among the iron rods in the backyard, she would no longer be alive.

Occasionally Ahmad cast a glance at her, like a fearful child check-ing to see whether the ghost he had seen was still hovering in the vicin-ity. But Hassan didn't look at her once. Seeing him, his clamped lips, and the line drawn along his jaw above his clenched teeth, she knew she had deeply hurt him, but she felt no remorse for doing so—only the sweet consolation of someone who deals justly with herself, an over-whelming feeling that rose and fell within her.

They raised the iron rods over the edge of the masonry walls and laid them crosswise at regular intervals, tying them with thin wire. Afterward they crowded steel struts into the room to support the wooden boards under the netting. When they had finished and consulted among themselves for a moment, they headed for the ladder, bidding her good-bye with a slight nod.

"Wait," she called to them. "You've earned your money." She fol-lowed them down the ladder and went into the house. When she came out, she put the envelope in Hassan's hand. Only after they had left without a word did she remember that she hadn't asked them to sign a receipt for the money, nor had she given them the wrapped parcels from the cupboard.

The next day, after leaving Udi with the baby-sitter despite a red-dish rash on his skin indicating that his diaper hadn't been changed in time, she was already waiting for them on the roof as though spoil-ing for a fight. Today, she thought, excited at the idea, they'll pour the concrete for the roof. The network of iron rods was prepared and the steel struts were in place. The wooden forms were raised, the buck-ets of gravel and sand were covered under plastic sheets, and the sacks of cement were arranged next to them. Today they would pour the roof, and the weather was fine. The transparent clouds didn't herald rain.

When she heard the sound of the pickup truck and leaped to the edge of the roof, it seemed that even before she could actually see them she had noticed his absence. Three men sat in the cab, but he wasn't one of them. Salah and Ahmad got out of the left door, wearing gray woolen hats. Then a man with a shaven head got out of the truck, look-ing like a fugitive she had seen in an Italian movie, who had made his way to a widow's home in a village and laid siege to it. In one glance she took in his black eyes, like the maw of a coal mine, his eyebrows meeting over the bridge of his nose. The strange feeling of an unpopular girl overcame her, like when all her girlfriends had been asked to dance, and she was left alone sitting by the wall, gazing at the legs moving in the dark.

"Where's Hassan?" she asked Ahmad.

"Hassan no come. This one come, Muhammad."

Observing them from her corner on the wall, trying to repress the desolate feeling that grew ever stronger within her, she watched them put on rubber boots and mix the cement with shovels, adding sand and gravel and pouring water, stirring it to produce a thick gray mixture in the square they had enclosed with wooden beams. Then Muhammad climbed up to the edge of the roof. Ahmad handed him bucket after bucket brimming with the gray concrete, and he swung and emptied them in big arcs over the network of iron rods, while Salah quickly filled in the space between the two wooden planks below, to stop the concrete from dribbling out.

Sitting erect on the edge of the roof, her knee swinging, her arms folded, she felt her disappointment give way to anger at Hassan's absence. Suddenly it became clear to her that he had come between her and them, serving as a kind of protective barrier from them. Here she stood exposed before the three of them: Salah stole furtive glances at her, as though already hatching a foul plot in his mind; Ahmad smiled directly at her, baring his yellow teeth like the fangs of a beast; and the new worker, standing high on the upper concrete band, his body tense, his hands on his hips, ogled her openly. From where she sat his figure looked frightening, and his shaven head resembled a crooked egg against the background of the sky above him.

She sat where she was for hours, not because of the anger that had gripped her the previous morning, which had made her decide to sit and see with her own eyes how well they would work under supervision, but rather out of fear to get up and raise her legs over the edge of the roof in front of them. They worked without stopping, diligently, bringing up the contents of the big pool of concrete and spreading it on the network of rods. From time to time they would confer with each other, exchange shouts in Arabic, sing a line or two, laughing out loud into their hands. And she, sensing they were laughing at her, was angry, insulted, and fearful. She watched them cook their meal, kneeling next to each other on the torn mat, tearing with their teeth at loaves of bread they held in their hands.

"What now?" She turned to Ahmad, keeping her voice steady.

"Now must dry."

"If it rains?"

"Two hours—good. Not two hours—no good."

"The roof is twenty centimeters?"

"Yes, yes," he said, and she thought that since the morning she hadn't heard them say "lady." She turned, pointed at the floor they had left spotted with cement. "Wash that down before it dries," she ordered, pretending she still had power.

"No dry. We put water."

She stepped to the edge of the protruding ladder and grasped the wooden rung and, as though incidentally, turned to them, "What's the matter with Hassan?"

"Hassan no come."

"I see that."

"This one Muhammad come."

"Will Hassan come tomorrow?"

"Tomorrow, tomorrow, tomorrow—Hassan no come."

"Did something happen to him?"

"He not here."

She carefully raised her legs, and when she had descended, even before her feet touched the ground, she heard their deep, guttural laugh, and she blushed. That was how men laughed at a woman when they spoke ill of her.

The next day, waiting at the window, she knew why her legs had taken her there, why she had arisen early to prepare the kitchen, why she had checked how much coffee was left in the bag he had brought with him from home.

Salah and Ahmad came alone. She, knowing in her heart she wouldn't see Hassan again, was glad the shaven-headed Muhammad wasn't with them. Swallowing her pride she went out and stood before them.

"Is Hassan sick?" she asked.

"No sick."

"He won't come to work?"

"He work someone."

"Why isn't he working here? Three will finish faster."

Salah, perhaps seeing through her deceptive sentences, smiled somewhere in the depths of his eyes, the mockery of someone careful not to be tripped up.

"He no want come to lady."

"He doesn't want to work here?"

"No want," said Salah, and she imagined she heard an echo of triumph in his voice.

"He doesn't want to get his money?"

"No want money, no want lady," he said. She no longer had anything to say after that sentence, but she spoke in her normal voice: "Very well, then finish by yourselves. You can make coffee in the kitchen if you want. There's still some of the coffee you brought."

Salah and Ahmad kept coming for a few more days after the concrete on the roof had dried, removing the steel struts that had held up the forms. They put in the door and bars over the window and broke through the upper room into the breakfast nook. She didn't ask about Hassan again, but they sometimes volunteered that they had seen him. She, stirred by the sound of his name, gave in to them and made the final payment before they had completed the work. Perhaps they would run into Hassan and tell him of her generosity. But they never came back. They left the walls unplastered and forgot their tools behind the wall. Shaken with fury, again pushing her baby carriage, she roamed among the construction sites and hired workers to finish the plastering, the tarring of the roof, and the installation of the electric wiring.

BY THE TIME Yoel returned she had a new hairstyle. The stairs had been installed, leading to the bright, pleasant room on the roof, with three barrels in the corners from which palm trees sent up sharp bayonets all about, their fronds growing like a magic trick. He stood in amazement before the new structure and then burst out laughing. "Well, I'll be . . . You leave a woman for two months, come back—and the world's changed!" On the roof, his arm around her shoulder in a gesture of respect, he wandered from one corner of the roof to another, inspecting the landscape and sliding his hand along the walls: "I didn't want to do it, I confess, but it's really nice. Was it very messy?"

"Not so terrible."

"You found good workers?"

Stroking the rough wall unconsciously, she said, "They were relatively decent, workers from the territories."

"What, Arabs?" he asked, looked at her reproachfully, turning solemn.

"Arabs. You can't find anyone else. But every day a Jewish foreman came to keep an eye on them, the one working in the building at Herzl Street."

"They behaved all right? They didn't make trouble?"

She took a quick, deep breath, with a whistling sound, and, restraining the whirlpool of emotions stirring within her, looked away, clearly seeing Muhammad standing on the edge of the upper roof, staring at her with hatred, and the flash in their eyes when she got up and stood in this very place and accused them; seeing Hassan's fists clench and the crease along the line of his jaw when he clamped his teeth shut, hearing the rumble of the men's laughter when she raised her legs to climb down the ladder. "They were fairly decent. Once Udi fell down and I was really alarmed. One of them picked him up so very gently and calmed him down, you wouldn't have believed it. He spoke to him softly and kissed his fingers. Then it turned out he had studied medicine for two years. He wanted to be a pediatrician but for some reason he didn't finish his degree. He has a baby Udi's age and another boy of four . . ." Suddenly she noticed the softness flowing into her voice, betraying herself to herself, and she added loudly, more stridently than she intended, "But once they made some trouble about the money and tried to trick me by putting in iron rods that were too thin. Arabs, you know . . ."

Translated from the Hebrew by Jeffrey M. Green

Apples from the Desert

ALL THE WAY from the Orthodox quarter of Sha'arei Hesed in Jerusalem to the great stretch of sand where the driver called out "Neve Midbar" and searched for her in his rearview mirror, Victoria Abravanel—her heart pounding and her fists clenched—had only one thing on her mind. She took some bread in brown paper and an apple with a rotten core out of her string bag and adjoined the blessing on the fruit to the prayer for travel, as prescribed. Her eyes were fixed on the yellowing landscape spread out in front of her—and her heart was fixed on her rebellious daughter Rivka, who had left the Orthodox neighborhood six months earlier and gone to live on a kibbutz of secular Jews. Now Victoria had found out from her sister Sara that Rivka was sharing a room with a boy, sleeping in his bed and living as his wife.

All through the eight-hour trip, she pondered how she would behave when she was face to face with her daughter: maybe she would cajole her as if she weren't angry with her, teach her about a girl's honor in a man's eyes, explain sensitive issues, one woman to another. Or maybe she would start out with cries of despair, shout out her grief, the disgrace that Rivka had brought down on their noble family, shriek like a bereaved mourner until the neighbors heard. Or maybe she would perform her mission stealthily, draw her daughter away from there with false news and then put her in her room under lock and key and obliterate all trace of her. Or maybe she would terrify her, tell her about

Flora, Yosef Elalouf's daughter, who fell in love with some boy, gave up her virginity for him, and then he deserted her, so she lost her mind and wandered around the streets, pulling little children by the ear.

On the road from Beersheva, she came up with something new: she would attack the boy with her nails, rip off his skin and poke out his eyes for what he had done to this change-of-life daughter of hers. Her daughter would come back to Jerusalem with her, which was what she promised her sister: "I'll bring her back even if I have to drag her by the hair."

From her sister Sara, Victoria already knew that her daughter was sixteen when she met him. He was an army officer and was brought in to tell them about military service for Orthodox girls. Later on there was a fuss about letting people from the army come and poison the girls' hearts, but the venom had already worked on Rivka. Cunningly, he'd sent her letters through a friend even after he had returned to his kibbutz. And she, the fool, who was known for neither grace nor beauty—even when she was a baby, people would mistake her for a boy—she fell for it, and when she was eighteen she picked up and went to him in the desert.

The further Victoria got from Beersheva, the more her heroic spirit deserted her and the pictures in her imagination made her sigh. What if Rivka turned her back on her and threw her out? What if the boy raised his hand to strike her? How would she spend the night if they locked her out and the bus didn't leave till the next morning? What if they didn't get her message? She didn't know anything about traveling, hadn't been outside of the neighborhood since the barren Shifra Ben-Sasson of Tiberias gave birth four years ago.

But when the driver called out "Neve Midbar" again and found her in his mirror, she got off the bus, pulling her basket behind her. She stood there in the sand, the dry wind striking her throat. How could you leave the pure air and beautiful mountains of Jerusalem—and come here?

By the time she came to a path and found a woman to ask about Rivka, rivulets of sweat were streaming from her kerchief. Victoria plodded on, looking dizzily at a woman whose arms were laden with rows of pots, one inside the other, her bare legs in men's shoes and folded army socks. Coming toward them on the opposite path was a girl, also wearing pants, whose hair was cropped short. "Here's Rivka," said the woman. Just as Victoria was about to say, "That's not the one I meant," she recognized her daughter and burst into a shout that resounded like a sob. The girl put down the laundry basket she was carrying and ran to her, her head thrust forward and her eyes weeping.

"What's this . . . what's this . . . ?" Victoria scratched her nose. "Where are your braids? And those pants . . . that's how you dress . . . oy vey!" Rivka laughed: "I knew that's what you'd say. I wanted to get dressed but I didn't have time. I thought you'd come on the four o'clock bus. When did you leave home? Six? Come on. Enough of this crying. Here's our room. And here's Dubi."

Stunned by the short hair, the frayed trousers with patches on the back, and the shoes spotted with chicken droppings, Victoria found herself squeezed in two big arms, a fair face close to hers, and a male voice said, "Hello, Mother." Her basket was already in his hand and she—not understanding herself, her hands suddenly light—was drawn after her daughter into a shaded room and seated on a chair. At once there was a glass of juice in her hand; her eyes looked but didn't know what they saw, and later on she'd remember only the double bed covered with a patchwork quilt and the voice of the giant with golden hair saying "Welcome, Mother." And as soon as she heard him say "mother" again, very clearly, she swallowed some juice that went down the wrong way and started choking and coughing. The two of them rushed to her and started pounding her on the back like a child.

"Leave me alone," she said weakly and pushed them away. "Let me look at you," she said after a moment. Once again she scolded Rivka: "What is this, those pants? Those are your Sabbath shoes?" Rivka laughed, "I'm working in the chicken coop this week. They brought in new hens. I usually work in the vegetable garden. Just this week in the chicken coop."

Weary from the journey, confused by what she was seeing, shaken by the vicissitudes of the day, and straining to repress her rage, which was getting away from her in spite of herself—and always remembering her mission—Victoria sat down with her daughter Rivka and talked with her as she had never talked with her children before in her life. She didn't remember what she said and she didn't remember when the boy who called her mother left, but her eyes saw and knew: her daughter's face looked good. Not since Rivka was a little girl had she seen her eyes sparkle like this. Even her short hair, Victoria admitted to herself, made her look pretty. Not like when she wore a skirt and stockings, with her broad shoulders, as if she were a man dressed up in women's clothes.

"You don't miss the neighborhood?"

"Sometimes. On holidays. I miss the Sabbath table and the songs and Aunt Sara's laugh. But I like it here. I love working outside with the animals . . . You, too, I miss you a lot."

"And Papa?" Victoria asked in a whisper into the evening light filtering in.

"Papa doesn't care about anybody. Especially not me. All day long in the store and with his books and prayers. Like I'm not his daughter."

"God forbid! Don't say such a thing," Victoria was scared—of the truth.

"He wanted to marry me off to Yekutiel's son. Like I was a widow or a cripple."

"Really?"

"Don't play games with me. As if you didn't know."

"They talked. You heard. We don't make forced matches. And anyway, Yekutiel's son is a genius."

"A pale, sick genius, like he sits in a pit all day long. And anyway, I don't love him."

"What do you think? You think love is everything?"

"What do you know about love?"

"What does that mean?" Victoria was offended and sat up straight. "This is how you talk to your mother around here?"

"You didn't love Papa and he didn't love you." Rivka ignored her and went on in the silence that descended: "I, at home . . . I wasn't worth much."

"And here?" Victoria asked in a whisper.

"More."

A question began to take shape in Victoria's mind about Dubi, the fair-haired giant, but the door opened, a light suddenly came on, and he himself said, "Great that you're saving electricity. I brought something to eat. Yogurt and vegetables on a new plastic plate. That's okay, isn't it? Then, Rivka, you should take Mother to Osnat's room. It's empty. She must be tired."

In the room that led out to the darkening fields, Victoria tried to get things straight in her heart. But years of dreariness had dulled her edge and yet she already knew: she wouldn't bring her daughter back to Jerusalem by her hair.

"Why did it take you half a year to come here?" Rivka asked.

"Your papa didn't want me to come."

"And you, you don't have a will of your own?" Victoria had no answer.

When Dubi came to take her to the dining hall, she poured all her rage on him, and yet she was drawn to him, which only served to increase her wrath.

"What's this 'Dubi'? What kind of name is that?" Anger pulled words out of her mouth.

"It's Dov, after my mother's father. The Germans killed him in the war."

"That's a good name for a baby, Dov?" She hardened her heart against him.

"I don't mind." He shrugged, and then stopped and said with comic seriousness, "But if you do—I'll change it tomorrow." She strained to keep from laughing.

In the evening, the two of them sat at the table with their eyes on Rivka as if she were all alone in the big hall, while she made the rounds with a serving cart, asking people what they wanted.

"You want something else to drink, Mother?" she heard him ask. She queried angrily, "You call me 'Mother.' What kind of mother am I to you?"

"I'm dying for you to be my mother."

"Really? So, who's stopping you?" she asked, and her sister Sara's mischievousness crept into her voice.

"Your daughter."

"How is she stopping you?"

"She doesn't want to be my wife."

"My daughter doesn't want to get married. That's what you're telling me?"

"Exactly."

As she was struggling with what he had said, he started telling her about the apple orchard he was growing. An American scientist who grew apples in the Nevada desert had sent him special seeds. You plant them in tin cans full of organic fertilizer and they grow into trees as high as a baby, with little roots, and sometimes they produce fruit in the summer like a tree in the Garden of Eden. "Apples love the cold," he explained as their eyes wandered after Rivka, "and at night, you have to open the plastic sheets and let the desert cold in. At dawn, you have to close the sheets to preserve the cold air and keep the heat out."

"Really," she muttered, hearing these words now and thinking about what he had said before. Meanwhile, somebody came to her and said, "You're Rivka's mother? Congratulations on such a daughter." And suddenly her heart swelled within her.

Then she remembered something that resurfaced from distant days and dimensions. She was fifteen years old. On Saturdays in the synagogue, she used to exchange glances with Moshe Elkayam, the goldsmith's son, and then she would lower her eyes to the floor. In the women's section, she would push up to the wooden lattice to see his hands that worked with silver and gold and precious stones. Something grew between them without any words, and his sister would smile at her in the street. But when the matchmaker came to talk to her about Shaul Abravanel, she didn't dare hurt her father, who wanted a scholar for a son-in-law.

At night, when Rivka took her back to her room, she asked, "You came to take me back to Jerusalem, didn't you?"

Her mother chose not to answer. After a pause she said, apropos of nothing, "Don't do anything dumb."

"I know what I want."

"Your aunt also knew when she was your age. Look at the kind of life she has now. Goes from house to house like a cat."

"Don't worry about me."

Victoria plucked up her courage: "Is it true what he told me, that you don't want to marry him?"

"That's what he told you?"

"Yes or no?"

"Yes."

"Why?"

"I'm not sure yet."

"Where did you learn that."

"From you."

"How?" Victoria was amazed.

"I don't want to live like you and Papa."

"How?"

"Without love."

"Again love!" She beat her thighs with her palms until they trembled—a gesture of rage without the rage. They reached the door. Victoria thought a moment about the bed with patchwork quilt and heard herself asking, "And the special bedtime prayer, do you say that?"

"No."

"You don't say the prayer?"

"Only sometimes, silently. So even I don't hear it myself," said Rivka. She laughed and kissed her mother on the cheek. Then she said: "Don't get scared if you hear jackals. Good night." Like a mother soothing her child.

Facing the bare sand dunes stretching soft lines within the window frame, as into the frame of a picture, Victoria said a fervent prayer, for both of them, her and Rivka. Her heart was both heavy and light, ". . . Let not my thoughts trouble me, nor evil dreams, nor evil fancies, but let my rest be perfect before Thee . . ."

And at night she dreamed.

In the dream a man approaches a white curtain and she sees him from behind. The man moves the curtain aside and the trees of the Garden of Eden are in front of him: the Tree of Life and the Tree of Knowledge and beautiful trees in cans of organic fertilizer. The man goes to the apple tree, laden with fruit, and the fruit drops off and rolls into his hands and, suddenly, the fruit is small and turns into stones. And Victoria sees handfuls of precious stones and gold and silver in his white fingers. Suddenly the man turns around, and it's Moshe Elkayam, the goldsmith's son, and his hair is in flames.

All the way back to Sha'arei Hesed she sat, her eyes still clutching at their rage but her heart already reconciled, her basket at her feet and, on her lap, a sack of apples hard as stones that Dubi gave her. She remembered her daughter asking, "You see that everything's fine, right?"—her fingers on her mother's cheek; and Dubi's voice saying, "It'll be fine, Mother."

All the way, she pondered what she would tell her husband and her sister. Maybe she would sit them down and tell them exactly what happened to her. When the bus passed the junction, she considered it. How could she describe to her sister, who had never known a man, or to her husband, who had never touched her with love—how could she describe the boy's eyes on her daughter's face? When the mountains of Jerusalem appeared in the distance, she knew what she would do.

From her sister, who could read her mind, she wouldn't keep a secret. She'd pull her kerchief aside, put her mouth up to her ear, like when they were children, and whisper, "Sarike, we've spent our lives alone, you without a husband and me with one. My little daughter taught me something. And us, remember how we thought she was a bit backward, God forbid? How I used to cry over her? No beauty, no grace, no intelligence or talent, and as tall as Og, King of Bashan. He wanted to marry her off to Yekutiel and they were doing us a favor, like Abravanel's daughter wasn't good enough for them. Just look at her now." Here she would turn her face to the side and spit spiritedly against the evil eye. "Milk and honey. Smart, too. And laughing all the time. Maybe, with God's help, we'll see joy from her."

And to her husband, who never read her heart, she would give apples in honey, put both hands on her hips and say, "We don't have to worry about Rivka. She's happy there, thank God. We'll hear good tidings from her soon. Now, taste that and tell me: apples that bloom in summer and are put in organic fertilizer and their roots stay small—did you ever hear of such a thing in your life?"

Translated from the Hebrew by Barbara Harshav

A Married Woman

ONLY WHEN THE divorce bill lay in her hand did Hannah Rabinsky remove her wedding picture from the wall next to her bed. Throughout the years that she and her daughter had been in and out of the Rabbinical courts, she and Moshe had been standing arm in arm above the well-polished German chest of drawers. He, erect and festive, eyes looking straight into the camera, and she, huddling into his tall shoulder, her eyes beaming. Now, while polishing the glass prior to putting the photograph in her closet, she suddenly stared at it as if seeing it for the first time. The bridal veil, borrowed from the photographer, may have looked like a veil from the front, with pretty beads on top and a lacy ribbon tying its edges, but from behind, hidden from the camera's eye, it had two unseemly threads dangling down her nape. The wedding gown she was wearing had been purchased by Moshe from a Polish noblewoman who sold her wardrobe for dollars right after the war. Looking at her straight shoulders, Hannah remembered how proud she had been of her handsome bridegroom and her fine dress. Two years later she had her picture taken in the very same dress by another photographer, this time on Allenby Road in Tel Aviv, with a baby in her arms, her swollen breasts protruding from between the buttons. The shadow in her eyes betrays the fact that nothing is hidden from them anymore.

As she was polishing the glass that covered her face, a sadness suddenly overcame her, for she had been so young then, so full of dreams, so grateful for the new world that suddenly greeted her with such warmth, and so trustful of the handsome man at her side.

"That's it, then," she said softly, like a weary traveler yearning to rest after a long journey.

"The hell it is," Pnina shot at her. Her back facing the backyard, leaning both elbows on the window sill, she glared at her mother. "You should've kicked him out of here, not given him a room to stay in, let alone the largest room in the house. This is not a divorce, this is a joke. You think you're through with him? You'll hear from him soon enough. I bet you anything he'll pretend to be sick," and her foot aimed a kick in the air toward the wall of the adjacent room.

Even without looking at her daughter's face, Hannah knew what expression it wore: two lines drawn from her nostrils to her chin, and her brow angrily furrowed. She was only eighteen, but her face was the face of a weary, miserable person. Since the day this kicking and screaming baby had emerged from her womb, Hannah tried in vain to appease her implacable spirit. "I can't throw him out now," she said softly, her face turned to her face in the photo. She saw him for the first time in the central railway station of Warsaw. He was tall and pellucid, like a stained glass figure in a church. The place teemed with shadows, and trains the color of ashes were spewing refugees onto the platforms. Some slumped by the walls, never to rise again. Others milled around in the crowd looking for lost relatives. Several survivors from the town of Sosnow gathered in an apartment near the station, which formerly served as the office of the Polish Ministry of Transportation. He addressed her by someone else's name and then led her to the apartment. And she followed him as if she had already foretold her future. In the apartment she made the acquaintance of the others. They spent the following days there like a colony of lepers. They were tongue-tied; sentences tumbled out of their mouths tortuously. From time to time, they would grope toward each other, trying, like children, to learn anew the language of a world that had been recreated for them. They were cautious with words, sensing how their wounds gape at the sound of voices, at the touch of a hand, at the blowing of the wind. And then, as if in reversal, people clung to each other as the blind do. Every night they had a wedding, attended by all their dead. It happened on Avram and Bina's wedding night. Moshe was sitting on a blanket he had spread on the floor, surrounded by people. Hannah was seated in the back, and she could not take her eyes off him the entire evening. His back was bent, his shoulders protruded as his arms clasped around his knees, and his neck and forearms looked as thin as a boy's who had undergone a sudden spurt of growth. Tremendous compassion and loving kindness impelled her to touch his back gently, to quell in him the overpowering sense of despair. Then he suddenly turned back and his laughing mouth asked, "Shall we get married?"

"I can't throw him out," she told her daughter again. "He's been living here almost eighteen years. Where can he go now?"

"All those places he used to go until now. Where did he spend the nights when he didn't sleep at home? Let him go to his women, to his drunken buddies, to his card games."

Everywhere, from Warsaw to Tel Aviv, women were attracted to him like butterflies, and with them the boozers and the cardsharps. Even when times were hard, his eyes were always smiling, his collar smelled nice, his cuffs were shining white, and his pocket always carried chocolate. When they settled in their two-room apartment in Tel Aviv, he showed no great alacrity in looking for a job. In the morning he would take a long time shaving, then go to the employment office, offer candy to the clerk, and sit there joking with him. But he never found a suitable job. A month after their arrival in Tel Aviv, after she had sold the necklace Moshe had given her as wedding present, Hannah found herself a position in a large shoe shop on King George Street, and from then on supported the family.

Whenever Moshe got lucky in his card games or in the wheeling and dealing whose nature she never discovered, he would show up like a bridegroom, bouquet in hand. On other occasions, he would rummage in her purse and take her cash.

On Saturday afternoons, after having spent the whole morning cleaning the house, Hannah would wash, dab her earlobes with perfume from a tiny vial she had brought from Poland, put on a blue dress with shoulder pads, lace collar, and pearl buttons, and go out for a walk in the streets with her shining husband and their little girl. People would turn their heads to gaze at them. Women would dart sideways glances at him, and his smiling eyes glimmered. But at other times, her mouth would be covered with the palm of her hand, so that the child would not hear her mother crying. On his return in the morning, after the first few nights he was absent from home, he found her pale and bleary-eyed. He always had a well-prepared and detailed story. Later, he dropped the excuses, and she did not want to hear them. He would come back after three nights' absence, his eyes bloodshot, his cheeks unshaven. In his sleep he called out strange women's names: Sylvana, Adela. The first time she was alarmed. She sat up all night on the edge of the bed deliberating what course to take. In the morning she saw him huddling against her in his sleep, his tattooed arm stretched over her brow, and suddenly she realized that this was her fate. She must spend her life with this man, and she was greatly relieved.

"I want to tell you something about those women, Pninele. What you see is not always the true story. It's true he likes women, but it's their fault. They cling to him, and he's the type who can't say no. People think he's so tall and handsome. A strong man. But the truth is, he's weak. I was the strong one. Always."

By the window, Pnina tilted her head to her bent shoulder, darted a quizzical look at her mother and said, "Well, if we're talking like grown-ups, then I think you're still in love with him. Honestly."

"And I can never understand why you hate him so much. Ever since you were a baby."

"I hate him because I know him."

And Hannah remembered. Right before Pnina's fifth birthday, at the breakfast table, Moshe asked, "What shall I get my prettiest princess for her birthday?" He said the word *princess* in Yiddish.

Without raising her eyes to him, Pnina said in a high, firm voice, "A bicycle."

Hannah was dumbfounded, wondering in her heart where the little girl had learned to express such determination so icily, poker-faced. "This is too much to ask, Pninele . . ." she started.

"No," Moshe stopped her, one hand stretched forward, the other pointing to the ceiling, as if on a theater stage. "Whatever my princess wants, my princess gets."

"But you know how much a bicycle costs," she said to him, then turned to Pnina. "Maybe a doll or a skirt . . ."

"A bicycle," the girl announced calmly.

"A bicycle is out of the question. It's too much money . . ."

"Enough, enough." His face contorted in disgust, as if he were tired of the argument. "A bicycle and that's it. No doll and no nonsense."

When he had left, she looked at her daughter sipping her tea, so erect and self-confident, and was terrified by her feeling of alienation from the girl.

"You shouldn't have asked for a bicycle, Pninele. You're a big girl now, and you understand that a bicycle is very expensive and we are not rich. You go with me to the grocery store, don't you? You hear me buy on credit, and Nissim does me a big favor, and I feel ashamed."

Pnina met her gaze and said, "He won't get it anyway."

They waited for him for two days. On the third evening, Hannah baked a cake, then watched the girl blow powerfully on the six flames, her eyes dry. Rosa, the neighbor from whom they had borrowed the candles, stationed herself at the doorway and said, "Bravo, bravo, what a strong girl."

Now Pnina was staring at her mother and the two furrows leading downward from her nostrils deepened. "Just don't tell me you regret the whole thing."

Hannah stroked the wedding picture with her palm and put it in a drawer. "What is there to say? It's over. I regret or I don't regret, what difference does it make?"

"You should have done it fifteen years ago. You didn't need him. You supported him."

"I didn't want to."

"Maybe you don't want to now, either."

When he faced the Rabbis, Moshe's visage was like that of a child who doesn't know what wrong he has done. His eyes, fixed on the beautiful fingers of his hands, were raised from time to time to meet her eyes, as if refusing to believe that the person he had trusted most in the world would thus betray him. "You are all I have," he repeated in front of the strangers; she could not restrain herself and started to cry.

And here Pnina addresses her in a harsh voice, "Admit that you didn't want a divorce."

"I admit it."

"Then why did you divorce him?"

"Because I had no choice. You're stronger than I am. Stronger than both of us."

Pnina, at sixteen, burst into a shoe shop and, in front of the owner's wife, lashed out at her mother's flushed face. "You think that you're kind and forgiving and that people don't know? Everybody knows! They're laughing. Laughing to your face and you don't see it. She's fourteen, maybe. Following him with that big belly. Her parents kicked her out of the house and he drops her here, drops her there. Soon she'll run after him with a baby in her arms. But he needn't worry. He doesn't give a damn! Whenever he feels like it, he can go home, where a nice woman awaits him, makes him the food he likes, irons his shirts, works like a horse for him. And pretends not to know anything. If she is a little suspicious or has an inkling of an idea, she forgives him right away. You can stay with him. I'll be leaving soon enough."

Rosa, the neighbor, pail in hand, passes her on the path to the garbage shed. She calls out her name, but Pnina does not respond.

"This whole arrangement isn't worth a thing. Now he has even more freedom. He's divorced and is entitled to come and go whenever he wants. And when he comes back, you'll rush to cook and wash for him. So why did we even bother?" After a short silence she added, "But if that's what you want, go ahead. I have done my part. Now I have to go because my ride to the kibbutz leaves in half an hour."

That's it, Hannah said to herself, watching Pnina's back receding down the path, kicking the myrtle bushes with the tips of her shoes along the way. The marriage wasn't really a marriage and the divorce won't really be a divorce. You have done your part. You wanted to do it since you were a little girl. You did it out of your strange love for me and your hatred of him. And to alleviate the hurt inside yourself, too. Who knows. Maybe it's my fault: there were many things I didn't explain to you. You said that I forgive easily. I forgive you, too.

Suddenly, a coughing sound erupted from the adjacent room, and Hannah tensed up, like someone hearing secret signals unintelligible to anyone else. Years ago, the Greek porter brought him to the door, and Moshe collapsed on the doorstep like a rag doll. All that night his coughing wrenched deeply, bringing forth faint echoes from his frail body. Then came hours of fever and delirium, words were uttered which she could not understand, and names of women from magazines: Clara, Suzanna, and Heidi stalked about the room like evil spirits. Then— as always—came the complete reconciliation and the promises and the good whispers. Now, too, she heard the crackling cough muffled by his fist. In her room, Hannah hurried to collect the divorce papers that Pnina had left on the chest of drawers. Now she'll go and check if there is anything left of the dark medicine that the German pharmacist on Ben Yehuda Street had concocted for him, which had been so beneficial for him in the past. And she'll make sure there are the right ingredients in the kitchen to make him chicken soup and homemade noodles. Honey and warm milk are good for his throat, and she'll also prepare some eggnog. She must rush to buy eggs and honey before Nissim closes the shop and darkness falls.

Translated from the Hebrew by Marganit Weinberger-Rotman

Hayuta's Engagement Party

FIFTEEN DAYS BEFORE Hayuta's engagement party, which was hastily arranged because of the youngsters' unexpected announcement, nobody had thought about the disgrace that Grandpa Mendel might heap on their heads. Everybody was busy with guest lists, musicians, food, drinks, dishes to borrow, neighbors willing to lend chairs and tables, and the presents the prospective bride might desire in case someone asked what to buy. Bella, Hayuta's mother, was appalled at the sight of the house: the stains on the green couch were so conspicuous; the drapes were frayed at the edges; the wallpaper in the dining room showed a faded line where the three chairs used to stand. Thus a list of fine upholstery stores was added to the existing lists, as well as the names of wallpaper experts.

In the middle of all this commotion, Bella suddenly remembered that she had not yet decided on the dress she was going to wear for the occasion. After rummaging through her wardrobe, and having tried on dresses in shops for two days, she came to the conclusion that the success of her dress depended on the style of dress Ran's mother—her daughter's future mother-in-law—was going to wear. She had already heard that the mother was a tall, pretty, well-connected woman. If she herself chose a frilly and elegant dress, Bella reasoned nervously, while her future in-law came in a tailored suit—why, she herself might look provincial while the other looked like a sophisticated woman of the world. On the other hand, if she chose a suit, while her in-law selected an elegant dress, then she would look stodgy and the other, glamorous. The choice of color was also a complicated matter. If she wore red and the in-law black, then she would look vulgar and the other, refined. If she wore black and the other red, why, she would look dreary and the other, lively. Other problematic questions concerned buttons, the length of the hem, and the width of the belt. The more she thought about these matters, the more hopeless they seemed.

Dealing with furniture, clothes, food, and invitations saved Bella from having to think about the cause of all this commotion: Hayuta, almost twenty-three years old, about to finish college, with perfect timing vis-à-vis the approaching autumn, and before wrinkles appeared at the corners of her eyes, managed to find herself a clever and vigorous husband and—so people said—from an educated and well-off family. Perhaps the full meaning of this engagement would only sink in later, after the party, when the guests had left, the band had packed up its instruments, and the hallway had been swept.

After several days of hectic activity, things were falling into place. The chairs and tables had been collected from the neighbors and a way had been found to arrange them in the backyard: the bulk would flank the garden wall, while the side rows would stretch diagonally like two open arms welcoming a child; the middle of the yard would remain empty. A representative of a catering company came and displayed an array of colored photographs featuring different methods of presenting the food.

Following lengthy deliberations, they decided to order the utensils, the meats, and the salads from him and to leave the baking of the cakes to the lady of the house, as that was her forte—this after reaching an understanding regarding the terms of payment. Inside the house, too, work progressed apace, despite the gloomy predictions. For a special fee, the workmen diligently applied themselves to the task. Even though Bella had not been completely happy with the choice of wallpaper, and maintained that the hasty selection produced a pattern that did not go well with the style of the chairs, it looked quite nice when she saw it on the wall. The question of the dress was also resolved. Since her daughter refused to cooperate in spying on her future mother-in-law, Bella hit on an ingenious solution and chose a dress that was both elegant and endearing: a blue suitlike silk dress with raised white piping and a little, pointed white collar.

Only then did she find the time to think about her father, Mendel. By a strange coincidence Hayuta, too, was thinking about him during her final exam in Jewish history. After lunch the two of them were ready to discuss him.

"If he ruins my party, I'll never forgive him, never!" Hayuta said, her mouth full of radish.

"You're right," her mother agreed.

"This isn't just another Seder or holiday meal," Hayuta explained as if facing opposition. "The whole family knows him by now, they know his history, and they forgive him. But Ran's parents don't know him, and his sister and some of their closest friends will be here, too. I don't want them to get the impression that there are strange people in my family. I'm telling you right now that if he does it in front of everybody, I'm just going to drop dead!"

"God forbid," exclaimed Bella, truly distressed. "So what's one to do?"

"We'll have to find some solution." Hayuta searched with her fork among the slices of cucumber, looking for radish rings.

"But we can't very well not invite him," said Bella in the tone of someone arguing with herself. "After all, such an occasion—his first grandchild is getting engaged. This is something very special for him, the dream he's always talking about—a large family. I don't see how we can not invite him. We'll never forgive ourselves afterward. Don't forget, he's already eighty-two. How many more parties like this will he be able to attend? What are we to do? Can we possibly not tell him?"

"We could send him on a trip," said Hayuta pragmatically, having just had a brainstorm. Bella looked at her daughter and shuddered: here she is, already getting rid of him like an unwanted object, with that typical nonchalance that this new generation has. Hayuta had already forgotten how he raised and coddled her, ready to give up his food for her. And all these years, when Bella herself was busy at the plant with her husband, Grandfather—no longer a young man—would take his granddaughter to ballet lessons and art classes, and wait for her patiently outside, rain or shine.

"Perhaps we could talk to him, explain that this time he has to control himself," Bella tried. "After all, he's not senile or anything. On the contrary, he's quite alert."

"Talking's not going to help, and you know it," Hayuta stopped her. "Would you be able to stand the suspense all evening? Just wait and see when he's going to start?"

"I'll convince him, you'll see. I'll explain it to him clearly. I have an idea: we'll seat him next to Shifra; she'll keep an eye on him and shut him up the moment he opens his mouth. Shifra won't let him talk; you can count on her. I think that's a good solution, what do you say?"

"I say I'm going to find out what trips the municipality is organizing for senior citizens. I saw an ad in the paper once. It's better this way, for him and for us."

Monsters, thought Bella in disgust as her daughter went to answer the phone. We are raising monsters. At first they look like babies, then like children, but behind the innocent facade—hearts of stone! I have heard of children throwing their old folks into the streets, waiting for them to die. Just like this—shamelessly to evict Grandfather from your engagement party!

AFTER HAYUTA HAD gone, Bella calmed down and had to admit to herself—there was no doubt about it, he would cause a disaster at the party. In sight of all the food, he just wouldn't be able to help himself. On such occasions, words just gushed from his mouth, beyond his control. In the last few years, the situation had worsened considerably. It seems that in his mind distant memories overcame those of yesterday, as often happens with old people. Up to about six years ago, he was really in good shape. Until then he did not talk about what had happened to him during the war. When he returned from the concentration camp to the house of the Polish peasant with whom he had entrusted his two children for four years, his little daughter Bella only barely recognized him. His face was emaciated, his cheekbones and nose protruding, and his hair was cropped short. At the sight of him the peasant woman crossed herself and said, "Mr. Goldberg, all night I dreamed that you were coming. Your children weren't sick even once! I took care of them as if they were my own!" He bent down and gathered the children in his thin arms; the rancid smell of his body hit them when he said, "We'll forget everything, everything. We'll look for mother and then we'll go to America."

However, they did not find their mother and they did not go to America. Years later he married another woman in Israel, and she raised the children as if they were her own; only when they got sick, she would urge them to get well quickly. Up until six years ago he never said a word about what had happened to him in the war. Once, in his room, she found a memorial book of survivors from a small Polish town, and between the pages, newspaper clippings announcing memorial services. His children never asked him what had happened to him during all those years when they were scrambling and shuffling in pig dung on the peasant woman's farm—as if all of them had vowed to force those memories to oblivion. When his second wife died, years after his grandchildren were born, he refused to live by himself and refused to move in with his children. He arranged a room for himself in an old folks' home. He would spend the Sabbath and holidays with his family, coming and going by bus. He would never let them drive him. He would talk with wit and animation about the economic situation, Russia and America, topical events he read about in the papers. But the war—as if part of him were dormant all these years—he never mentioned.

The change in him, Bella calculated, occurred six years ago. The tables laden with meat, fish, chopped liver, glazed carrots, black plum pudding, triggered something inside him, like a coded message. A secret door to the memories of the war—what had been shrouded in blissful oblivion for decades—suddenly burst open forcefully. It all started on the eve of Rosh Hashana. Around the table laden with food, everyone raised their glasses, and Mordechai, Bella's brother, turned to their father and said, "Dad, now say a blessing for a good year."

The old man turned a little pale; he was already sensing something buckling inside. He raised his glass to the expectant eyes and said in Yiddish: "May we have a happy new year. A year of peace and family bliss and many happy feasts. I want to tell you something—and I'm glad we are all gathered here together and the children are listening. During the war—for four years I did not eat any meat. We all looked like skeletons, you could see every single bone in our bodies. When rumors started to spread that the Americans were coming, the Germans became nervous and we had even less to eat. When we saw a German starting to run, Shloyme Bermanski and I pulled a sausage from his belt. I smelled it once and started to throw up, but Shloyme started eating like a pig. He ate the whole sausage, and half an hour later his eyes bulged and he fell dead, even before the soldiers arrived." Around the table, everybody looked at him, flabbergasted. Bella and her brother exchanged astounded looks. Yehiel, who had come from Netanya with his wife and children, fidgeted uneasily. Shifra, Mordechai's wife, looked around her in disgust, as if an ill omen had been introduced in their midst. The old man, however, oblivious to the silence around him, raised his glass and added, "Let's have a happy new year. And let the children grow—that's the main thing. *Lechayyim!*"

The people echoed *lechayyim* faintly and raised their glasses to their lips. The embarrassment lingered in the air for a while, as often happens when a shock dispels, but as the evening progressed toward the plum dessert, the tension subsided gradually. When the host told a story about a newlywed who, on his honeymoon, went to borrow a newspaper from a neighbor and returned only at dawn—everyone laughed loudly. When dessert was served, the memory of Grandpa Mendel's embarrassing moment had dimmed. Yehiel and his wife started singing in Polish about a girl with a long braid who goes to wash her hair in the river and is watched by a boy behind a blackberry bush who does not dare to declare his love. Perhaps it was the dessert or the mention of the blackberry song, or perhaps something else altogether, but Grandpa Mendel rose to his feet again, lifted his right arm, as he had done earlier when he was holding the wine goblet in his hand, and said, "In the camp, every day two or three people would die in our barracks. We used to drag them to a corner. Those who died during the night were already cold. Those who died in the morning weren't quite so cold. But those who died in the evening had started to smell by morning . . ." Shifra rose to her feet and stood, rebellious, in front of him, and then defiantly left the table and went into the next room. The old man followed her with his eyes and resumed his speech. "Once I found a potato in the pocket of one of them. We used to look in their pockets; we would take sweaters or socks off them. What use are socks to them now? I have no idea how he got that potato. He didn't work in the kitchen. I asked around, but nobody knew. And I couldn't figure it out. Where did he get that potato?"

His son Mordechai tried to shush him. The initial astonishment was over and now he could find words more easily. "Dad, this is a holiday.

We want to celebrate and eat and not remember such things. On holidays one should be reminded of happy things."

"But where did he get that potato, I'm asking you. Maybe you read something; maybe you have an idea."

"No, I don't. Look, Bella is bringing in the cake. Look at that cake! This is a sign that we shall not lack cakes all year!" He bent toward Hayuta, who was then in her senior year of high school, and said to her jocosely, "Isn't that a sign that we shall not lack cakes all year?" But the cloud was already hovering over them; even the children sensed it.

The years that followed hardened their hearts gradually. It became a habit; over the laid tables on Sabbath and holiday eves and birthdays, Grandpa Mendel would tell them about people who dropped dead in the streets of the ghetto and about other passersby who trampled them or robbed them of their shoes or rolled them to the side with their feet and covered them with newspapers. He told them about those who died of starvation, with bloated bellies and sunken eyes; about the man who put an end to his misery by throwing himself on the electric fence and, in a second, became a piece of charcoal; about the man who came to the camp and saw his younger brother hanging on the gate; and about the man who sorted the victims' clothes and found his wife's dress with pearls embroidered on the front, the dress he had bought her when their son was born, and which you couldn't mistake because the hem had torn and was repaired with red thread—and when the German saw him linger over the dress in his hand, he suspected him of trying to steal the pearls and hit him on his neck with a whip; and about the boy who carried the bodies to the crematoriums who found his mother among the dead. They let him talk, blocking his stories from the path to their hearts. Whenever he rose to his feet and lifted his right arm with the goblet in his hand, they knew that the moment had arrived. The children would go out to play; the hostess would start clearing the table so as not to waste time. The others would start whispering or drifting into thought, letting the next few moments pass, like a raging hurricane that would soon blow away, like an airplane that zooms overhead and takes its roar with it.

While other members of the family were resigned to these descriptions of hunger, death, and putrefaction as part of holiday celebrations, his daughter-in-law Shifra rose up against them. "He is ruining my evening," she would complain, knowing full well that her words reached his ears. "We have suffered enough, and we have heard enough. Don't we have Memorial Day and Holocaust Day and commemorative assemblies and what have you? They never let you forget for a minute. So why do I need to be reminded of it at every meal? I don't understand how you can go on eating so heartily when he goes on and on about festering wounds, blood, and vomit—but that's your own business. As for me, the moment he opens his mouth, the holiday is over." And she would slam the table with her fist. Bella, on the other hand, was especially attentive to her father. When preparing a meal in her house, she would listen from the kitchen; when they visited others, she would listen from her seat at the table. Suddenly a window opened for her, a key to the riddle that had haunted her all those years.

Had he erased from his memory everything that had happened to him in the four years she and her brother spent in the pigsty of the Polish peasant? For a few moments she found herself walking in the village roads, smelling the sty as if it were a reality and not a distant memory. She felt the wet snouts of the piglets in the palm of her hand, their skin hardened with mud. Had her father forgotten the death and the fear and the hunger? How would he lock them in his heart and never mention them for forty years? And now, how had his locked memories awakened in him, in the presence of all the abundance and the songs and the conciliatory atmosphere that permeates the illuminated rooms on holidays? It's a psychological mystery, Bella concluded, whose resolution can perhaps be found only at the level at which man is totally denuded—he will take it with him to his grave.

But this time, she admitted to herself, it was a difficult situation. How could they not invite Grandpa to the engagement party of his beloved granddaughter, who was named after his wife, Haya? On the other hand, how could they jeopardize the whole party, perhaps even Hayuta's own future, and cause the family to irrevocably lose face in front of all their guests—and in front of the new in-laws?

Toward evening she hit on another idea and was about to suggest it to her daughter, but Hayuta preempted her by saying, matter-of-factly, "I spoke with Ran. He says we have to invite him."

"Did you explain the problem?"

"Yes. He says it wouldn't be civil not to invite him."

"And what if—"

"I've already spoken to him."

"To Ran?"

"No, to Grandpa."

"You spoke with Grandpa? When?"

"This afternoon."

"And?"

"I explained to him how important it is for me that everything goes smoothly."

"And?"

"He promised he wouldn't say anything except 'lechayyim' and 'all the best.'"

Bella sighed with relief and leaned back in her chair. "I really think this is the best solution. We would have felt awful if we had sent him away on a day like this. Is that what he said? Nothing except 'lechayyim' and 'all the best.' Well, you've got to hand it to your Grandpa, he's certainly got a sense of humor."

"And you've got to hand it to his granddaughter; she knows danger when she sees it. I'm going to stick to him like glue all evening— to be on the safe side."

"Everything will be fine." Bella smiled and touched her chest with a fist. "My heart tells me so."

THE NIGHT OF the party the air was exceptionally pleasant. It was no longer the end of summer, though fall had not yet started—those in-between days of beauty and clarity. Bella, who had finally begun to grasp how momentous the occasion was, was circling like a sleepwalker among the elegant guests, all strolling about with wine glasses in their hands in the soft little halos of light that the round garden lanterns were shedding on the lawn. The rapid flashes of cameras added a touch of importance to the atmosphere. She scrutinized her in-law from the corner of her eye, pleased to notice that she was indeed rather tall, but also excessively skinny; the front of her dress, which had layers of folds to camouflage the flat, boyish chest, apparently did not fulfill its function. The rest, too, turned out to have been a false alarm; the in-law's pink dress was too pale, and its sash was tied in such a complicated knot that it required constant tying and retying.

Walking around the garden as in a dream, Bella experienced a happiness almost palpable. Everything seemed to be perfect: the immaculately set table, the bowls that kept refilling as if by magic, always looking as if the table had just been laid; the small band playing pleasantly, loudly enough to be heard, yet softly enough so as not to drown the conversation. Hayuta followed her grandfather with her eyes, like a trained hunter. Even when she turned her back to him, responding to well-wishers, she still sensed his movements.

The old man looked radiant and festive, responding to those who greeted him and patting children's heads. Once in a while, when Hayuta thought he was talking too much, she made her way to him, as if by chance, brushing by his back, listening. At one point she sensed danger and stiffened. He was facing the set table, looking at the guests loading their plates with food. She recognized the look, the raised hand, which always heralded the lofty words. He opened his mouth to talk, but was pierced by her harsh look. Across the long row on the table, he suddenly smiled at her mischievously, as if caught red-handed, and called, "*Lechayyim,* Haya'le, *lechayyim!*" And then he added, as if reminded, "And all the best!" And he laughed like a child who had managed to fool an adult.

Hayuta joined in his laugh, relaxing for the first time since the first guest had arrived. She raised a hand holding an imaginary goblet to him and called, "*Lechayyim,* Grandpa, and all the best!" The photographer, from his vantage point by the door, caught them in his lens, standing face to face saluting and toasting each other across the table. He darted his flashes at them and smiled, contented, seeing the finished product in his mind's eye.

From then on, Hayuta felt at ease as she mingled with the guests, catching a glimpse of her grandfather in the crowd from time to time. For a little while the photographer took her and Ran away from the guests and seated them on the slanted garage roof that was covered with sprawling ivy. He shot them facing each other, in each other's arms, until Hayuta remonstrated, "Enough with this kitsch. This is so banal!" And she waved her hand at the camera in protest, and pulled Ran by the arm.

From the roof she suddenly saw her grandfather. He was staring at the people huddled around the table. The meat platters had been removed and were replaced by plates of cakes. People were helping themselves to pieces of cake, and from where she was standing, Hayuta could discern the excitement on her grandfather's face vis-à-vis the new extravagance, the new commotion around the table. His eyes shone with a familiar light, and his arm, though no longer holding a glass, raised by itself. His other hand thumped on the table, drawing the guests' attention. People were looking at him from all corners of the garden; several came closer, waiting respectfully for him to talk. He waited a minute for the conversations to subside, like an expert orator, and then began. Silence fell on the garden, as before an important announcement.

"Grandpa, no!" Hayuta yelled from afar, from her shaded corner, and he raised his face to her, straining his eyes to see her beyond the peoples' heads, near the darkening ivy.

Suddenly he ducked and disappeared from view. Hayuta could see the sudden commotion in the crowd, people pushing and gathering to the empty place he had just occupied. She tore herself from Ran's arms and rushed there, tearing through the barrier of people around him, but by the time she got there the table had already collapsed, the strawberry, cheese, and chocolate tortes, and the tall, layered cake were lying ruined on the grass, and her grandfather rolling among them, his face and his suit splattered like an actor in an old comedy, who had just been hit by a cream pie.

In the bedroom, they could hear Mordechai's voice trying to stave off the guests who came to inquire about the old man. He sent them back to the table, which had been hastily restored, and to the band, which had resumed its playing. "He got very excited, now he's resting. No, please, don't disturb him. I'll tell him. He needs his rest now. He'll be okay. Please go on dancing." His voice, and the music and the murmurs of the people, came from a great distance.

Inside the room it was very quiet. Hayuta, with the wreath of roses still resting in her curls and her face very pale, took out a tissue from a pop-up box, which spewed out thin rectangles one after the other, and handed it to her mother. Bella dabbed her wet face and wiped the jam and the chocolate chips that had smeared the front of her dress and her white collar when her father was carried inside and she held his head close. Then she took another tissue and very gently, as if she could still inflict pain, wiped the anguished face, which knew no final release, and the handsome mustache, and the closed eyes, and the lips that were tightly pursed under a layer of sweet frosting, firmly treasuring the words that would now never bring salvation, nor conciliation, not even a momentary relief.

Translated from the Hebrew by Marganit Weinberger-Rotman

Excision

WHEN HENYA EXTRACTED the sharp scissors from the green plastic sheath with the picture of the dissected chicken sketched on it, her eyes started glazing, and when she put her hand to her granddaughter's head and parted the shining, golden hair, which tumbled like curled laces under the clicking scissors, her face had already turned into a mask.

"Come closer to the window, baby, so that Grandma can see better and won't hurt you. Grandma loves you and never wants you to feel pain. Bend your head a little so that Grandma can do it properly."

There was a note of urgency in Henya's voice and the child, sensing the importance of what was being done to her, stood for a long time motionless and obedient, her head bowed, her hands tucked behind the belt buckle of her short dress, and her eyes staring at the long blonde clumps of hair piling up around her sandals.

"We'll do this properly," Henya whispered promisingly to the pale, slender nape exposed to the light. "Nothing will be left on your sweet head and all the dirty stuff will drop off." Her left hand burrowed in the small child's extraordinarily long hair, and her right hand quickly manipulated the scissors; her body was arched like a bow over her grandchild's head. Thus she worked with a frozen glaze, like a woman possessed.

The parting between the two golden curtains was getting more and more jagged until at last the entire head was shorn; short stubble, like mown stalks of wheat, stood on the pale scalp, exposing the tender white skin that had not seen the light since the hair first grew on it.

Henya emitted a feverish breath and her whole body was seized by a tremor. She returned the scissors to their sheath, dropped exhausted into a chair as if after great exertion, drew the grandchild to her, hugged her with all her might, and covered her nape with kisses, as if they were about to part. Her voice regained its soothing tone, despite the turmoil that had overwhelmed her. "Everything will be all right now, baby. You don't have to worry anymore."

The child raised tender hands to feel her head and recoiled from the new sensation. Then she looked at the heap of hair on the floor and turned her head away, her face contorted with crying. "You cut off all of my hair. Now I look like a boy."

Henya pulled the child to her bosom and stroked the anguished face. "We had to do it, baby."

"Why?"

"Because of the note from your teacher. You remember she pinned a note to your shirt collar? That's what it said. But now everything will be fine. Your hair will grow quickly and be very, very clean."

The girl ran to the big mirror in her parents' bedroom and returned to her grandmother sobbing. "I look ugly without my hair. I don't want to go to school like this. They'll make fun of me, 'cause it's ugly. It's even shorter than Hedva's hair. I'll tell my mommy on you. She won't talk to you, and then she'll stick my hair back on."

Behind the glazed look, Henya's irises started flitting. "Baby, come here to Grandma. Closer, closer to Grandma. I want to tell you something. I know tomorrow is your birthday and you're a big girl now and you understand a lot of things. So now I'll tell you something that only big children can understand, and then you'll see that we had to do what we did."

THE FIRST TO see it was Zvi. For a moment he stood there flabbergasted, his head tilted back as if he had been slapped. Then he looked as if he were about to burst into tears: his lips were sucked in and his eyes clouded over. He lowered the cardboard box he was carrying and put it on a bench in the hallway without taking his eyes off the girl caught in Henya's arms, as if trying to figure out what a strange child was doing in his house being embraced by his own mother. Then his gaze wandered to the puddle of golden hair and his hands shot to his head, clutching his temples.

The girl tore herself from her grandmother's arms and started to cry, her little hand groping on her scalp. "Daddy, look what Grandma did to me; she cut off all my hair, and it's not nice at all. The children will say I look like a monkey."

Henya rose briskly from her chair and spoke to her son as she used to when he was a child, "Zvika, come with me. I want to show you something."

Zvi put his hand on his daughter's head, and his palm, feeling its way like the palm of a blind man, stroked the coarse, straight spikes on the child's head. "Mother, I don't know what came over you. This time you're really out of your mind."

"Look what it says here." She held the note before his eyes. "Read for yourself and then tell me if it isn't a shame and a disgrace that a thing like this should happen in our family."

Zvi read the note, and his hand wandered in the air and stopped on his brow, as if he were struck by an excruciating headache.

"This is a note from the teacher," he said. "She sends such notes to all the kids every Friday."

"You didn't read it, Zvika! Read it first. Read carefully what it says."

"I already know it by heart. Every Friday I fetch Miri from nursery school and she has a note like this pinned to her collar. It always says the same thing."

"Zvika, it says she has head lice."

"I know."

"What do you mean, you know? As if it was a normal thing in our family. And the teacher knows and anyone who sees the note on the child's collar knows. People will talk. There are people here who know me from abroad."

"Mother, this time you really went out of your mind," he said. The girl wailed suddenly, frightened by the shouting between her father and her grandmother. She pressed her cheek to his thigh and hugged his waist.

"Look what you've done to her. She had the most beautiful hair in the school. We've never cut her hair since she was born. And you knew it, you were so proud of her hair. How could you do this, explain to me, how?"

"But Zvika, she has head lice!" Henya's eyes turned into two black rings in her face. "What does it matter if the hair is pretty or not if you have lice?"

"And now you argue with me. You refuse to realize what you did, and you're sure you're right. Don't you know that all the kids have lice? It's an epidemic. You yourself told me last month that you saw on television how they declared a nationwide campaign to wash all the children's hair that day, so that they wouldn't reinfect each other. Ziva washes her hair every week and treats it with a special chemical, and still she picks it up from the kids in her nursery school."

"Zvika, listen to me. I know what's good for my children. I've been through a lot and I know. When you've got lice, no chemical and no washing will do. The best thing is to crop the hair right away, down to the roots. Every hour there are more and more eggs and every minute counts."

"Cut it like this?" he asked, his voice on the brink of crying, and he pointed to the head clinging to his thigh. "If you decide to cut it, why like this, in a fit, why not at the hairdressers, in a straight line, so that it will look pretty?"

Henya looked at her grandchild as if seeing her for the first time: the shorn stumps of hair, the shrunken head, and the tender neck that looked like a plucked chicken's. Her head was still bent toward him, as if trying to explain. Henya suddenly started to cry and to emit a strange sobbing sound, like a person who was born without the ability to cry but has learned to fake it, to reduce the distance between themselves and other human beings.

"It really didn't come out so nice," she sobbed. "It should have been more straight. But I was so agitated, I didn't pay attention. Will you forgive Grandma for doing such a poor job, baby? Will you forgive Grandma? You know, Grandma only wants the best for you, don't you? You know I have only Zvika and one Miri in the whole world."

The child lowered her eyes, unwilling to look at her, and a moment later turned her back to her, tightened her grip around her father's waist and buried her face in his trousers. When Henya put out her hand to pat the shorn head, the small body trembled, as if scorched by fire.

"It will grow again soon, baby," Henya promised her, her heart sinking at the sight of the recoiling girl. "You'll again have the most beautiful hair, and, more important, you won't have lice."

Zvi was staring at the felled hair scattered on the floor, beneath the window, like wisps of light. He said in a lifeless voice, "I really don't know what to do about this. Come with me to the other room, Mother. Ziva will be here soon; she only went out to order the birthday cake. What she will do when she sees this I really don't know. She'll blow her top. You'd better not be here at all. Go in there, and when Ziva gets here I'll take you home as quickly as possible."

IN HER SON'S study, with eyes staring at the darkness, Henya heard her daughter-in-law screaming, her granddaughter wailing, and her son trying to intervene, to explain, but his voice was drowned by theirs.

"Why should I care about that now?" she heard her daughter-in-law. "So what if that's what they used to do in the camps forty-five years ago. The world has advanced a little since then, and we are not in the camps now. Look at your daughter! Look at her! Tomorrow is her birthday. On this side she is completely shaven. And look here, she has a scratch. She cut her skin! Her hands should be broken so she'll never touch a pair of scissors again! Get that woman out of here or I'll kill her with my own hands. And tell her never to set foot in here again. I never want to see her face. Never again in my life!"

Zvi's voice struggled and rose, and for a moment sounded loud and clear and dominant in the adjacent room, but Ziva's voice immediately overpowered it: "Stop it, it won't do now. I'm telling you, it only makes me madder. I don't want to hear about it anymore! Those stories are prehistory by now. I told you not to ask her to baby-sit for us. She's crazy. You must realize that your mother is crazy. I told you a long time ago. She lost some screws in her head in the Holocaust. Look at the catastrophe she brought on us. A catastrophe! I'll never let her near my child. And I don't want her to come here again. If you want to see her, you'll have to go to her house. She's crazy and you should put her in a nuthouse. Any doctor will agree to commit her right away. Look what she's done to our daughter. You remember what a pretty girl you had? Look at her now. She'll suffer for this all her life. Look here—and there. Turn around, Miri, so that Daddy can see. Can you take a child into the street like this? What shall we do with her? Put a wig on her? Shave her head? It will be at least a year before it looks okay. I want your mother out of my house now. I don't want her to stay for the birthday party. Anyway, we must call off the party."

Suddenly the screaming stopped and Miri's shrill voice was heard turning into a sob. "Do you hear what your child is saying? She knows what the lice did when people died in the camps. A four-year-old needs to hear such things? Is this a story fit for her age, I ask you? I want my child to hear stories about Cinderella, not about Auschwitz!"

THE TANGLE OF the voices stopped at the door of the study and Henya was enveloped by deep silence. The death rattle of the boy who was hanged by his feet in the passage between the men's and the women's camp had stopped a while ago, and since then only distant barking and rustling of leaves broke the silence now and then. In the corner of the barrack, near the only window overlooking the woods beyond the electric fence, a woman was tossing on her berth and groaning in her dream. The woman sleeping next to her moaned and turned too, so as not to find herself without the sack that served as a blanket, trying to warm herself against the nearby body. Henya raised her hand and with nailless fingers scratched her head; it made a dry, crackling sound, like a wooden floor scoured with a coarse brush. Her skull was itchy, the flesh of her nape inflamed, and she felt tiny bites in her armpits. In the morning, she will find that her neighbor on the other side, the one who had ceased to dream many weeks ago, died in her sleep. For weeks her face had borne the look of the dead, yet on the morning of her death she looked more alive than ever, serene, her eyes staring at the ceiling with a sort of curiosity. When the women hurry in the morning to line up in front of the barracks, the lice will start to leave the dead body; they will look like a black dotted line cutting across the forehead, feeling their way toward another body, looking for a new life for themselves.

Translated from Hebrew by Marganit Weinberger-Rotman

Written in Stone

FROM THE BOTTOM of the carved steps where she had stopped her car and for a long moment continued to sit motionless, more tired and sweaty than usual after the two-hour drive, Erella could no longer see the faces of the women crowding the windows of the house on the hill. There had been a time when she used to gaze intently through her windshield, squinting through the afternoon glare and the thick foliage of the fir trees, seeking the square window and the women whose eyes flashed daggers at her from faces enclosed in dark kerchiefs.

But she no longer lifts her eyes to the windows. Leaving the car, she will start climbing the stairs with her eyes on her feet. Without seeing them, she'll know that they are looking at her. She will feel the harsh touch of their gaze on her body, clinging to her forward moving legs; taking measure of her dress, her shoes, her hair; weighing her walk, searching the contours of her belly for signs of new life. When she raises her eyes she will see them draw back and drop the curtain and she will know: they are waiting for her, each back in her corner, crouching on the frayed mats with eyes like hidden traps.

She will pause for a moment in the doorway, standing erect in the framed light, her eyes adjusting to the dim interior. Huddled like large dark birds, the women will examine her through the slits between folded arms on their knees. And nailed to the cross of their searing gazes, she will know: this is how her guilt is scoured and cleansed. Consumed by this fierce, malevolent fire, all her sins are purged and she is purified.

WHEN THE ROOM becomes visible, she will see that, as always, the corner near the niche is empty. Like a reserved place—she will tell herself with relief. Like a cursed place—her darker spirit will reply. And she will enter without a greeting and go to the low chair by the niche that has been her place every year since the very first days of mourning. She will sit and, as always, she will fold her hands and drop them like objects in her lap. But then she will remember the wedding ring that Shlomi gave her eighty-three days before he died, and she will meticulously place her hands on her knees, displaying them, so that the adorned finger will be visible to all. Then, of their own volition, her eyes will move to the window, to the mulberry tree in the backyard, and she will remember how there, with the twisted trunk against her back, Shlomi placed hesitant hands on her shoulders and kissed her for the first time.

The men will cast quick glances from the doorway of the next room. Among them she will recognize his brother, who was a boy in those days and by now had grown into a man. His resemblance to Shlomi will set her heart to sudden pounding. And he, as always, will steal a look, see her, and clench his lips as if stifling a cry. The women sitting along the four walls will regard her darkly. The hostility in their eyes and in their huddled bodies had not diminished over the years. But by now it was tinged with curiosity at the sight of the fair woman who came back every year on this particular day, which they observe like one of the seven days of mourning, as did their ancestors in their distant land. In the twelve years that passed she had never missed coming. In the third year she arrived shaking with fever and sat slumped in her chair, breathing heavily, with her mouth open like a thirsty dog. The women watched her in silence through the years, seeing her waist thicken, her ankles swell, the creases at the root of her nose deepen, the gleam in her hair fade. They watched her as she sat among them like one who had come to claim her share, as if telling them without words: he was mine, too. You will not shut me out of the memories. Your hate comforts me on other days. Sometimes I think that maybe I come here for his mother, for his image that lives in her memories, for her endless pain—the pain that, without her knowing, yearns for my pain like a lost brother. If she would tell me to leave, I would go. I would stop ingesting the flames that flow out from you to me. I, too, would be relieved by this. For I, too, do not really know what binds me to this place as if by a vow.

The women will not approach her. They will gaze from a distance at the ring coiled around her finger. The youngest of his mother's sisters will turn her head and spit on the floor. After a while, one of the girls will be sent over to the visitor, carrying a pitcher of water and a heavy glass on a tray. Erella will whisper her thanks, pour herself some water, return the pitcher to the tray that the girl will leave at the foot of the chair, place the full glass in the niche, and never touch it again. Thus she will sit for a very long time, her eyes fixed on the bright mulberry leaves. From time to time the silence will be pierced by sounds slipping their restraints and bursting forth from the women's mouths. His oldest aunt will raise her shattered voice in a ululating, shrieking lament, her throat swelling like the throat of a crowing rooster. And always there will be the muted words of hate, always directed at the stranger, even when no one will look at her.

"We had a flower, a flower," one of the women will grieve, and Erella will lift her gaze back to the tree, detaching herself from the sounds of lament, thinking of fresh mulberry leaves and the silkworms that used to cocoon in the corner of the white shoebox with the red label: "Paris Fashions for Children," and below, in smaller letters, "Recommended by Orthopedic Surgeons for Healthy Feet. Leather Uppers, Leather Lining, Leather Soles."

His sister, Gila, was the only one who welcomed her. If the young woman was home when Erella arrived, she would hasten toward her. They would embrace in the doorway and then settle in the corner by the niche, talking in low voices. Gila was eight years old when Erella married her brother. During the weekend visits they would play together for long hours. Before and after the Sabbath, Erella would help Gila with her Hebrew and math homework. After the tragedy, they took care to keep the girl out of the house during the memorial observances. But when she grew older, Gila would spend the day with the women, waiting for Erella, and the two of them would draw harsh looks as they sat, forehead to forehead, whispering in the corner. As their conversation grew longer, the women would try to interfere: Gila would be called upon to make tea, to serve cakes to the men, to bring cooking oil from her aunt's house across the road. Until her return, Erella would remain alone, feeling how the dark spirit that had been troubling her for days was subsiding. Soon it would leave her body empty and tired from the conflict that had raged inside it. After twelve years it was still without victory or defeat—hurt enough to seek its dignity, alive enough to revive and regain strength.

And all the while, even while gazing at the mulberry tree, out of the corner of her eye Erella will follow the woman who had been her mother-in-law for a full summer and the beginning of one fall. She will see her sitting still as a statue in her black garments, her mouth clamped shut and her eyes on the mat. In all the years since she learned of her son's death in a bunker near the Red Sea, she kept her animosity toward her young daughter-in-law barricaded within her silence, its force undiminished. For seven years she did not say a word to the young woman. And then, on the seventh year, when Erella went up on the roof for the first time and was found swooning, the old woman offered her a handkerchief dipped in ice water and said, "Not good you come here," and then turned and walked away without another word. But when Erella left the house that day, the old woman lifted her eyes to follow the pale ankles that were encased in tight stockings. In the five years that passed since then, the silence between them remained unbroken.

When the sun crosses the meridian and the shadows of the trees start creeping eastward, Erella will rise. Her emotions drained and her heart light, she will leave without saying good-bye, sensing the eyes stabbing at her as she descends the steep stairs. And then, quickly drawn back to her other life, to the gray-eyed girl who was with her and then was gone, to the first man who waited for her in their house and to the other man who replaced him, she says to herself, "Enough! This was the last time! I will never come here again." And, with an intoxicating sense of freedom, she thinks: If I ever drive on this road again, I will not lift my eyes to look for the house on the hill. Whatever is left in me is mine. I will do with it as I wish. I no longer have anything to do with these women who sit in a circle like the mourners of old, whispering insults into their cupped hands.

But at the end of every summer it would suddenly stir again, like an internal organ growing toward her throat. This overwhelming yearning for something that, so it sometimes seemed, had caused her to start missing it even as it was happening. The pain had receded over the years until all that was left was the memory of pain, and it, too, was dissipating into the passing days. And every year she would be surprised again by the awakening of that distant ache that had been coiled so carefully within her through winter and spring and summer; and stirred only with the blowing of the autumn winds, knowing its seasons like the migrating birds who launch into flight when the right wind comes.

Twelve years, the first five of which she had been alone—a war widow, trapped in the net of furtive glances that accompanied her everywhere. And in the remaining seven years, twice a wife. And in all those years of going back to school and making a home and having a baby and loving a man and parting from both of them and loving another man, the yearning subsided within her, drawn to the brink of oblivion by some miraculous force. But with the onset of autumn it would come upon her like a seizure, bringing with it the memories with their colors and odors and touch. Then she would retreat to other realms, saying little, shutting herself in her room, complaining of fatigue, escaping into sleep. She would neglect the shopping and stop doing housework. Her husband, who after the first year no longer questioned it, allowed her to stay in bed for days, prepared the meals, and drove their daughter—when she was still with them—to the baby-sitter or his parents.

And even though he didn't know what it was about, he knew nothing about it, he learned that when she returned from Galilee in the evening, she would be herself again. And, lying in bed with her eyes closed, gathering strength, she was already familiar with the signs: her body was preparing itself for war. Two days from now she would stand face-to-face with Shlomi's old mother, her mother-in-law for eighty-three days. Since the day they had faced each other over the pit in the military section of the cemetery, locking glances at the moment when the guns roared their salute, the old woman had said nothing but the five words she uttered when she went up on the roof and placed a cool handkerchief on Erella's forehead.

At night she would feel it stir, fluttering inside her like a fetus. The memories would stream from all directions, converging on her like living creatures: Shlomi, the youngest Ph.D. candidate, crossing the campus lawns, immersed in his thoughts, staring at his shoes, passing all the young women stretched out on the grass with their faces to the sun without seeing them; Shlomi alone in the computer room long after it was officially closed, facing the clever metal monsters in the great silence, conversing with them in their own language; and Shlomi with her on the balcony of her room, gathering the purple jacaranda flowers that had dropped into the grooves of the shutter and then, with the flowers still in his hand, kissing her like a young boy. And she, younger than him but already a veteran of love, laughing at him when he said, "I don't have much to offer you." Jokingly, she replied, "Is this a loan application or a marriage proposal?" And Shlomi, as she last saw him, cramming his books into the military pack, saying with a smile, "I spoke with my Aunt Geula yesterday. She called from the pay phone and I could barely hear her. She says that my mother has been having dreams ever since she heard about this reserve duty. Everybody there is very superstitious, you know. For every move they have good omens or bad omens, depending on the mood. Anyhow, my mother asked my aunt to call and tell me that it is forbidden to leave a bride a month and a half after the wedding. She consulted the rabbi on the matter. And, you'll laugh, but I can't get this nonsense out of my head. I know that I'll have a quiet time down there and I'll be able to finish my paper and be rid of this year's reserve duty at the same time, but logic doesn't seem to apply here. Besides, I've gotten so used to your exercises in the morning. Do you think I'll be able to stand not seeing you exercise for ninety days?"

"I hope they'll at least let you come home for Yom Kippur." She did not join in his joking.

"Yom Kippur is definitely out. I checked. I get leave on the following weekend. Anyhow, I'll write to you a lot."

"Every two hours, like you call?"

"Every half-hour, since I'll be holding a pen anyway."

"The weekend after Yom Kippur doesn't make much sense. It's so close to the end of your service."

"I'll talk to them about it when I get there. That always works better than on the phone. But I spoke with my reserve officer and she promised me the weekend after Yom Kippur. That's all I know now."

But on that weekend her life had already come to a stop. Two days after his interment the mail brought his letter, surprising her with expressions of affection he found difficult to make while he was alive. And when she saw them in writing, it already seemed that they had been sent by a stranger.

Afterward she gave his good clothes to his nephew and packed his books and sent them to the university library. She only kept his wedding shirt, carefully ironed and hanging in its place in the closet. From there, she embarked on a new life and a split occurred within her. The part of her life that contained Shlomi and Shlomi's death left her and went in a different direction. The new part of her life emerged from the point of amputation: a moment before she saw him in the campus cafeteria, walked over, looked at the tray he was carrying, and asked, "Excuse me, is that stuff safe?" How she found the strength to truncate herself at that precise place and reconnect to her life exactly where she chose, she did not know. But it was clear to her that this had occurred. And only infrequently—now that she was fully caught up in her new life, cutting her hair, planting roses in her garden, loving people, and carrying babies—when she heard a sound or saw a sight or caught a smell that she had known in the amputated chapter of her life, a tremor would go through her, like a dull echo of memory, as when very old people remember their youth.

FROM THE DOORWAY, even before the dim shapes solidified and took on human form, she saw: there were fewer mourners. The room that the men always occupied was empty. Apparently, not enough men had come to form a quorum for the prayer and they had gone to the synagogue. The women, whose number hadn't diminished, received her in silence when she entered the small room. As always, she allowed the moment in which she stood within the blazing pyre of their gaze to pass, and walked over to her chair by the niche. This time her body was heavier than usual. She was tired and weak from the climb and she felt dizzy. Her stomach was also sending out signals from deep within, and it felt as though there were rocks in her breasts. She was unable to lower her body gracefully as in previous years, and flopped into the chair as if she had been pushed. As always, her hands folded themselves in her lap and then, as if remembering, she extended her fingers and cast her eyes around, gazing at them as they gazed at her. She recognized all except two: neighbors, or perhaps new in-laws. Strange, she thought to herself, this year it seemed as if the intensity of their hatred had also diminished, adjusting itself to her own waning strength. Spots floated before her eyes. When the girl with the pitcher comes over, she thought, I'll drink and ask her to refill the pitcher. Her throat was parched. For two months now she had been perpetually thirsty. Out of the corner of her eye she saw: his mother was sitting in her usual place with her back to the wall. The rough gray blanket had slipped from the corner of the mattress, exposing the worn striped fabric. Their eyes connected for a moment, and then the old woman dropped her gaze toward the fingers that were spread on the young woman's knees. She has aged, Erella said to herself and scrutinized the woman: her head was tucked between her meager shoulders and a kerchief, knotted at the temple, covered her forehead, exposing a small face whose deep creases were evident even in the dim light.

In the early days, twelve years back, they still had the strength. Shlomi's proximity infused them both with power. In the distraction that comes with dreams, he seemed very close then, present inside each of them as they clashed and battered each other without words. And each, in her own moments, would tumble into lucidity as into a trap. But on the fifth day, one day after her parents went back home and left her there, Erella's spirit faltered. This was evident in the way she sat, her head on her knees, rocking silently like a man in prayer, allowing the grief to seep into her without protest. And the words *war widow, war widow*, stalked her like a terrifying shadow. For two days the bride waited for the heavy woman to rise and gather her into the arms that used to cradle Shlomi when he was a baby. Of all the people who hovered around her, amid the great silence and the wailing laments, she wished only for that hand, craving the touch of its parchment skin, pleading silently for it to come, to soothe the sudden loneliness, to dispel the horror and that terrible swell of longing. But the woman did not rise. She kept swaying in her place, as if a great wind were blowing, her eyes stricken.

Many years later, those days of mourning would return to haunt her dreams: the men sat in the living room and recited psalms. Old men in dark garments came in and sat down and got up and left. Some would approach her haltingly and whisper, "May you know no more sorrow," like an incantation or a fragment of prayer. And in the other room the women huddled on mats along the walls. From time to time one of them would emit a long keening wail, like a lost bird, and all the others would join in at once. Then, gradually, the voices would subside to a murmur. Until the next scream. It seemed to Erella that people were performing a slow dance before her. She saw a woman whose shoulders were covered in a fretted scarf edged with three silver stripes, and she remembered the scarf from her wedding. A woman entered the room with curls of smoke spiraling up from her hands. Erella watched her in wonder until the woman put down the two cups of coffee she was holding. The mouths that had been wide open on her wedding night, with hands drumming on them to produce the festive shrieks, were open wide again, and harsh screams were being ripped out of them as if their vocal cords had been twisted. A girl approached her and bent forward, as if bowing in a game Erella and her girlfriends had played as children. She removed Erella's sandals and replaced them with cloth slippers, explaining in whispers the prohibition against leather shoes. And later, when Erella's fingers tried to hold together the frayed edges of the tear that had been made in her blouse at the cemetery, a woman darted from one of the corners, as if she had been watching all along, waiting for Erella to do so, and ordered her to leave the ripped blouse alone.

And so she sat on her chair by the niche and watched the people perform their rituals. On the first day, a skeletal man dressed in black came in and placed on the table an egg, some small olives, and a loaf of bread with a cracked crust. He then withdrew to the doorway and waited. When the mourners finished eating, he carefully gathered up in his bowl-shaped palms the eggshells, the pits, and the crumbs, then walked about the room and tossed everything he had collected into the corner behind the television set. From that moment, Erella no longer sought to understand their ways and allowed them to do with her as they pleased. She didn't inquire as to the meaning of the skeletal man's actions. She didn't question why they ate lentils every day, and why a tall woman hurried in and wrenched a baby from his mother's arms, took him outside, and placed him on the steps by the door, and why they pressed dirt and prickly weeds into her hand and ordered her to toss them behind her as they left the cemetery.

During the first days after the funeral his mother would moan and drop her head on her knees, or let it fall backward and dangle as if her neck were broken. The women would converge upon her, splashing water on her face and slapping her cheeks to revive her. She would push the lentil dish away with the back of her hand. Then, on the third day, the mother suddenly fell silent. She lifted her head, gathered her hair into the black kerchief that was tied under her chin, and stared at a fixed spot on the mat all day long. And, in the evening, when she began humming to herself a muted melody that might have been a prayer, or perhaps a lullaby, Erella buried her face in her hands and wept.

From time to time, as if by some conspiratorial sign, the women would pierce Erella with their stares. And she knew: they were cursing—hurling ancient Arabic incantations at her. Great pain is inflicted by a language whose words are unfamiliar but are clearly laced with hate. His mother's eldest sister grew daring from her age and told her plainly, "With your own hands you killed him. To let him go was like sending a child alone to the sea. To study quietly, you told him. That's how he died . . ." Facing the silent young woman, she continued to rage, raising her voice and drawing worried looks from the men in the next room: "The government killed him. The professors. They came and took him away, twelve years old. We had a flower here. A good boy. Not yet Bar Mitzvah. The professors took him saying, 'Gifted. A genius you have. He will bring you great honor. He'll live with a good family in the city and be in the university, studying.' What honor? What genius?— They took him and they killed him!" The other women joined in with muted whimpers.

"If they hadn't taken him—he would have stayed here with his family." The aunt raised her inflamed voice higher. "He wouldn't have gone to study there on Yom Kippur. He would have prayed here with his people in the synagogue. These people took him alive and brought him back dead!" She slapped her hands together to signal termination as the last word burst from her mouth. The women joined in a chorus of murmurs and his mother dropped her head to her chest as if she'd been struck.

Erella's parents and her aunt came to sit with them during the first three days of mourning. They would arrive in the morning and every afternoon would return to their hotel in Tiberias to eat and rest. Her father sat in the living room with the men like a foreigner who had wandered in and was forced to stay. With the unaccustomed skullcap perched too far forward on his head, he spent most of the time staring at the floor or at the windows. The two women came with him. Her mother had removed the silver beads from her good black dress in order to give it a more modest look, and her aunt wore a dark silk scarf on her shoulders like an ornament. On the first day the two women appeared in the doorway and hesitated, as if weighing the appropriateness of kneeling down on the mats together with the others. After a moment of confusion and a whispered consultation among three young women, two chairs were brought in. The two light-skinned women sat down, facing the row of women crouching with their backs to the wall, their eyes level with the soft white thighs that showed between the seats of the chairs and the hems of the skirts. From time to time her mother and her aunt would exchange whispers and try in vain to strike up a conversation with the hostile women opposite them. When the dark women burst out with sudden shrieks, the light-skinned women would shrink back in their chairs, alarmed. They tried to draw Erella to them but she was immersed in herself, endlessly twisting the wedding ring on her finger. At times their scouting gazes would capture the eyes of the father in the next room, and they would exchange embarrassed looks as if saying, "What are we doing in this place?"

On the fourth day, after the morning visit, the three of them departed and drove back home. Erella marshaled her strength until the end of that night, resisting the onslaught of whispers and murmurs and laments. During the entire fourth day Erella did not take her eyes off his mother, as if pleading. If she would only reach out to her, talk to her with her eyes, allow her to enter her grief, to share her burden of sorrow. But the woman did not acquiesce. At the dawn of the fifth day Erella gathered her belongings, and, without brushing her teeth or combing her hair, and without saying good-bye to anyone, she made her way among the women who were strewn at her feet like corpses, sleeping on the floor, wrapped in old army blankets and tattered children's covers. She left the house, went down to the main road, and took the first bus back to her parents' house. As the bus pulled away, she did not lift her eyes to the house on the hill, and she did not go back there thirty days later for the traditional memorial. She spent that day in her clean bed, in her bright room, among all her childhood dolls, burning with fever, crying out for Shlomi in delirium.

Then came the long years of silence in which nothing changed except

the markings of time: rain, flowers, falling leaves, the rising and setting of the sun. Every morning she would get up, wash, eat, go out,
and come back—pushing herself with her last spurts of strength to yet
another place, hoping that there the circle of silence would be broken and she might be stimulated to return to the land of the living.
In those days she spent many hours in the cool, dim offices of ther-
apists, learning to resolve things in a new language: emotional defi-
ciencies, loss trauma, guilt feelings, ego reinforcement. She also
learned this: it was the annual encounter with his family, to which she
was inexorably drawn time after time, that enabled her to withdraw
from the memories, from the man she never had time to know, until
only the memory of their love remained, detached, like an unfulfilled
promise. And as the years passed, Shlomi drifted away from her
toward the women kneeling in the room by the mulberry tree—toward
his mother, who followed her with her eyes and never said a word.

And once, in the ninth year, when she was on her way out, Erella
paused for a moment before the old woman who was huddled in her
corner. She wanted to bend toward her and say, "There is a new war
going on. That war is already history. You hate me because I knew your
son in a place where you did not. Well, neither of us knew him. Like
a man who made a date and never showed up. Maybe I come here
every year to ask your forgiveness. Maybe I want you to forgive me
for having something of yours that I took without your permission—
and then lost." She did not know if any hesitation was apparent in her
stride. She walked on, not finding the strength to say the words.
Descending the steps on the hillside, she promised herself: "Next year
I'll talk."

THIS YEAR THERE is a great heaviness in her body. Every part of her
seems cast in iron. Even her eyelids are weighted down, shuttering her
eyes as if fending off the light. And the autumn heat wave is more oppressive than usual this year. The girl with the water pitcher hasn't shown
up yet. Gila isn't here. Maybe she'll be back from an errand soon, or
maybe she couldn't get leave from the army. Erella closed her eyes, her
mouth open, feeling the fullness permeating her body in a gentle flow,
and the first ripple of waves at the pit of her stomach, in the place where
she imagines the beginning of a swaying momentum, like an emer-

gent whirlpool, forming from the springs that flowed ceaselessly within her and drawing them to greater and greater depths.

The intense heat brought with it a memory that had eluded her for years. On the way back from their last visit here, the heat was as heavy as it was now. The flowering squill stalks erupted from the fields behind the cemetery like drawn swords. And Shlomi, his eyes on the open fields, the fields of his childhood, heard her say, "Your mother is not exactly in love with me." And after a while he answered, "We have to give her time. It's very complicated for her. When she sees you she understands how far I've strayed from what she wanted me to become. To her, you are the embodiment of this discrepancy."

"And where are you in this discrepancy?" A taunting note in her voice.

"When I'm with you I'm connected to you, and when I come here I'm connected to this place. A man of two opposing worlds." He flashed a bitter smile. "This could be an interesting case for a psychologist: splitting a personality under controlled conditions. Take a twelve-year-old boy and transfer him to a totally different environment. Emotionally, he belongs to his first environment; mentally, he is part of the second environment—a perfect experiment in creating a split personality under laboratory conditions."

"And if you had stayed here," the teasing was gone, "what would have happened to you?"

"Maybe I would have been happy. The happiness of innocence that is blissfully unaware of other possibilities," he recited with exaggerated drama. "Maybe I would have become a teacher. A Bible teacher. A senior Bible teacher. Even a principal. The principal of a religious school. I probably wouldn't have had a split personality. But when I think about it, I realize that I wouldn't have gotten to know you. And that would be too bad. That would be the most difficult thing for me to give up."

The ripples in her stomach had become pounding waves. And she answered the man who lived in her memory: "But if you had stayed here maybe you would still be alive. It is possible to live without me, you know. I'm speaking from experience: I myself lived without me for many years."

She struggled to calm the growing turbulence inside her, drawing long, rhythmic breaths. For a while it seemed that the swaying in her stomach had subsided. But suddenly a cascade erupted within her. She squealed, jumped to her feet, and ran from the room. By the time she reached the toilet, her dress and shoes were splattered with vomit. Slippery slime dripped between her fingers and she felt engulfed by the stench from her mouth. She threw the puddle of reddish vomit from her cupped hands into the toilet and wiped her fingers on rough paper from a roll on the floor while continuing to spit sour specks into the foamy water. Careful not to touch anything, she retreated to the sink and scrubbed the spots of vomit off her clothes with soap, absorbing the water with the rough paper. She washed the front of her dress over and over again until the fabric reeked with the smell of cheap soap and the dress was completely soaked.

She opened the bathroom door and hesitated. Despite the repeated rinsing of her mouth, she could not get rid of the sour taste. And it would be impossible to go back to the room in her wet clothes. The decision came suddenly: she would climb up the ladder at the end of the hall and go out on the roof. There the breeze will dry her clothes and she will be able to look out and see the tips of the gravestones in the cemetery. She groped through the dark corridor, found the ladder, and placed her foot on the bottom rung. A rustle came from behind her and a dim figure appeared at the end of the hall. Even before the contours of the silhouette became defined, Erella knew: his mother. And a chill rose in her like an omen.

The woman approached without haste and Erella found herself thinking: She's so small. All these years Erella had been watching the woman huddled on the mattress without noticing how much she had shrunk, as if her bones had shriveled and her flesh had contracted. The woman stopped in the square of sunlight that came through the opening to the roof, and Erella saw that her eyes were as golden as her son's were—not black as she had remembered, but flecked with luminous gold. The woman did not speak and kept her lips pursed as if determined to remain silent. And Erella, mortified by the stench emanating from her clothes and her mouth, aimed her breath away from the woman, and was annoyed by the note of apology in her voice when she said, "I didn't feel well. I thought I would go up—"

"Not good you to go up," the voice was rough and dry, devoid of the gentleness it possessed for others.

"There is more air up there—"

"Not good you on the roof."

"My dress," her voice was suddenly desperate. "My dress is all wet. I thought that the breeze, up there—"

"Not good you up there in wind with head open like that," the woman raised her hand in a hostile gesture.

Erella felt the anger surge within her, just like the wave of nausea that had crested inside her earlier. She had rehearsed this scene many times, but the words that came out were not the ones she had prepared. The old woman was supposed to stumble over broken sentences, to apologize tearfully for her cruel silence all these years. Erella was supposed to deliver her lines in a firm, demanding voice, like someone about to see justice done. She tightened her grip on the ladder, feeling that the long contest was about to be settled right here. She placed her foot on the bottom rung and was overcome by dizziness.

"I also want to see the grave from the roof," she tried to infuse her voice with determination.

With a sudden wild motion, the old woman grabbed Erella's arm and clamped her black fingers onto the pale, soft flesh.

"Not see grave. Not see nothing. And you, not good you go up now. Now need be very careful. That's what. What is dead—need be dead. And what is living—need be living."

You are trying to tell me something. What is it that you are trying to tell me? Erella pleaded through her dizziness, like someone who is trying to grasp something important but does not understand the language in which it is being said. What are you trying to tell me now? Erella felt that it was because of this sealed thing, dangling in darkness just beyond her reach, that she had been drawn to this place for the past twelve years. Why did you leave your mattress and follow me out here? Why are you grasping my arm so tightly? What is it that you are trying to prevent me from doing?

"That's what you wanted to tell me?" she cried out. "That I should stay out of the wind?"

"Stay out. Be careful. Need to be careful now. There are things that don't help be careful. And you are like this. I come to give something."

She thrust her hand into a pocket, groped inside the quivering cloth, and pulled out a brown military envelope, folded in two. She offered it from a distance.

"A letter?"

The old woman released the envelope when Erella grasped it from the other corner.

"You read here. Not go from here."

Erella turned the letter over in her hands as if cuddling a living creature. Shlomi's handwriting, the same writing that covered the many pages piled on the desk—his unfinished dissertation. The letters were so even and cautious, as if the writer had been trying to guard a secret. And on the envelope, her old name—like the name of another woman—and the address to which she had returned once more to get her things, subsequently taking great care to avoid, never passing by the entrance or under the windows that faced west, where she and Shlomi would press together and watch the sun set.

Her knees buckled as if she had been running for a long time. She kneeled down on the floor to relieve the pain. Her fingers pulled a sheet of white paper out of the envelope, a page from a military communications pad, and the lines streamed out to her in fluttering fragments.

> Erellinka,
>
> I put the letter that I wrote yesterday morning in the mailbag and the helicopter took it in the afternoon. I'm writing this with a terrible feeling. I've been walking around with this awful feeling for two days now. Last night I had a horrible dream. I'm afraid that something will happen to my mother. I know that it will be hard for you to do what I ask. Please do what you think I would have done. I am saying this because, in many ways, you know me better than I know myself. The guys here are preparing for the fast. I'm not planning to fast this year. I'm trying to study, but I'm not getting much done. In my wallet I have that old yearbook picture that you gave me. When I miss you a lot I kiss it when no one is looking. The first chance I have, I'll get another picture. I know this one by heart already. I love you and I miss you and I hug you from afar.
>
> Your split man on a distant shore.

The tears that started rolling down the length of her nose made reading difficult, and she was rocked by an unprecedented current laden with cargoes that had been dredged up from the deep. She was there, yet she was not there, like a person seeing words that she had read in a dream. He had wanted to tell her something in this letter but never got to send it. If she had known about this from the start, she would not have sat still all these years, waiting for the old woman to embrace her. Maybe she would have gotten up and approached her mother-in-law. Maybe her heart could have withstood the ordeal of crossing the distance between them. And all the while she was calculating: the letter was probably found among his personal effects and given to his mother. But his mother couldn't read Hebrew. Someone must have read the letter to her. Erella was suddenly embarrassed by the strange eyes that had seen, "I love you and I miss you," and then she was overcome by rage at this tiny woman who, for twelve years, had denied her the last letter her beloved had written to her.

"You saw?" She heard dimly.

"I saw." She wiped her wet face with her hand and clasped the letter tightly.

The old woman took a step toward her and held out her hand. Her palm was surprisingly pink.

Erella laboriously pushed herself off the floor and stood up. "I should have seen this twelve years ago."

The old woman stood very straight, her head lower than Erella's chin, and held her hand out with fingers extended. Erella swept the letter behind her back and her neck arched as if prepared to do battle: "Why didn't you show it to me then?"

"No need you see," the old woman said quietly.

"No need!" she cried. "You decide on your own what I need and what I don't need? This letter is mine!"

"Not good for wife to see letter from when husband is dead."

"Not good?" Erella mimicked derisively. "Maybe you just wanted to keep it for yourself. Not good for wife to get letter? And for mother to get letter, that's good?"

The old woman blinked rapidly, but her voice remained steady: "A mother, her son dies—she dies. A wife, her husband dies—she lives."

"I didn't live when it happened." She could not stop the tears that were suffusing her voice and her rage. "What do you know about what I felt? You never asked me, not once. How do you know what I went through? I was only twenty-one."

"I have husband and he died," the old woman said dryly. "I was seventeen and have two children."

Erella glanced at her, wiping her face with her hands again, surprised at the direction things had taken. "What do I care about your stories and your dead husbands?" she wanted to say. But her heart was sinking.

"Shlomi not know. I not tell. Nobody from my children I tell. Only now I tell you this: my husband's mother came and took his things, everything, everything, the clothes, the prayer book, his shoes. She said to me, 'You get married and bring children. What is dead goes to his mother.'"

Erella found herself examining the dark face as if seeing it for the first time, looking directly at her and suddenly knowing with a certainty that stunned her: she withheld this page from me out of concern for my peace of mind. Out of concern for me. And, as if to verify this, she asked, "And what made you decide to give me the letter today?"

"Today you are living. Today there is life in the stomach. Twelve years makes no difference."

Erella gasped. It wasn't noticeable yet. Even her husband's parents didn't know yet. And her hands instinctively moved to stroke her stomach.

The old woman tapped her hand over her heart and her mouth opened wide with pleasure. "You thinking: from what she knows the baby? From my heart I know! This is my heart here. Before five years I know. You go up on roof and fall down." She looked at her closely. "Is true you go up on roof with baby in belly?"

"It's true," Erella whispered. "I went up on the roof and fainted. That was exactly five years ago."

"And the baby, he die!" the old woman announced, her eyes shining.

She died, Erella wanted to correct her. She was beautiful. We called her Shlomit. The bad signs appeared at the end of her first year and nothing could be done. And the silence that came between them afterward, moving them about the house like strangers, as if they had never laughed together. And the long hours she spent sitting on the baby's chair, her knees hurting from the low crouch, staring all around at the toys she couldn't bring herself to give to other children. And during that pregnancy, like now, in the second month, before anything showed, she had come here.

"How did you know?" she whispered.

"You tell me. With your eyes you tell me. Want to, don't want to—don't matter what you want."

You are a surprising woman, Erella wanted to say. In other times we might have grown closer. We might have greeted each other as we passed. And I have learned something today: All these years you wanted to protect me in a way that is strange to me. And all the years that you sat there—refusing to acknowledge me, avoiding my eyes—you were measuring my strength, waiting until I was strong enough to face the letter that would thrust me into a forbidden place. Instead she said without raising her eyes, "From the moment you saw me, you didn't want me."

"Sure I don't want. I look at eyes, I see: this is not good for my boy. You are Shlomi's death."

Erella, profoundly shaken, tried to hold on to the momentary alliance so swiftly disrupted. "How can you say such a thing! You have no right to say this!"

"Why I can't?" the voice replied calmly. "Me—my boy is dead—I have right for everything. Now I say this: You sit here. Rest. Not come in room. Sit here. When the eyes dry—you go home. Here not good place. You go and not think about here. And take Shlomi's ring off finger. Not good for baby in belly his mother a little dead."

A short while later, by the doorway, the woman pried the letter out of Erella's stiff fingers and pushed her toward the door with surprising strength. Erella turned to her, wanting to see the eyes again, Shlomi's eyes with amber flecks floating around the irises. But the woman, as if hiding, pulled the kerchief forward over her head to keep her eyes shaded and said, "Not good in sun and not good in wind. And not good in car, too. Now you need strength. And if a girl—not to give name Shlomit. And if a boy—not to give name Shlomi. This is name written in stone on grave. New baby need new name, good name. Shlomo was name of my first husband. Enough Shlomo!"

As Erella walked carefully down the steep stairs, her hand pressed against her stomach, the realization came upon her: today she had been set free! This woman had the power to release her from the vow that neither of them had ever understood. And she had done it. The old woman had let her go. And the scream that had been locked in her bones—echoes of which she had hurled at herself, at the men she loved, and at the dead girl—was separating itself from her at this very moment.

She felt the old woman's eyes on her back, and she was glad that she had chosen to park the car in the shade of the huge oleander, out of reach of the snooping eyes peering from the windows. She was glad that the cemetery trees could not be seen from this place. For she was already caught up in a new feeling that was throbbing inside her, making her dizzy. Her stomach was a lump pulling heavily toward the ground, and the soles of her sandals seemed to strike roots that were ripped out with every step she took. And at the same time, an ascending thrust welled up inside her, drawing her entire being upwards, like a bird preparing for flight.

And when she was on firm ground again, at the bottom of the many steps, she turned her head and could not see the windows or the house. She stretched her arms sideways and spun around in a jagged circle. Then she raised her hands toward the sky, like a farmer welcoming the first rain. And she was ethereal and glowing, as if her body were made of light.

Translated from the Hebrew by Gilead Morahg

The Road to Cedar City

A SHORT WHILE after the axle of their car broke down, on the shore of Otter Creek Lake, the three of them were making their way to the Merchant Trail of Utah Travel Agency, located on the corner of Elm Street and Washington Square in Antimony. They were crossing a shady avenue of canopied plane trees whose leaves were almost all gone, for it was the beginning of fall. Yehiel Harari and his son, Yuval, were marching forward with long, springy strides, chatting and laughing out loud. Shoulder to shoulder, they carried large, seemingly weightless, vinyl suitcases, as the white tennis shoes they had bought at Macy's bargain basement for three dollars a pair crushed the fingerlike leaves underfoot.

Trailing behind them, at an ever-widening distance, Hassida strained to keep up with them, panting audibly, feeling the slight, familiar dizziness that always preceded a hot flash and an acute pain in her depleted lungs. The avenue, all covered with withered plane leaves, looked to her—as often happened in her dreams lately—like an expanding ocean, separating her from her husband and son. She stopped in her tracks, hesitantly, her eyes following their receding backs, for she could not bring herself to trample the dead leaves that lay on the ground like severed hands; so she slowly made her way among the layers of leaves, clearing small islands with the tip of her shoe, straining and exerting herself, yet barely moving ahead.

She watched them from afar as they reached the end of the avenue, emerging from the shade of the trees into the light, dropping the suitcases at their feet, and turning their faces to her. When she finally came within earshot of their voices, her husband eyed her, his head cocked to one side, like a teacher commiserating with a failing student, and her son, planting both hands on his hips in a gesture of reproach and impatience, shouted to her, "So what is it now, Mom? You've already made us carry your suitcase, so you have no more excuses. What's the problem now? Why do we have to stand and wait? Don't you see, you're holding us up all the time!"

She noticed two schoolchildren, in visored caps and blue blazers with red and white insignia embroidered on their lapels, staring at her curiously and snickering. She felt her chest contract at the affront, and her vocal cords strained to the point of bursting. "Even when you were a little kid, I never spoke to you like this," she wanted to tell her son. Her eyes smarted from trying hard to contain her tears. But instead of scolding, she called out in a clipped, shrill voice, to overcome the distance, "I must rest a little, I am awfully tired. You two go ahead, and I'll catch up with you in a little while. I'll find the office. I've got the address in my purse."

"Sure you will," Yehiel called out tauntingly. He bent down and picked up a suitcase in each hand, "just as you found us in Yellowstone!" Yuval, who was about to resume his walking, his back turned to her, the handles of the bags in his hands, now dropped both bags to the ground and shrieked with laughter. His father joined him instantly, roaring out loud and putting down the suitcases at his feet.

Hassida watched them across the path of dead leaves, their figures becoming distorted by the moisture in her eyes. She remembered with horror those moments in the park before they found her, panic stricken like a trapped animal, straying on a narrow wooden bridge that connected two tracts of smoky terrain that looked like the frightening picture she remembered from her childhood, the picture that used to hang in her grandfather's study, and underneath it, in dark, slender letters the inscription: *Dante's Inferno.*

She sat down in the middle of the avenue, on a white bench with curled armrests and ornate iron back that reminded her of the lawn chair at their home in Jerusalem, and surrendered to the hot flash. The gold and copper hand-shaped leaves lay at her feet; she watched the receding backs of her husband and her son, and she sobbed inwardly, inaudibly, her spirit giving way to her physical frailty. Since her childhood, since the summer her grandfather suddenly died shortly after he had taken her by the hand to show her a slowly opening evening primrose, she had not felt so forlorn as she did on this trip. And yet she had been planning this trip in great detail for several years now, until she wore down the travel agent whose office she used to visit at the start of every tourist season, and he no longer welcomed her.

Here, in this strange and magnificent landscape, she saw, as in a polished mirror, what had eluded her at home: They no longer belonged to her, those two men who had suddenly turned against her, becoming her enemies. They ganged up on her, forming a strange, malicious alliance; they no longer bothered to conceal their invidious mockery, they taunted her mercilessly; they left her prey to the gazes of strangers, passersby, hotel clerks, and saleswomen. As if all the years that she had mediated between them—the times she interceded, cajoled, and scolded, mitigated the animosity, contained the raging storm— were suddenly obliterated. As if the father had never insisted on evicting his son after he had failed an electronics course, and then, for an entire year, refused to exchange a word with him. Every Wednesday she would pack candy and detective stories in a cardboard box and go visit him at his boarding school.

The realization first hit her at the airport, a short while after they had left the house, and she was appalled: here she was exposed to the world like a snail wrenched out of its shell, entrusting herself to the mercy of her husband and son, expecting them to protect her, while they, sensing excellent prey, stealthily, quietly surround her, conspiring against her: bawling her out for being too neat and meticulous; making fun of her hair, messed up by the wind at the airport; letting her drag her huge suitcase with the broken buckle; ignoring her when she waved her arms at them from a distance. A few days later, they began to exchange smirks whenever she stopped to look at shop windows, or when she wanted to visit one of the great department stores, or when she pressed a coin into the palm of a monkey perched on the shoulder of a clown in the street.

At times, with vague misgivings already gnawing at her heart, she watched them from afar as they laughed themselves silly, slapping each other on the back like bosom buddies, and almost burst out crying. And all the while, a distressing thought ate at her heart: she should be happy with the new intimacy that had sprung up before her eyes between the two men she cherished most in the world. Did she not pray at night that the two would find a way back to each other? Did she not make vows impossible to keep? And now, all she wanted was to kindle a fight between them, to see them beat each other senseless, to force them to call her back to be the mediator between them, as before.

Once in a while, she would rouse herself from her distressing thoughts and tell herself, "This is all nonsense you're putting into your head. It's been a year since you were called upon to make peace between them. Remember? Not since last Passover, when they went out on a hike together to Wadi Amud." One night, Yuval said to her quite pleasantly, "What's going on, Mom? Why are you so serious? We want to laugh a little and you frown at us all the time like a teacher of disturbed children. What's wrong with laughing a little, eh?" And then she shook herself and thought, "I'm being silly, spoiling this wonderful trip for everybody. They laugh, they enjoy themselves, what's the harm in that? Father and son on vacation." But the next morning, when she woke up, she found Yehiel watching her. He told her softly, "You're depressed all the time, Hassida. You even sigh in your sleep. Let's take you to a doctor to prescribe some medication. There are excellent drugs against depression nowadays." She sat up in her bed, remembering the moment in her dream when she was about to be thrown into a lunatic asylum, and shrieked, "I won't let you take me to any doctor. No way!" and she burst out crying.

One afternoon they left her alone in a motel at the outskirts of Jackson. When she woke up from her afternoon nap, her limbs heavy and sweaty, she noticed that the rented Plymouth was gone from its parking place under the window, and her heart raged as if an ill prophecy had been fulfilled. Still groggy from her sleep, she darted to the closet and cried with relief when she found their suitcases there. They had not even taken the video camera, she realized. For the next five hours, Hassida paced back and forth along the porch in front of the motel, her steps reverberating in the air. She ignored the quizzical yet discreet glances of a large black man who was raking leaves with a tiny, toylike rake. Suddenly, when he was close to her, he dropped the rake and took out a metallic object from his pocket. He stretched his hand and offered her candy in a small tin box. Recoiling, she cried out, then declined vehemently, and then, seeing the miserable expression on his face, she apologized.

In the golden light of early afternoon, she saw the Plymouth wending its way through walls of dust that the tires stirred up in the dirt road. Hassida ran toward them as if to throw herself under the wheels, sobbing and flailing her arms; her legs buckled under her as if her knees were broken.

"I thought something terrible had happened to you," she shouted, realizing that she could not tell them the truth. When the car pulled up, she pounded with her fists on its metal fender, lowering her mouth to the crack in the window. "I was going out of my mind here. I wasn't sure who to call first, the police, the hospital, or the consulate."

They looked at her, amused—sitting motionless, their shoulders touching—and let her shout and pound on the front window. "What could possibly happen to us, Mama Hassida? You have here an officer in the Israeli Defense Forces and a judo champion."

She stretched her hand to them outside the windshield, and her head dropped. Yehiel smiled an insincere, conciliatory smile, lowered the window, and said, "Hassidale, we just went to see a lassoing contest, lariats, ropes, that sort of thing. You said yesterday you were not interested."

"You could have left me a note." She saw the black man standing erect, watching her intently. She pulled her upper body from the front of the car and smoothed her disheveled hair.

"But Hassida, the pen was in your bag and you were sleeping so peacefully, like a baby, we didn't want to wake you up." His voice sounded unctuous, evasive. Offended, she did not respond. She had a feeling they were mocking her. Helplessly, she looked at the two men, who were smiling at each other. Then they both rose and came out of the car on the driver's side. She felt certain then; they were lying to her face. She craned her neck toward them, her eyes wild and her voice shrill. "I know where you went!" she shrieked. Peering at Yuval—staring him right in the eye, as she used to do, for many years, to check if he were telling the truth—she said, "You went to hookers!"

They were plainly and genuinely stunned. Yehiel and Yuval

exchanged glances, restraining themselves for one moment, watching the grins creep onto each other's faces, then burst out in yelps of delight. From that moment on, whenever the question "Where have you been?" was asked, the answer came right away, with a laughing snort, "With hookers!"

In the last week, she became very dejected. Even the decorated stores, the museums, the polished sidewalks, and the beaming faces of passersby no longer attracted her. She now, deliberately, shunned other Israelis whenever she heard them speaking Hebrew, whereas earlier she would gladly strike up a conversation with them, exchanging information about hotels and stores. Every few hours, she would surreptitiously take out a small photo album from her bag and stare at the pictures she had brought from home. When she could no longer tolerate Yehiel and Yuval's taunting, she would go to the ladies' room, and, in the dim light, try to discern the features of the people in the photos, and her heart would grow heavy. Then she would flush the toilet to drown her groaning. Every other day she called Israel to hear her granddaughter's voice, and for a long time afterward, she just sat there motionless.

In her dreams she often saw Yuval, always a child of five, feverish with meningitis. And she, looking young as in the old photographs, dozing at his side, or when awake wiping his face with one hand, while the other lies trapped between his feverish palms. Then his withered face no longer came to her in nightly visions, but during the day; she saw Yuval at his Bar Mitzvah celebration, minutes after a bitter quarrel with his father, his face pale as if painted, delivering his speech in front of the guests, pledging allegiance to his family and to his country, and all the while his eyes remain fixed on her. And she, fearing his tongue might slip, silently recites the words of the speech that she knows by heart.

Then other scenes, with other people, rolled before her eyes. One in particular made her heart ache: Yehiel comes home from the battlefield, his eyes burning, his face gray and dusty, and he takes her in his arms, like a hero in a Western.

Where are you now, the man I loved, the child who was only mine? When did you depart from me, and why? She spoke to them in her mind while her eyes flitted over foreign scenes, alluring billboards written in English, and a McDonald's Big Mac held in the palms of her hands. Yuval's mischievous face popped in front of her: "Mama Hassida, you're daydreaming again!"

Now, in the midst of the plane tree avenue—feeling calm after the hot flash subsided, yet exhausted from the heat, from the bottled-up fury, and from dammed-up tears that threatened to gush out—for the first time in her life she was frightened of them: They are conspiring to drive her out of her mind, to have her locked up in prison in a strange country so they can be rid of her and go home without her. With her out of the way, Yuval will be able to bring his girlfriend to his room not only on Friday nights but at all times. And Yehiel will get rid of her very easily; one little note from the rabbis and he is free to marry his secretary—the one who, when he talks to her on the phone, his voice suddenly changes—and the two of them will sit holding hands under the pergola with the vine that she planted eighteen years ago when she came back from the maternity hospital, and which she had cultivated lovingly all these years. It all started at home—a picture flashed in her mind and her cheeks turned red with excitement—poring over spread-out road maps; that's when they hatched the plot, and now she is caught in the gin.

Tomorrow, when she talks to her daughter, she will reveal their plot to her, and make her swear to come and rescue her if the other two return without her. And she made a note to herself not to accept any drink from them; they might slip her some medication. She hesitated a moment before adding: or perhaps poison.

From the distance, she made out the intersection where her husband and son had made a right turn. She decided to get up, climb over a low brick fence, and walk carefully along the paved sidewalk that led to the intersection. Thus, she would bypass the path and would not have to trample with her shoes the leaves that looked like supplicating hands.

IN THE COOL and pleasant office of the travel agency, where the walls were suffused with a faint odor of wood and cigars, Yehiel greeted her with an amused look. "So help me, Hassida, you made it! And in only forty minutes. We're really proud of you. Aren't we proud of Mommy, Yuvali? Now, listen to what's going on here. This is Mr. Williams. He has some good news for us."

The agent, with gray temples and a tan like a model in an advertisement, smiled when he heard his name and furrowed his brow. He straightened his collar, rose from his chair in a gesture of respect, and said to Hassida pleasantly, "Good morning, Mrs. Harari. I hope you're feeling better. I was telling Mr. Harari and your young man here what good news I have for you: ten minutes ago, I received an answer from the head office in Salt Lake City. The company will collect the car from the place where it broke down. I hope you appreciate it, because you were not supposed to drive on a dirt road. It says so specifically in the contract that you, Mr. Harari, signed. But the head office decided not to hold you liable. Please see it as compensation for any inconvenience you may suffer due to our inability to supply you with another car at this location. The nearest place you can get a car is St. George, but we'll provide the transportation there. I'm sure you'll find this arrangement to your satisfaction. We've got you a minivan that will take you to St. George. There will be a short stopover at our office in Cedar City. Only one other couple will join you in the minivan. Now, here's the good news: your fellow passengers are also from Israel. A young couple from Jerusalem. I'm sure you'll have a pleasant ride with our company. Your driver, by the way, is our most popular driver. He's a very friendly guy and one of our most experienced drivers."

Hassida, her lips pursed, her eyes circling the room, deliberately avoided looking at the agent. Directing at him the anger accumulated inside her against the other two, she said testily, in Hebrew, "I thank him very much for the good news. I can't stand Jerusalemites."

Yehiel Harari put on an indulgent smile, the kind of smile he wore when imitating their neighbor, Mrs. Reisman, in front of his children. "Hassidale, maybe next time you'd better stay home with the cats. These trips seem to have a bad effect on you. You become terribly unsociable. Unlike you, I rather look forward to meeting some people from home. Maybe they'll tell us what we've missed. And you'll notice, this is not just a couple from Israel, but from Jerusalem, our capital. Just imagine, there's a chance they can tell us how our soccer team is doing. Maybe they even know Yuvali's girlfriend. We'll be able to hear something about her family tree."

Pouncing at the opportunity offered her to vent her fury, Hassida lashed out at her son, with a dash of her old spunk creeping into her voice. "Judging by the mess she leaves behind her in the room, I can tell you all you want about her family tree."

From the corner of her eye, she noticed that both of them were startled by her vehemence. Since leaving home they had grown accustomed to the humble voice coming out of her mouth.

"Hassidale, you're becoming too cynical," Yehiel said, affecting great concern. "The air here is unsuitable for your delicate respiratory system."

"I can't stand Americans," she said, finding a new outlet to vent her distress, yet still not daring to look her husband in the eye. "Look at this fool standing here with a stupid grin on his face."

"He may understand what you're saying, Ma. America is full of Israeli emigrés," Yuval chimed in with a thought of his own, using the same singsong that his father adopted when talking to his three-year-old granddaughter.

"Israeli emigrés don't have such a stupid smile." She got carried away, unable to stop.

The agent, his smile fixed like a permanent facial feature, sensed that they were talking about him, and apparently decided that the family had debated long enough, and here was his cue to step in and announce, "I sincerely hope that you will accept our offer. You see, Antimony is a very small town, and our office represents most car rental companies. But none of them will let you pick up a car here and drop it off in St. George. We could, of course, take you back to the main office in Salt Lake City, where they will give you another car, if that's the arrangement you prefer."

"All right, all right." Yuval smiled at the American over his parents' head, and the agent broadened his smile and looked at Yuval, who then added in Hebrew, "As long as you stop blabbering."

"And what about the lady?" The agent assumed a solicitous expression without erasing his smile. He tilted his head toward her to indicate that she had his undivided attention.

Hassida hesitated. For the last couple of weeks she had not been required to make any decision regarding herself. In another era, in another country, in another atmosphere, she was capable of quick decisions. People were impressed with her ability, would come to seek her advice. Here, she seemed to have lost her powers; she was totally unskilled.

Like Samson after his hair was shorn: the image flashed through her mind from the Bible lessons she used to teach.

Yehiel laughed. "The lady is homesick," he took the liberty to speak for her.

"That's the big problem with these trips." The agent grew serious at once and almost sighed, but the corners of his eyes kept smiling. "You can't take your home with you."

"The lady is homesick for people, mostly," Yehiel explained seriously, darting a look at his son over his wife's head, to see if he was on to his mockery.

"In that case," the agent beamed with genuine glee, "she will certainly enjoy the company of the couple from Jerusalem. Just by chance I found out," he tilted his head as if apologizing for sharing a bit of gossip, "that the gentleman from Jerusalem is a nuclear engineer."

"You mean people from Jerusalem who are also intelligent," Yehiel said to the agent seriously. "That's very rare."

Hassida let out a low cry and hastened to cover her mouth with her hand. She walked over to the other end of the office and sat down on a chair, as if to proclaim her separation from the other two. She struggled to stop herself from saying the sentence that was forming in her mouth: "I hate both of you, hate both of you, hate both of you." She felt the words draw back to the edge of her gullet, then sucked into her throat, seeping through the sides of the larynx and permeate her inside like poison. Facing the quizzical eyes of the three men, she heard herself apologize in a submissive voice, "I'm sorry, I'm terribly sorry. I am very tired."

THEY HAD A light lunch at a Chinese restaurant, where they ate from shining china plates with dragons wiggling along the edges. Every once in a while, as if by accident, while talking, Yuval reached his fork into his mother's plate, angled a pineapple ring, and landed it on his own plate.

Her fingers were about to grab the dragons' backs, ready to push the plate toward him and say, "Take the whole plate!" But then she thought better of it and decided to let it go, and instead fixed her gaze on an extremely obese black woman in overalls who peered at the plastic food displayed in the restaurant window under the menu.

In the afternoon, in the back seat of an orange minivan with sail-boats painted on each door and an ornate logo spelling "Otter Creek Lake Transport," Hassida, her unreleased anger turning inside her like a viper trapped in a narrow cage, leaned her stiff neck on the soft head-rest and closed her eyes, abandoning herself to the artificial coolness that felt so pleasant on her skin. The men sitting at her side were por-ing over a huge, intricate road map spread on their knees, their fin-gers following the red arteries. Through their mumblings, she could hear the excited voice of a radio announcer permeating the car. "From now"—the woman on the radio announced after a short drumbeat, like a circus fanfare—"until midnight, listeners are invited to come along with the roving microphone on a grand tour of all the departments of a new shopping center that has opened today. Rogers and Binder will be the biggest shopping center in the area. It's located on the highway between Kingston and Circleville. At the opening cer-emony, the mayor of Circleville, Mr. Jonathan Martin, will inaugurate the place. At his request, he is now visiting the book department." At the mention of the word *mayor* the raging serpent inside her became subdued. She remembered when she first learned the word: freshman year in high school, in a story about a poor crippled boy who defeats a rich arrogant boy in a contest and earns the blessing of the mayor. The story was taught in class about the time that her father had an acci-dent. She had to leave school for two weeks, and when she came back, the class was studying another story. *Mayor*—it was a greeting from a distant era. Except that Mrs. Jacobs, the British teacher, pronounced the word differently from the word repeated on the radio.

The drumbeat was heard again, and through the sounds on the radio came Yuval's incredulous and chagrined cry, "My God! Look who's com-ing!" Alarmed, Hassida opened her eyes, chasing away the image that began to form in her mind of Mrs. Jacobs standing at the classroom door, her mesh basket full of exam papers. She followed the men's eyes to the lawn beyond the parking lot.

In the gleaming light were three figures crossing the lawn into a shaded lane. On the right marched the broad-shouldered, energetic man who, a short while earlier, had introduced himself as the driver of the mini-van. He was carrying a suitcase held together by a makeshift belt of incongruous colors. He was talking to the young man at his side, dressed in a long-sleeved shirt despite the muggy weather, who was also carrying a suitcase and an overnight bag on his shoulder. A step behind them, barely discernible from inside the minivan, taking small, hasty steps, as if trying to catch up with her companions, walked a young woman with a baby in her arms. She was wearing a light pink dress, buttoned up to her neck with a row of pearl buttons, sleeves cuffed at the wrist. Her hair, black and gathered behind her ears, was covered with a gauzy white kerchief.

"Israelis from Jerusalem, my foot!" blurted Yehiel Harari. He craned his head and rose from his seat, touching the ceiling. "They brought us Arabs!" he said in disbelief, and tilted his head to look at his son. "To come all the way to America, spend eight hundred sixty-seven dollars before travel tax, all for the honor of sharing a cab with Arabs!"

"Nuclear engineer!" Yuval burst out laughing, throwing his head back.

"Intelligent, and from Jerusalem—and an Arab to boot!" Yehiel added incredulously.

"And a nuclear engineer, no less! Just the right profession. Maybe he expects to find employment at the nuclear reactor in Dimona."

"The reactor in Dimona! That's a good one." The father slapped his son's knee affectionately, peering outside at the approaching figures coming down the avenue. "I hear there are openings at the reactor in Iraq."

"In Iraq! That's a good one!" Yuval roared, shaking his head in glee. "That was clever of you, Dad."

At the edge of the chiaroscuro shadow thrown by the plane trees, the driver halted, putting down the suitcase to free both hands to explain something to his companions that required wide swinging of his arms.

The couple, both much shorter than the hulking American, listened attentively. The woman nodded politely; she still kept a step behind them, rocking the baby gently in her arms. All at once, they raised their heads and looked at the minivan. The driver picked up the suitcase and started walking at a brisk pace, the couple following him in single file.

"Here is the Harari family, and this is the Haddad family," the driver announced formally, having pushed his body inside the van and turned off the radio. Then, patting the seat with his hand, he invited the new passengers to sit down, looked benignly at all five of them, and said, "They told me at the office that both families are from Israel."

While he was stashing the suitcases in the empty compartment at the rear of the van, the couple stood by the open door, looking uncomfortably at the street, peering at the store signs above the van, averting their eyes from Yuval, who was eyeing them curiously from the back seat. Then, without saying a word, the man took the baby from his mother's arms, and the woman lowered her head and climbed to her seat. At the same time, as if by accident, she turned her eyes and, with a motion that could be construed as part of the process of sitting down, she nodded silently at the three who watched her silently.

The man, whose face at close quarters looked more tired and wrinkled than was suggested from a distance, handed the baby back to his mother, got in, sat down next to her, and slammed the door forcefully. By the time the driver took his place, all the passengers were settled in their seats, keeping quiet. The man and the boy in the back, their mirth now tinged with embarrassment, smiled at each other encouragingly, yet sat taut and waited to see how things would turn out, the mockery gone from their eyes. Hassida felt something stirring inside her, beginning to burgeon and grow, a sensation she remembered from her youth, like a body preparing itself for an adventure, and with the stirring came that special tingle that signals the recognition of danger. The couple in the middle seat sat there like strangers; they kept quiet and refrained from looking at each other. Even their baby, unlike most babies, did not utter a sound when transferred from lap to lap.

"I hope we have a pleasant ride," bellowed the driver at the people in his rearview mirror. "If everything goes smoothly, we'll get to St. George at six. The distance from here to St. George is about a hundred and fifty, a hundred and sixty miles—about two and a half hours. In Cedar City we'll take a short break, and from there to St. George, it's exactly fifty-four miles—less than one hour's drive. We are now taking Route Sixty-two, which will bring us to Highway Fifteen." His voice sounded strong, excited, and upbeat.

When the vehicle got on the highway, wending its way through columns of moving cars, the silence in the van became oppressive. Hassida, huddling in a corner, kept a distance from her husband and stared, fascinated, at the shining threads in the young woman's scarf, noticing the strange position of her shoulders, which looked immobile. She felt she could pick up in her own body the tense muscles of the young woman in front of her: the axis spanning the shoulder blades, cutting through the nape and causing pain at the point where it joins the neckbone; the tense tendons in the upper arms shooting pains all the way down to the little fingers, and the arrow shot from the neck along the spine all the way to the toes. From the tension in the woman's body, Hassida was also able to deduce the strain in the body of the young man sitting next to her; his neck looked nailed to his shoulders, and only his eyes (judging by his profile, which was all she could see from her seat) nervously followed the cars passing by the van.

The driver turned on the radio, settled back in his seat, and said with pride, "Today is the opening of a big shopping center on Route Eighty-nine. This program is heard all the way to Arizona. It's all they've talked about here all month."

In a pleasant, solemn voice, flowing smoothly like a recording, a watch salesman enumerated the various kinds of children's watches on sale in his department: a Miss Piggy watch with hour and minute hands, in a lavender case with a color-coordinated band, $16.47, reduced from $19.99; Donkey Kong watch, showing hours, minutes, and date, with a black plastic band, $14.97, reduced from $22.95; Mickey Mouse watch, shock-resistant, silver-plated case and black band, $19.97, reduced from $29.95; Smurf watch, displaying blue numbers on a yellow background, silver case and blue band, $19.97, reduced from $22.95; Holly Hobby watch, golden case with vinyl strap, $19.97, reduced from $29.95; alarm clock playing the theme song from E.T., showing time and date, hands glow in the dark, $19.97, reduced from $29.95; alarm clock playing the theme from *Star Wars,* hour, minute, and second hands plus date, $19.97, reduced from $29.99.

The announcer with the mellifluous voice now called out number forty-three, and a faint gasp of surprise could be heard in the distance. Her voice rose over the commotion, "Here's the gentleman who won the watch! Come here. Please, sir. You can choose any watch you like from the display in the window. Do you have grandchildren, sir? What did you say? We can't hear you. Do you have grandchildren? You don't, sir? What did you say, sir?" She emitted a laugh that was surprisingly hollow considering her rich voice. "Ladies and gentlemen! I'll repeat what the gentleman said, because it's worth hearing. He says he has no grandchildren because his daughter is too lazy." Faint sounds of laughter rose and subsided as the young, excited voice triumphed, "May we hope, then, that this watch will rouse your daughter from her laziness, sir? Maybe, you say. You're willing to try anything, you say. Terrific, sir. We wish you all the best, sir. Please, a round of applause for this kind gentleman! Thank you, you're very generous. And now to our listeners. Good afternoon, listeners, I hope you'll stay tuned. We wish you could join us here, so you, too, could see this wonderful place for yourselves. But, for those of you who can't be here, we'll give you all the details. After the next song, we'll visit the candy department, and there, I can promise you, sweet surprises await you. It's my pleasure to tell you that among the forty-two couples getting married next month at Old Mason Hall, a seven-layer marzipan wedding cake will be raffled off. So stay tuned, listeners."

The driver, beaming with delight, turned down the radio, adjusted the convex mirror above his forehead, and turned to the people reflected in it. "That's Glenda Anders," he pronounced the name reverently. "She's great, isn't she? She probably doesn't remember me, but we met twenty-five years ago when I played baseball with her brother, Charlie Anders. She was just a little girl then, but she insisted on sitting in the front row and wanted to know everything about the game." He burst into laughter, engrossed in his own story. There was no reaction. His gaiety and good humor did not dispel the tension in the van; rather, paradoxically, it intensified the mounting estrangement, as if he were attempting to divert attention from an impending disaster.

"Great talents don't just happen," the driver continued, still raising his voice, though Hassida seemed to detect some signs of distress in its raspiness. "You can spot them at an early age."

For the first time, the driver peeked nervously at the silent people in the mirror. His brow furrowed a little, clouding the mirthful expression he still struggled to maintain.

"Is everything okay?" he asked, scanning them one by one in the mirror. Even those who met his roving gaze did not respond.

"You're all very quiet," he suddenly boomed at them reproachfully. "I know from experience that Israelis are not usually very quiet. Just last week, I had an Israeli couple who wanted to know the price of everything."

It seemed to Hassida that the young woman recoiled a little, scrunched her shoulders, as if lashed with a whip. The man at her side, looking tense and nervous, glanced at her for the first time since entering the van, and then averted his eyes again toward the moving traffic, as if he were charged with the urgent task of locating a certain car. Yehiel was shaking the tip of his foot, as he always did when he was at the end of his tether. Hassida, fearing the mounting tension, glanced at the rearview mirror, looking for help, but when she encountered the driver's eyes lurking there, she hurriedly looked away.

Then the driver said in an apologetic, somewhat alarmed voice, "I hope you're not offended. I didn't mean it in a negative way when I said that Israelis are not usually quiet. I meant just the opposite, I really did. I happen to like people who are not quiet. I myself am not a very quiet person." He smiled, ready to enjoy his own pleasantry, yet again he found himself alone, confronting the speechless passengers. A note of pleading crept into his voice, like an entertainer in front of an unresponsive audience, when he said, "You'll see for yourselves during this ride that I'm not a very quiet man. So when I say that somebody is not quiet, it isn't an insult. I definitely mean it as a compliment."

A little farther along the way, he suddenly said into the heavy silence, as a last-ditch effort, without looking at them in the mirror, "I hope you understand English," then glanced at the mirror to catch Hassida nodding slightly.

"I'll speak more slowly," he smiled hesitantly, confident now that he had figured out the cause of misunderstanding, and, mollified by the initial reaction, taking it as a good omen. "Tourists often tell me that I talk too fast. I don't mean to imply that your English is not good enough. Far from it. Actually, I was talking earlier with the two gentlemen, and your English is truly excellent. I'm really surprised at how good it is. But I thought maybe you couldn't follow me because I talk too fast. So let me tell you a story. About a month ago, I had some British tourists in the van, and they asked me to speak more slowly. So you see, I didn't mean to imply that your English isn't good enough."

The houses by the road now stood wider and wider apart and the patches of green between them expanded until only a few houses could be spotted in the middle of large fields, and in the distance only clumps of treetops alternating with roofs. A big bridge with directional signs loomed ahead as the minivan turned onto a broad highway. On both sides of the road, the sloping shoulders were covered with lush green grass, the color of fresh foliage. To her amazement, Hassida noticed a man working at the roadside, pushing a blue lawn mower. The man soon vanished, replaced by stretches of manicured lawns along the highway.

A young woman's voice came out of the radio, sounding thin and coy, telling the listeners that she had just bought a birthday present for her husband, a pendant in the shape of an eagle. The pedantic voice of a saleswoman immediately followed, enumerating the pendants sold at a special discount owing to the grand opening. "We have pendants in the shape of an oil rig, Italian horn, horseshoe, rowboat, lady on the moon, owl, clown, teddy bear, girl with parasol, girl sitting down. All items will be sold at cost, today only! Prices range from $49.97 to $147.90."

"I happen to like Israelis," the driver said as soon as the price list had ended. "Of all the foreign tourists that get to this part of the country, I like the Israelis best. And believe me, we get tourists from more countries than you can find in the atlas. The British really are polite, but—excuse me for saying so—they're just too bland. The Germans are also polite, but they have absolutely no sense of humor. Besides, I can't forgive them for the Second World War. The French—I'll let you in on a secret—at the office they know better than to assign me to a French group unless there's absolutely no alternative. But the Israelis are my favorites. You guys catch on quickly. And besides, you're the best soldiers in the world. If I were young today, I would join your army. Not that I'm so keen on fighting, but if I had to serve in the army at all, I'd choose the Israeli army. What do you say, kid? Am I right or not?" He peered in the mirror, meeting Yuval's eyes. "Of course, I'm right," he added without waiting for an answer. "You did a bang-up job in Entebbe. I read all about it. I know all the details. Not many Israelis know as much as I do, I'll bet. I read every line and every word. That was some operation! Just like in the movies. Sneaking in with planes, in disguise, consulting with a general who knows the airport, using a black Cadillac identical to the one belonging to Idi Amin, then loading all the hostages on the plane and flying home. There are no words to describe it! Fantastic! It's not just the courage you displayed, it's the planning. Jews have brains—there's no denying it—the best in the world. That's what I always tell my wife. And they have more guts than anyone else in the world. Whenever I hear that a kidnapped airplane has been released somewhere in the world, I don't need to hear the rest. I know right away that it's the work of the Israelis. I always say: In war, the soldier's brain is more important than the weapon he's carrying. If you don't know how to use the weapons smartly, what's the use of stocking them in your arsenals? Take Russia. The Russians keep sending arms to the Middle East, but what good are new Russian arms to the Arabs, if they don't know how to use them, right?"

He glanced at the mirror again, seeking confirmation, and caught Yuval's eye. "Right?" he called to him. "Isn't that so? Listen to this— it was a week ago. I was driving an Israeli tourist, and he told me that during one of the wars they found warehouses full of Russian arms. Brand new, still in the boxes, with instructions in Russian. None of the Arabs knew how to use them. Not even their generals, can you believe it? Not even their generals! And you know what?" Here the driver burst out laughing, tilting his head backward. "You know what? They weren't even smart enough to destroy it so that it doesn't fall into the hands of the Israelis. So what happens next is obvious: the Israelis win the war, capture the warehouses, get all the treasures out, and what do you suppose they do? They take the Russian weapons, upgrade them, and use them against the Arabs. Smart guys, the Israelis, right, kid?" In the mirror he sent Yuval an encouraging smile. "Bet you agree with me. You don't look like someone who takes off his shoes and runs away barefoot." He looked at them mischievously.

"You wonder how I know about the shoes, eh?" He thumped with both hands on the wheel, enjoying the surprise he was about to spring on them. "I learn everything from my passengers! One of them told me about the shoes. Rows upon rows of shoes that were found in the desert. You know better than me how backward those Arabs are. They left the shoes behind and ran away!"

The driver leaned forward, trying to catch the eye of the passenger in the center row, but the man was looking outside the window intently, his face inscrutable. "What do you say, Mr. Haddad? I know a lot about Israel, don't I? I bet you know the story about the shoes. I'd guess you probably completed your military service not so long ago— six, seven years, I would say, not more than six or seven, right?"

Amid loud applause, the radio announcer now cheerfully invited the listeners to visit the music box section at the music store, and the driver's attention was captured. He turned up the sound, and the passengers could clearly hear the hoarse voice of a man describing the music boxes and reading their price tags. They could also hear the wooden boxes being placed on a glass surface: a hand-painted clay statuette of a colt with reins of silver threads playing the theme from *Cabaret,* $26.84, reduced from $29.95; a ceramic musical windmill, with rotating wings, playing "White Christmas," $13.94, reduced from $16.95; a china figurine of a lady with a unicorn playing "O, Danny Boy," $26.74, reduced from $32.95; a blue angel with golden wings holding a hand-decorated harp playing "Für Elise," $11.97, reduced from $14.95; a silver-painted watermill cottage with a spinning wheel, made of all natural materials, $13.97, reduced from $16.99. As soon as the man was done, the melody "White Christmas" was heard, and the driver turned down the sound.

In the back seat, her body aching from trying too hard to relax, and dreading the sweet melody like a bad omen, Hassida thought to herself, "Something is going to happen now. Perhaps a tongue of fire will leap from the engine and blow up the car and all its passengers. Perhaps the car will veer into the grassy shoulder and the driver will suffer a stroke. That will certainly put an end to his chattering."

"I like music boxes. I have a small collection of them. So anyway, that's what I always say," the driver continued, picking up where he had left off in a cheery, lively tone, "Arabs are Arabs. They leave their shoes behind in the middle of the war and run back home. Hiding in their tents until the was is over. No wonder they are in such a sorry state— that's no way to run a war!" He raised his voice in admonition, shaking his head vigorously. "They're bound to be defeated. In all the wars—they were always defeated. And there's always a war in your part of the world. Never a day of peace, never a dull moment. Every other day, a soldier is buried, young men are getting killed all the time. I heard there's a cemetery on the road to Jerusalem—the entire mountain covered with tombstones of soldiers. But in Israel, you don't have wars like our Vietnam War, do you? You don't have the time for such long wars. You only wage short wars: one week, two weeks—you finish them quickly."

Hassida noticed that Yehiel's foot had stopped fidgeting. He was either ready to pounce, or he had disengaged himself, as he would often do when she was talking to him—his ears listening, but not his heart. Suddenly the driver emitted a loud laugh that jolted her.

"I've also heard," he said, smacking his lips lightly, "and this has nothing to do with the wars—that the Israeli girls are the most beautiful in the world. Prettier than the Italians or the Germans. I heard this so many times, it must be true. What do you say, kid? Is that true? I'm asking you, in particular. You look to me like someone who knows about girls."

The driver bent his head and peered keenly into the mirror. "Why do you turn your head and grin? Are you embarrassed?" He straightened, taken aback. "I'm sorry if I embarrassed you. It's a private thing. If you'd rather talk about wars, that's fine with me. Wars are just as interesting as girls. And I'm a hundred percent sure that . . ."

The baby, his head on his mother's shoulder, his temple against her neck, began to squirm, emitting choking sounds, flailing his arms, then spitting up a viscous yellowish discharge that stained his mother's dress. The air in the narrow confines of the car immediately filled with the distinctive, sweet smell of baby vomit. The young woman gave a cry of distress and turned her head to her husband, whispering a spate of Arabic words. Hassida heard the familiar words that she could not decipher, and, watching the frightened woman's profile, she noticed how young she was, the soft features of a young girl still clearly discernible around the mouth and eyes. "She cannot be much older than Yuval," she reflected.

The young man took out a cloth diaper from the travel bag at his feet and handed it to his wife, who wiped the spit off the baby's face and clothes and off the sleeve of her pink dress. The driver, his nostrils contracting on account of the stench, offered politely, "If you need water, sir, I can stop. I have a water canteen in the car, and if you need anything else, we're not far from a gas station." But the man seemed not to listen. Once more, the girl turned to her husband, asking something, and he shrugged and made a gesture indicating he did not have whatever it was she was asking for.

Yehiel, who had been sitting with folded arms, bound like a man restraining himself from bursting out, now released his arms and turned his face away from the foul odor. Hassida winced; his patience must be at an end. Suddenly she remembered something; she pulled her bag from a ledge behind her seat, took out a few small tinfoil squares she had saved from the plane, and handed one to the girl over her shoulder. The girl looked at the square with the logo of El Al Airline written on it in Hebrew, and without moving her head raised her eyes to her husband. He motioned imperceptibly with his eyelids, like a secret code, and the girl stretched her hand and gingerly took the wet towelette that Hassida had unwrapped. She nodded thank you without making eye contact, then turned around and wiped the baby's face gently. The fresh fragrance quickly permeated the car, and the baby's whimpering subsided.

"Did you see what a noble soul your mom is?" Yehiel asked his son in a loud voice, masking his sarcasm with feigned praise.

"A real Hassid is our Hassida," Yuval retorted, and the two of them convulsed with laughter.

At the sound of laughter, the driver threw them a glance in the mirror and seemed to spring to life. "Is everything all right with you two?" he chuckled.

Yehiel rubbed his hands together, and Hassida trembled at the familiar gesture; he was signaling to himself that the battle was afoot. "Tell us some more about wars. It's very interesting, all the stuff that you know." Hassida saw her husband's chin rise and noticed the excessive politeness in his voice, masking the restrained malice.

"You're interested in wars, sir?" the driver beamed at him. "If you don't make wars, at least talk about them, right? I understand you, sir. I like this stuff, too. War movies, accounts of battles, news reports from the war zone—that's what interests me. At home I have books about the Vietnam War. I know whole pages by heart. We have some Vietnam vets in our town. They know they're always welcome in my house. Whenever they feel like it, they can come talk to me about their war experiences—and have a cold beer. So where were we with your wars? Yeah, we said you always keep the wars short. Call up your troops quickly—well, your entire country is in the army—cross the canal, surprise them, catch them with their pants down, capture the Russian hardware—that's how you guys operate. No fuss, no muss."

He glanced in the mirror and caught the nodding acquiescence of the passenger in the back seat. He finally seemed willing to engage in a lively discussion of the topic. Encouraged by this passenger's reaction, the driver sought in the mirror the eyes of the passenger in the middle seat, but the man avoided his searching eyes.

"What do you say, Mr. Haddad, am I right?" the driver pressed on, but the man would not meet his eyes, so he was obliged to turn his attention back to the road and focus on the trucks he was passing. But a little farther on, he resumed his patter. "You don't need to be so modest, Mr. Haddad. If there's anything life has taught me, it's: Don't sell yourself short! Where praise is due, learn to accept it."

The faint voices on the radio reported that the visit to the auto center was about to end. The driver, his face registering his disappointment, hastened to turn up the sound in time to hear about velvetlike synthetic car seat covers with cotton lining, guaranteed to maintain their shape, on sale for only $23.75. He turned down the sound when music was played.

"That's it," he declared resolutely, "I'm going to change the seat covers. Come back in a week and you'll see new seat covers. What do you say, Mr. Haddad? Sorry to ask so many times, but I really want your opinion on this. Am I right about the quick wars you guys fight?"

From her seat behind him, Hassida noticed how the man's neck stiffened and sank, like a tree trunk, between his shoulder blades. His wife raised her eyes to him, a worried expression on her face. The man, however, was staring at a car with a stack of bicycles tied to its rack and pretended not to hear.

"Don't you agree with me, sir?" the driver urged, eager to humor his passengers, thinking he had given them the opportunity to be proud without sounding arrogant.

This time the man reacted instantly, "I don't think you're entirely correct." At the sound of his voice, Hassida thought, "Judging by the accent, he must have left Jerusalem years ago."

"I'm surprised to hear you say that." The driver pretended to take offense, making a very long face designed to stoke the debate. "What am I incorrect about, sir? I'm curious to hear your opinion."

"In the small details, sir." Hassida noted how his squared jawbone hardened his features.

"Give me an example, sir. Please elaborate," the driver egged him on.

"In the October War, for instance, it wasn't the Israelis who first crossed the canal."

"Why do you say that, sir?" the driver asked reproachfully, as if to encourage him not to underestimate himself.

"Because in the October War, the Egyptians crossed the canal and caught the Israelis with their pants down, to borrow your expression."

A quaint pleasant feeling permeated Hassida's body, and while she was wondering what had brought it about, she already seemed to know. She grasped the menace in what was taking place: the man's elegant phrases, his pleasing voice. She did not comprehend the words; only their sound reached her like music with all the notes correct. And she knew that war, whose memory weighed on her heart like a rock, was now hurled only at Yehiel Harari, not at herself. Being estranged from her husband for many days now, she felt she would be out of harm's way. Whatever threatened him, she realized, did not automatically compromise her, as had always been the case in the past.

"Don't be so hard on yourselves," the driver said in a conciliatory tone.

"I'm telling you the facts, sir," the voice sounded more robust, and Hassida listened attentively, sensing the warmth spread further through her body.

The driver was taken aback. Confused, his mouth agape, he looked like someone rudely interrupted in the middle of his speech.

"Is that what really happened, sir?" he asked with feigned incredulity.

"Yes, sir, that's how it happened. It started on what the Jews call Yom Kippur. It's a holy day for the Jews. On that day, they fast and hope that God will answer their prayers. They were not prepared for an attack, and they didn't get organized fast enough."

"Is that how . . ." the driver checked himself before charging again. "But in the end you won, didn't you, sir?"

From the corner of her eye, Hassida watched her husband's face. She recognized the glint that flickered in his eyes when he glowered—a special alertness, the joy of entering the fray, was manifest in his upper body, which bent forward, his shoulders pulling up, his back stretching uncannily.

"In the final analysis, nobody has won yet. Whatever looks like victory is only temporary." The man continued to look through the window, and his words, which were uttered without emotion, had a saddening effect on Hassida, as would happen to her whenever she heard old people cry.

"But you didn't lose," the driver protested. "We have an Israeli on my wife's side of the family, who was a paratrooper in your first war, and I know all about the other wars, too. You were always the victors."

"Some victories only look like victories."

"But you always win, sir," the driver tried to convince him. "Maybe you have lost some small battles, but in the end you always win."

The man seemed to have lost interest. For a long time, there was no answer, and then the driver said, "But you always beat the Arabs."

"In the final analysis, everybody loses," the man said in a tired voice, and for the first time looked at the mirror. "Israel loses soldiers in the fighting and achieves less than it would at the negotiation table."

Yehiel leaped forward, his neck turning red. "I will not allow you to spread Arab propaganda here, if that's what you intend to do," he lashed at him in Hebrew and leaned so far forward that his chin almost touched the scarf of the woman in front of him.

The young man pounced on him in a flash, his body lithe and cat-like, his eyes burning, as if he had been waiting for these words to hit him in the back since the moment he got into the car. For a second, Hassida thought she saw the glint of a knife in his hand, but it was only a wedding band on the clenched fist he laid on the seat between them. Alarmed, she stared at the face distorted by internal turbulence, the eyes narrowed to two blacks slits, and the delicate beauty that she thought she had seen in it earlier had vanished.

"You had better realize right now that here you are a very small master. You are in a truly free country, and it is not your country. You can't call the police and have me thrown in jail without anyone knowing. Here the law is the same for everyone."

Her heart trembling at this development, Hassida noted to herself quickly: "He speaks good Hebrew for an Arab, even for an educated one; only the accent is unmistakable." The words sounded heavy in his mouth, and he shot them like bullets with restrained animosity. "Here there's one law for an Arab like me and for a colonel like you, Colonel Harari." Hassida flinched; her hand shot to her chest. How does he know the name? Even though she did not feel close to her husband anymore, it was her name, too, that came out of his throat, sounding so distorted and menacing.

The young woman batted her eyelashes quickly and looked at her husband, terrified. Yehiel Harari thrust himself backward and cleared his throat. Hassida, who knew her husband's mind, tried to follow his line of reasoning, to quickly figure out: how does the young man know her husband's name and rank? True, the name is written in the passport, but not his military rank, so this could not be obtained from the clerk. He must have met him in Israel. Yehiel's pictures had been in the papers several times, but he looked different in his army beret; only someone with a phenomenal memory could recognize him from those blurred photographs. The Arab must have encountered him somewhere in Judea and Samaria when her husband was there on duty. His contacts with the Arab population were a matter of routine. Hundreds of people filled the courtroom every day. Thousands knew the military prosecutor, knew about his contacts with the military governor. As if looking through her husband's eyes, Hassida now scanned the man's face, gauging the danger—a face with no distinguishing marks. Yehiel would not have been able to recognize him out of the hundreds of faces that crowded the courthouse every day. Even going through the file of cases retained in his mind would probably yield nothing: trials involving a land deal, a murdered Yeshiva student, a knife thrown out of a bakery, a robbery of Jewish-American tourists, and letters threatening the life of a moderate Arab mayor. "You are not in Israel now, Colonel Harari," the young man hissed maliciously, crushing the name between his teeth.

"I don't know how and for what purpose you obtained my name, but in my presence, you will not say that Israel has not done its best to reach an agreement by peaceful means."

Hassida turned to look at her husband in amazement. The pale crescents climbing up his neck testified to the turbulence inside him, yet his voice remained clear and its tone as resolute as when he talked to his subordinates. For twenty-five years, since the day she first saw him in the kibbutz breaking in a wild mare, she had been amazed at his ability to control and command.

"No, sir, that's not true." The polite tone did not disguise the aggressiveness, only underscored its restraint. "This is what you've been telling the world all these years, and the world believed you. All the media are in the hands of the Jews anyway, and our cries are never heard. But the world is not that stupid. It is beginning to see the truth."

"We were always willing to sit down and talk with you. But you had a problem with 'honor.' Only when you thought you had beaten us, in seventy-three, did you agree to sit down and talk."

"Who is this 'you' you're referring to?" the man thrust his neck as if ready to bite. "Who do you mean by 'you'? The driver here thinks he's talking to Jews. And who do you think you're talking to? Who's this 'you' you're talking about?"

The young woman looked at her husband pleadingly, a hangdog expression in her eyes, the corners of her mouth drooping. She tried to catch his eye, as mute people do when trying to communicate their thoughts. Responding to this mute plea, Hassida said, "Do me a favor, Yehiel, and stop it. I'm begging you not to answer." She touched his arm, but he brushed her hand off without looking at her, and remained stiff, his eyes narrow.

The young woman turned her head and threw a glance at Hassida, as if forming a secret pact with her, entreating, "My lips are sealed, please act for both of us."

"Mr. Haddad," Hassida bent her head forward. Her voice came out clear and pleasant, the way she used to talk to her children when they were young. "You're on a trip with your wife and baby. Don't spoil it."

Without looking at her, Yehiel said, "I'm asking you not to interfere," and Yuval moved his lips inaudibly to say, "Stay out of it."

"I'm not on a trip, lady," the young man said, with the weary voice of an old man, "I don't know what it means to go on a trip. They used to talk of the 'Wandering Jew'—today we have Wandering Arabs. And don't address me as 'Mister.' 'Hey, you there, Arab'—that's good enough for me."

"As a 'Wandering Arab,' maybe you could explain something to me," Yehiel continued, trying to regain the upper hand.

The young man pursed his lips, turned his back to them, and fixed his gaze on the changing landscape. Numerous roads flowed under a huge bridge, like gathering rivulets. Then he said, as if to himself, "It doesn't matter anymore. And here I don't feel like explaining anything to you. As soon as I saw you, I remembered where I saw you last. People say it's a small world, and that's true. This could only happen in a story. To find you at this remote place! You, of all people. To be reminded of things I thought I was beginning to forget. It's better to forget. This American here really riled me, talking about wars as if it's like going for a spin in his car. As soon as we met, he mentioned Jerusalem. You have no idea what it means to be homesick for Jerusalem. But it doesn't matter now. I'm not your enemy anymore. Lately, we have become allies. Now you are your own enemies. What you see now coming to an end is already dead, even though it claims to be still alive."

Hassida trembled, and her hands shook on her knees. Her eyes were wide open as if witnessing a terrifying vision. Yehiel—his eyes darkened, his face grim—tried to hurl a rebuttal at the man, but the latter sank back in his seat and did not respond. Whereupon Yehiel, too, leaned back to signify his withdrawal from the fray. His pale jaws indicated to Hassida that he was still agitated. Was he upset because the mission was unaccomplished? Was he alarmed by the man who spoke like a prophet, who knew his name and army rank?

The driver, who had been following their argument, trying to catch a familiar word, to understand the exchanges, to see how things would turn out, now decided it was time to reconcile his impassioned passengers and said, smiling, "I hope no war breaks out in my van. Because a war between two Israeli warriors is a dangerous thing." He looked askance at the mirror, caught Yuval's eye, and called out, "And what about you, young man, are you a soldier yet?"

Yuval, perturbed by what had transpired between his father and the Arab passenger, hesitated for a moment, unsure whether it was proper for him to reply to the driver. He darted a look at his father's frozen face, then slowly, as if reciting a rehearsed line, he said, "I'll be a soldier next year."

"Congratulations!" the driver beamed at him. "I feel safe with you guys. Two and a half soldiers in my car. You're not offended by me calling you 'half a soldier,' are you, young man?"

Yuval twisted his lips to form a smile. He seemed ready to chat a little in English. But at that moment the woman on the radio announced a visit to the jewelery department, and the driver hastened to turn up the volume and listen intently. A young man enumerated, grandiloquently, the selection of jewels displayed on the special discount shelf: a man's ring with sixteen diamonds and one large ruby stone for $2,550; a diamond-studded tie pin for $199.90, marked down from $350; a man's quartz watch, with diamond-studded face and leather strap, $499.90, down from $700; diamond and emerald ring for $1,699.99, down from $2,550; groom's fourteen-karat gold ring, $29.90, down from $45; thirty-inch-long gold and cultured pearl necklace, which can be separated into twenty-three-inch strand and a seven-inch bracelet, $799.90, down from $1,200.

When the visit to the jewelry department was over, the driver peered in the mirror and saw the boy and his father immersed in a book. The woman in the back seat was watching the scenery. The young mother was lulling her baby to sleep and her husband was looking out the window. From the groan of distress the driver heaved, Hassida concluded that he had given up on his passengers and resolved not to waste his energy trying to entertain them. A pleasant lassitude descended on her—her body eased of its tension, her muscles relaxed—like the pleasurable glow after a climax. Trying in vain to account for that sensation, she said to herself, "Things happen in foreign parts that the old logic cannot account for. Here one needs to muster a new kind of logic. Nothing is as it used to be, neither people nor their thoughts." Even her heart seemed to beat to a new rhythm. "Here one has to erase what was before, like in a child's game, and start afresh."

The announcer on the radio bade good-bye to the jewelry department and moved on to the gardening department. In a monotonous voice, a salesman rattled off the prices of garden tools, fertilizers, flower pots, sprinklers, spades, rakes, and seasonal plants that were on sale in his department. After a chat with an ancient woman who was buying petunias and extolled their virtues in a hoarse and trembling voice, the salesman selected the song "Keep the Change," by a local singer, and the driver hummed the tune with obvious delight.

Suddenly, as they were passing the exit sign from the highway to the town of Summit, a log rolled off a lumber truck in front of them. The minivan driver, the words of the song still on his lips, tried to brake, then swerved away from the log, but not far enough, and the van, its tires shrieking, jerked and ran over the log.

The baby woke up and started to cry. His mother rummaged frantically in her bag and took out a milk bottle wrapped in a diaper. She shook the bottle vigorously, put its nipple in her mouth to check temperature and flow, and then gave it to the baby. Her head bent, her hair spread over it like a veil, her eyes radiating softness and joy, she looked at her child gulping his food. The young father turned his head to look at his baby, and the gloom and anger in his eyes gave way to that special tenderness reserved for people looking at their children. The two whispered softly, and they exchanged words above their son's head. The woman smiled, a dimple appeared in her cheek, and her husband's eyes sparkled.

Hassida peered at them surreptitiously, as if intruding on a private prayer. The couple's shoulders were close; it was the first time since they entered the minivan that they touched each other. Their heads close, they watched their baby suckle noisily. "This is the most beautiful sight in the world," Hassida told herself, feeling a radiance permeating her, as if she had witnessed a rare vision. "Of all the sights I have seen in America—cities, waterfalls, wide highways—this is the most beautiful." She dimly remembered the sensation of holding a baby in her folded arms, its sweet smell, the warm soft touch when it pressed against her body. For a moment, it seemed as if it were not she who had experienced all this, but another woman, who faithfully reported it to her until it became a faded memory and all the details were absorbed in her.

"Why are you glowing with pleasure, Hassida Harari?" Yehiel's whisper in her ear, like a venomous hiss, hit her in the most delicate part of her meditation. She turned around, startled by the mean spark in his eyes.

"You sure look in fine shape," she lashed at him, trying to answer malice with malice.

"Why shouldn't I be in fine shape?"

"Because you almost suffered a heart attack an hour ago." She felt the agitation that breeds toxicity.

"People recover from heart attacks, too," he grinned, "so what are you so pleased about?"

"Why does it bother you?" she managed to remove the apology from her voice.

"When women glow with pleasure, I start to worry," he chuckled. "The next step is usually crying. And when women cry, I am lost. Do you hear me, Yuvali?" He raised his voice and turned his shoulder around. "You must realize that glowing with pleasure is never the end. It's a sign that something else is brewing, but what it is, that's a big mystery. Still, crying is better than laughing. You should learn from your dad's experience."

Suddenly Hassida noticed that they were going through the main street of a city. The driver said with apparent relief, "I hope you don't mind if we stop here for half an hour. We always make a stop here. Our travel agency is next to the passengers' lounge. You can use either the passengers' or the office bathroom. There's a cafeteria on the corner, if you want something to drink. We're leaving in half an hour. Please be ready on time. I hope you've enjoyed the ride so far. Have a nice break."

IN THE PASSENGERS' lounge, Yehiel browsed in a travel guide, Yuval watched a group of boisterous kids sprawled on the floor, and Hassida sat on a bench that was joined in the back to their bench. She looked over people's heads at the Arab woman with the baby in her lap. The baby was facing the table, and together they unwrapped a package. Suddenly she heard her husband's voice.

"Do you know why your mother is not sitting with us and is turning her back to us, Yuvali?"

"Because she's ashamed of us?" he burst out laughing.

"No, Yuvali, try again."

"Because she forgot to buy us mints and feels bad about it?"

"No, Yuvali, try again. But I'll give you a hint: it has something to do with shopping."

"Something she did not buy at the drugstore?"

"Something she did buy at the drugstore."

"But she didn't buy anything."

"Didn't buy anything for us. That doesn't mean she didn't buy something for someone else." Hassida felt herself being drained, like a container that has been cracked at the bottom and had all its contents flow out. She heard their voices, the tone of mockery, petulance, resentful banter, but the words did not reach her heart. At the table across the lounge, the mother and child had removed the wrapping paper and discovered a colorful box. At another table facing them sat the father, looking irate, smoking a cigarette and blowing the smoke toward the window.

"Who is that someone she bought it for?"

"Try guessing again."

"Somebody at home. A present for our neighbors."

"Well, you could say that. A present for our neighbors is right. Which neighbors?"

"I don't know. You tell me."

"Guess again."

"Mrs. Medini?"

"For the Arab baby, Yuvali."

"The Arab baby!" Accusingly Yuval turned his face to his mother, but from his seat he could see only her hair and the tip of her ear. "Is it true, Mom?"

She did not answer. She looked ahead at two young women in identical dresses who passed by each other, exchanging hostile looks.

"You bought something for the Arab baby?"

"Listen to what Colonel Harari says," he pulled his son by the arm and directed his words toward his wife. "Colonel Harari understands Arabic, among other things, and in the cab he heard the Arab woman asking the nuclear engineer for some money to buy the kid something to play with, and the nuclear engineer, who also happens to be an Arab, tells her that they don't have money and there's no room in the suitcases anyway. Then Colonel Harari sees the Arab woman enter a drugstore and two steps behind her walks Private First Class Hassida Harari. Twenty minutes later, PFC Hassida Harari comes out of the store and tells her son that she has forgotten to buy him the mints. However, three steps behind her is the little Arab woman carrying a package the size of a rocket that she can barely hold in her hands. Now that package is on the table over there, and what does Colonel Harari see? It's a game of shapes like the one our Hadassie has. Do you have any idea how much a Fisher-Price toy like this costs?"

"Six bucks."

"Try fifteen. So what do you say, Yuvali? Should we dock it from her allowance?"

"I think this is very serious!" Yuval said.

"I agree with you there!"

A hot flash came over Hassida, but of a totally different kind than the ones she had been experiencing lately, not inducing weariness but rather invigorating. Her eyes flashed, and her accelerated breathing sounded like the rumble of bubbling water to her ears. Her husband's voice sounded distorted, as if emitted by a faulty transmitter.

"You see what a smart daddy you've got, Yuvali? Your mom does-n't appreciate it. But there's no denying that she made a very good choice. This game she bought helps develop the baby's intelligence. With such an education, he has a good chance of understanding the Russians' instructions on the tanks."

Hassida rose from her chair. The hot flash spread though her body like fire. She heard a polite voice asking, "Mr. Harari?" She turned her head to see a man wearing a cap with the words "Merchant Trail of Utah" on its visor. The man consulted a binder of documents he was holding, and said, "Mr. Harari, regarding your request for another vehicle, we're always glad to oblige our customers. Of course, we can't delay Mr. Haddad, so he will continue in the mini-van. We can put you on a bus that leaves here in seventy-five min-utes, if that's agreeable to you. Your rental car will be waiting for you in St. George."

"I hope our fellow travelers this time are Eskimos," Yehiel Harari said to his son when everything was settled and the travel agent had left. "There are a few questions about building igloos that have been bothering me since I was fifteen. What do you say, Yuvali, we have an hour to kill. Want to talk about wars?"

"Mom, what are you doing?" Yuval yelled suddenly, causing his father to turn his head.

Hassida was holding the handles of her suitcase and dragged it a few paces. Then she quickly turned back to grab her handbag from the bench. "I've been entertained enough for one day," she said, panting, feeling the flames inside her subside, her voice sounding new and strong both to her and to them. "I hope you have a good time with the Eskimos. I'll be waiting for you at the office in St. George because I am rid-ing in the minivan."

"Mom," Yuval said, and for the first time in many days his voice was without a trace of derision, "you can't travel alone with the Arabs!"

"I traveled alone with you two. I'll be fine with them."

Yuval turned to his father, fear in his eyes. "Dad, do something!"

"The two of you have done enough," she called to them, getting farther and farther away. "I want to breathe some fresh air by the window. Besides, I have to make sure the baby puts the pieces together correctly."

Translated from the Hebrew by Marganit Weinberger-Rotman

"What Am I Speaking, Chinese?" She Said to Him

ELIYAHU YITZHAKOV, THE real estate agent, donned his professional welcoming demeanor for the woman. She had attracted his attention from the moment she stepped out of her car, scanned the signs on top of the building, and made her way to his office. A picture immediately popped up in his mind: a black marble floor, a wide staircase leading all the way to the roof, French windows in the living room. Quietly closing the door behind her, the woman walked in, bade him good morning in a pleasant voice, peeled off her gloves, and glanced at the office walls. Eliyahu Yitzhakov eyed her with pleasure as she quickly took in the photographs presented to him by building contractors to hang in his office: pictures of unfinished structures, surrounded by scaffolding; photos of completed buildings; and one photograph of a house undergoing renovation—draped in purple plastic sheets, like a gigantic gift-wrapped birthday present—that he himself had snapped somewhere in Germany. It did not escape him how her eyes lingered on an enlarged newspaper photograph in which he and the mayor were shown shaking hands at a presentation ceremony of "Business of the Year" awards.

When she sat down facing him and turned her eyes on him, he shot a quick look, like a seasoned hunter, at her fingers as they trailed the gloves across the desk, and said hurriedly, "I have something just for you, ma'am. Exclusively handled by my agency. It's a penthouse not far from the beach. Imported tiles, black marble floor, completely furnished, leather upholstery in the front room, irrigation system on the roof—super luxury!"

The brim of her hat shaded her eyes a little when she turned her head politely and smiled furtively—a smile that made him uneasy, as if she were remembering a private joke. A slight hostility arose in him, but he quickly allowed himself to be seduced by her pleasant voice.

"I'm interested in the apartment at thirty-four Ha-Mered Street."

He recoiled in his impeccable imitation leather executive chair, his face registering insult, his mouth contorting in an affected disgust, leaving no doubt as to his reaction. "Ha-Mered Street! It's nothing but a dump next to the junkies' park."

"I saw your agency's sign on the window."

"Thirty-four Ha-Mered Street." He correctly read the determination in her voice and now tried another of his tactics: he leaned forward in a gesture that suggested intimacy and intoned mellifluously, "Thirty-four Ha-Mered Street is not a place for a classy woman like you."

"Why is that?" the secretive smile was back on her face.

"I know how to read people," he explained earnestly, ignoring the amused smile that lingered in her eyes. "Like a good matchmaker who knows how to introduce the right people, I know, as soon as I see someone, which apartment will suit that person's soul. I once saw a woman from behind; she was standing nearby, looking at a jeweler's window. There and then I knew I had the apartment for her. I went out and asked her if, by any chance, she was in need of an apartment. To this day, whenever she passes by, she comes in and thanks me for the apartment I found for her. So you see, even by looking at a person's back, I can find them the right apartment. Ha-Mered Street is not for you. Look —" he spread the palms of both hands in front of her, as if to underscore his total honesty, "I'll tell you the truth: the owner of the apartment on Ha-Mered came to me and said he had this place on Ha-Mered street. As soon as I heard Ha-Mered I said to him, 'I don't want it. Go to another agency.' But he insisted and gave me exclusive rights. So I said to him, 'I'm not committing myself. I once handled an apartment on Ha-Mered Street,' I told him, 'and couldn't get rid of it for half a year. Finally sold it to a couple of blind people.' But you— you'd be wasting your time going there. Better let me show you the penthouse."

Twenty minutes later he stood in front of the ground-floor apartment, struggling with the old lock, applying his weight in an attempt to force the door open. The door gave suddenly, and he was hurled inside the apartment, immediately assaulted by an overpowering moldy odor. He hurried to a window, fiddled with its rusty handle, and opened the shutter.

Only then did he turn to her to invite her in, except that she was already inside the apartment, at the entrance to the room adjacent to the kitchen, her gloved hand still on the doorknob, tilting her head upward to study the ceiling.

Even before discovering her motive, his senses told him that this did not bode well. "Let's start with the living room," he suggested, trying to steer her toward the best room in the apartment, but she did not react and just stood there, looking upward, focused, her neck stretching. Then, without moving her head, she removed her hat with her free hand, and the fair hair that was trapped under the hat fell straight onto her shoulders, like plastic fibers, the strands in the middle of her back amazingly long because of the backward tilt of her head. He wondered what was drawing her attention up there, so he came closer and peeked and immediately realized where the moldy smell was coming from, and also knew he would have to lower the price of the apartment.

"It doesn't look good, but it's only a minor plumbing job. Nothing serious. It wasn't here a month ago." The smell of her hair hit his nostrils as he craned his head above hers.

She grinned, remembering the first time she had seen those stains.

"Just one month?" she said, unable to contain her derision.

"One month and one hour," he tried to impress her with an old joke that often stood him in good stead.

She did not respond; her memory became clearer and sharper, carrying her back to the moment that had haunted her for many years: the morning following that awful, sleepless night. As soon as her parents had left the house, she leaped out of bed and sneaked into their bedroom like a thief, looking for the stains her mother had mentioned while sobbing. There were two gray spots in the corner of the ceiling, resembling two unmatched eyes with pale pupils, perhaps the result of a shoddy paint job.

Across the ceiling, she now noticed some black, sooty squiggles surrounded by flecks in all shades of gray which looked like a series of X-ray images laid side by side.

"This looks older than one month," she said in a broken voice, devoid of any argumentativeness. Her neck still craning, she wondered how her mother was able to predict the longevity of those stains as she wept on that terrible night, long after midnight. "How can you tell me that it will disappear? These stains will be here long after I croak."

"You can trust me, ma'am. I have experience in such matters. This happened a month ago—two months tops."

"More like twenty years ago," she chuckled, her head still tilted backwards.

He stood behind her, sensing his anger welling up at her persistent examination of the stains. Suddenly it occurred to him that her purpose in lingering there was to bring down the price of the apartment, which was already low.

"Listen," he shouted in her ear, "I'm going to see a house nearby. I have some business there. I'll be back in half an hour. You can look around as much as you want in the meantime."

At the door he heard her say, "What, you're leaving me alone here?" Before slamming the door he announced harshly, "I have a good eye for clients. You'll end up buying the penthouse. But if you enjoy peering at stains on the wall, ma'am, be my guest."

As soon as he left she was overwhelmed by an eerie sensation. Alone in the empty apartment, she suddenly found the silence oppressive, like the silence she recalled from the nights at the rural summer camp, when she used to lie on a mattress she could never get used to, listening intently to the ominous lack of sound, imagining beasts lurking in the dark, moving swiftly, furtively, on padded paws, making their way toward the innocent, unsuspecting prey smiling in its dreams. Now she found herself roaming gingerly around the apartment, feeling her way, absentmindedly caressing the walls, the panels, the bathroom tiles, searching for old clues, for kind regards from the girl who used to live there, who dreamt a lot, secretly imagining her future, not knowing that the imagined future awaited for her in the bosom of coming years, never guessing that one day—like a visitor from another planet—the heels of her boots would click on the very floor she used to wash every Friday after school, and that she would recognize the exact spot where water had stubbornly gathered in the dining area near the crooked tiles, but would then search in vain for the pale squares left on her bedroom wall by her kindergarten and elementary school pictures, for marks left by hooks that supported shelves laden with her textbooks and the junior encyclopedia that her father bought second-hand. Only the stains that her mother mentioned in her weeping remained. She went back to the old bedroom and stared at the ceiling.

Had she not requested a reading lamp for her fifteenth birthday, she would never have heard the weeping. But she did request a reading lamp, and when they brought the lamp home, wrapped in brightly colored paper, they realized that the light socket was hidden behind the wardrobe. Her mother immediately declared, in her razor-sharp voice, "The Wise Men of Chelm: first they buy a pig, then they find out it isn't kosher."

Her father hastened to say, before her face could register her disappointment, "Actually, it's time we shifted this wardrobe. I always thought it was in the wrong place."

She emptied the shelves and the drawers of the wardrobe, and her father strained, his face flushed, to turn the wardrobe around and push it toward the opposite wall. Light burst from the window that had been hidden behind the wardrobe for years, and filled the room. Without much effort, the two of them moved the bed to the wall where the wardrobe had left a pale square. Her father plugged in the lamp and turned it on. Like witnesses to a magic trick, the two of them marveled at the bright shaft of light that fell on the sheet.

She spent that afternoon replacing her belongings, one by one, in the wardrobe, in a meticulous new order: one drawer for socks, one drawer for stockings, another drawer for underwear, another for handkerchiefs and her white scarf, a shelf for school shirts, a different shelf for everyday shirts, and a shelf for the two dress blouses. Then she got down on her knees and diligently polished the floor tiles, placed a small rug near the bed, smoothed its fringes, laid her slippers precisely in the center of the arches in its pattern, shampooed her hair, combed it until the strands looked like flax stalks, and then snuggled under her blanket and lay in bed reading until late at night, her face turned to the window, her eyes above the book, observing the drapes, puffed by the wind, looking like a pregnant belly.

At midnight the voices started coming through the wall; she reread the last line on the page and her heart sank at the thought that the neighbors might be turning up the volume on their radio, as they had been doing since their last quarrel with her mother. But then she recognized her mother's voice, and then her father's, and even before catching the words, she was horrified at the realization that all those years the wardrobe had served as a buffer that absorbed their voices, and that from now on she was doomed to hear them.

"I need it, Marilla," her father was saying.

"I can't today." Her mother's voice sounded sharp and metallic.

"That's what you said last week, too."

"I've told you before and I'm not going to repeat myself like a parrot."

"You won't even have to take off your nightgown."

"No."

"Do it tonight and I won't ask again until next week."

"Cut it out."

"I'm begging you, Marilla."

"No, period."

Even before she connected the words together to understand the exchange between his failing voice and her relentless one, she knew what they were talking about, but part of her kept on reading, pretending to her own ears, clinging to the letters sliding down the page. When she reached the bottom line she realized that she had not understood anything and started over again, struggling hard to be engrossed by the story, terrified by the voices now rising anew beyond the wall.

She scrunched up in bed and turned off the reading lamp, hoping that the darkness would drive away the sounds, but the voices only got louder and stronger.

"I don't know what to do anymore. I can't restrain myself any longer."

"Then don't. I can't stand the pain."

"You said you'd see the doctor."

"It's not going to help. You don't go to the doctor for something like this. It's a question of age. We should quit doing it. Full stop."

"I had a minor accident with the new machine today."

"This too is my fault?"

"I've been edgy the whole week."

"You're edgy? Well, I'm edgy too! You think I should do things for you—while you do nothing for me. I can't stand these stains. I told you so a month ago."

"What stains? There are no stains here. It's something in the plaster. The painter must have done a poor job."

"What am I speaking, Chinese?"

SHE TRIED TO force herself to fall asleep, conjuring the image that always brought her calm before slumber: she is swimming in placid water, with measured motions, gliding like a dolphin on the smooth, shimmering face of the water over a murky bottom, and then sinking, sinking into the inviting blue, forever deepening and darkening.

Suddenly she was roused from the depths, wide awake, all her senses alert. For the first time in her life she heard her mother crying, and immediately recognized the sound as if she had heard it often. In the dark she saw the curtain float into the room and heard her mother's sobbing and her father's voice: "Now it's the stains. Last month it was the tap in the bathroom."

An unidentified sound came from beyond the wall, like people wallowing in rustling sheets unrolled from huge bolts. Her mother's voice declared, harsh and devoid of tears, "And paint the ceiling, for God's sake. You can see these stains in the dark."

Silently she got up, went into the bathroom, locked the door, filled the tub, muffling the gushing water from the tap with a towel, undressed, and submerged herself in the water. She washed her hair, dived and surfaced, rubbed her ears, her nape, her temples, scrubbed her skin so raw that it looked infected. She combed her wet hair once more, then tiptoed back to her bedroom, wrapped herself in the blanket, pulling the cloth over her head. She lay thus for several hours, waiting fearfully for the voices behind the wall, but she heard nothing and fell asleep, only to wake up alarmed, watching the window getting lighter and brighter. In the morning, when her father came to wake her up, he found her lying in bed, her eyes open, red, and he said immediately, "I can tell by your eyes that you've been reading the whole night. So this is what will happen with the new lamp? You'll just read on and on and on?"

"I want to put the bed back," she said, her voice sounding sick to her.

"Now, when the wardrobe is finally standing in the right place?"

"I want to sleep on that side," her high voice sounding foreign even to her own ears.

"But there's no socket to plug in the lamp," he contended logically.

"Then I won't read!" she rebelled.

"You must read a lot," he said softly, lovingly, caressing her hot forehead. "There are still so many things you have to learn."

IN THE MORNINGS after her experience she would sit with her parents in the kitchen, the three of them eating silently, their elbows touching, her eyes focusing on the bread, the butter, the jagged knife, not daring to look her parents in the eye.

On Saturdays breakfast was even harder for her, but as she sat hunched over her slice of bread, diligently spreading the margarine, she was surprised to hear them discussing mundane affairs in their normal tone of voice.

"This notice from the post office about a parcel has been lying here for two days. You've got to go to the post office."

"Maybe it's not a parcel. Maybe it's the tax authorities again."

"We got a letter from the tax authority just last month."

"So maybe it is a parcel."

"Don't they have anything better to do at the tax authority than to write to us? They must employ a special clerk just for us."

Her knife stopped spreading the margarine and she froze, somehow expecting to hear a continuation of the previous night's conversation: her father saying again, "Just once," and her mother immediately shooting back, "That's what you said on Monday. It took you half an hour."

"Why don't you see the doctor?"

"I should see the doctor? I must be speaking Chinese."

THE DOOR TO the kitchen porch, long exposed to the rain, was peeling, and its pane was cracked. She tried to open the blind, pulling hard on the threadbare cotton strap, but the blind refused to budge and remained stuck crookedly in its rusty casement. She peeked through a gap in the slats and saw the back of the neighboring house, a patchwork of peeling plaster; her eyes were drawn to a line of striped kitchen towels hanging out to dry along the ground-floor balcony.

Sometimes she would remember the young couple that used to live there at the time, their bedroom window facing hers. She remembered the laughter that emanated from there in the nights, sending strange shivers down her body, from her throat to her toes. Sometimes, in the morning, on her way to school, she deliberately stopped and waited for them to get to their motorcycle, which was always parked in the same spot, leaning against an electric pole. She pretended to busy herself with the buckle on her schoolbag, watching them from the corner of her eye as they climbed on the bike, the woman hugging the man from behind, clasping her hands over his fly, the two of them becoming one unit, like stars in a movie preparing for the final scene when a helicopter rescues them from the jungle. Many years later she used to talk about them to men she loved, always whispering, always with the longing that accompanies a belated realization.

The first time she heard their laughter, she was sitting with her mother in the kitchen. She was peeling cloves of garlic while her mother furiously chopped cabbage for pickling, her hand clutching the big knife firmly, pounding the sharp blade very close to her fingers. Suddenly a peal of laughter was heard, sounding fresh and surprising. The two of them fell silent at once. Her mother stopped in mid-motion, pricking up her ears as if she had been issued a declaration of war. She stood still for a moment, then braced herself and said to her daughter, "Don't go out." She burst out of the kitchen onto the adjacent porch.

"There are small children here." She heard her mother's voice outside, and she quickened the rate of her garlic peeling. "You should be ashamed of yourselves!"

When her mother came back into the kitchen her eyes were glaring, her face flashed with fury.

"Who were you talking to?" her daughter ventured to ask.

"Talking? Can you talk to them? Animals!"

"Why did you tell them to be ashamed of themselves?"

"They know the reason very well."

Outside a young voice was heard derisively, "Lady, we are terribly ashamed!" The blood rushed to her mother's face.

Another peal of laughter was heard and her mother rushed outside to the porch, brandishing the knife in her hand. The girl rose, the garlic skin in her palm, gingerly walked to the door, and peered out. On the balcony opposite she saw the man and woman, looking like a pair of high school kids. The woman was hanging out laundry, bending toward the taut clotheslines, intoxicated with her laughter, curls cascading over her face and down to her neck. The man was standing behind, bent over her, hanging the laundry above her head.

The girl stood there, half hidden, smiling at the sight of the handsome couple hanging laundry together, like a four-armed creature: two arms placing a blue T-shirt on the line, and two arms clipping clothespins on it, moving in unison, like synchronized rowers in a rowboat.

"Pigs!" her mother shouted at the top of her voice, flailing the knife; the girl recoiled and sat back in her chair in the kitchen. "Only pigs carry on like this!" Her mother slammed the door, her eyes bulging in her face.

Years later, while she was shaking a rug over the balcony railing, her husband came behind her, lifted her skirt, and pressed against her bent body, whispering in her ear, "We're like Napoleon, capable of doing several things at the same time." In that instant, the scene flashed through her mind, as if splashed on a giant screen, and for the first time she realized why the skirt had flown up the young woman's back and why the laughter had burst from behind the curls. "What's the matter, lady? Come over and look. All we're doing is hanging out the washing together. We're trying to save precious time."

THE BOTTOM CABINETS and the marble counter in the kitchen had already been replaced by subsequent tenants, but the upper cabinets, ordered by her mother a few years before they left the apartment, were still in place. One by one she opened the cupboards, finding them empty, and remembered the flowery wax paper her mother used to replace every spring, and the muslin ribbons along the middle shelf behind the glass door where the beautiful crystal goblets were displayed. During Passover holidays, she would help her mother in the kitchen, polishing silver candlesticks, peeling the old wax paper off the shelves, scraping hardened glue with a knife, scrubbing the shelves with a wooden brush and laying them on the floor to dry. During the hours they spent together, her mother worked diligently and efficiently, her lips pursed, constantly carping about the glue that dried too slowly, about the inferior paper that could not be cut straight, the dishonest merchant who had sold her defective lace ribbons. Bitter and cantankerous, she would settle accounts with the greengrocer who sneaked a rotten eggplant into her bag; with the neighbor who saw a sheet blowing by his car but did not bother to pull it out of a puddle; with the insolent couple, new neighbors, who had no shame—day and night you can always tell when they were at home, carrying on loudly; with Father, who would not lift a finger around the house—"Just look at the grimy door frames that he claims are perfectly clean."

When her father's name was mentioned, she bent herself farther over the shelf and worked more industriously, shrinking as if to protect herself, listening to her mother fuming: "He doesn't understand anything; it's as if I'm speaking Chinese to him"

Now, standing in front of the empty cabinets, she felt sorry for her father, for the pointless bitterness her mother had injected into her life, for the poison she had accumulated in her heart over all those years, letting it fester and bubble like boiling lava, locking her heart even against rare moments of sweetness. Suddenly she remembered one Saturday night: her father came out of the shower, clean and fresh, a towel around his shoulders, looking like a poster advertising summer holidays; his face was so happy and he looked so handsome with his hair brushed back, his hands stretched out, singing an aria from some opera loudly and terribly off-key. He approached her mother, hugging her from behind; but her mother recoiled from him crossly, wiped her nape where he had dripped on her, smoothed the blouse he had wrinkled, and snapped, "Why are you shouting in my ears?"

Even in old age, her father never ceased to woo her mother: always bringing her flowers and small gifts, never begrudging her refusals, and all the years trying to reconcile his daughter's heart to her, telling her, his voice full of affection, "You have no idea how beautiful your mother was. Even after the war, when sometimes you couldn't tell who was a man and who was a woman, only she, with her gray eyes—like a butterfly."

So why does she cry in the night? The question tore from her but halted at her twisting mouth. In its stead another sentence came out, with a smile that replaced the contorted lips: "Daddy, I'm sure you don't mean to say 'butterfly.'"

"But it's so hard to love her," her father continued his train of thought. "So don't be angry if in the end she won't let you have a party here. She doesn't know how to give of herself."

SHE WAS IN her parents' bedroom, her eyes staring at the ceiling, when she heard the key turn, and there was the real-estate agent standing in the doorway.

"You're still looking upward?" his eyes rounded in amazement. She stared at him and suddenly burst out laughing, the kind of carefree, gay laugh she used to emit when her children were small and surprised her with newly invented words or an unexpected, clever act. It was the first time he saw her shed her sardonic grin, and he joined in her mirth.

"At this rate, it'll take you a month to inspect the apartment," he said, glad to hear her laughter grow. "And maybe six months to inspect the penthouse." He was encouraged by the laughter, which had become compulsive. The anger he had felt toward her disappeared and he was filled with kindness. "Now I have all the time in the world for you. I'll show you the apartment tile by tile. I can see that you like ceilings, so I'll show you ceiling after ceiling."

"I really want you to show me something," she said, her laughter slowly subsiding. She leaned forward, lifted her right leg, and standing on one leg, her chin touching her knee, started to undo her bootlaces. Her long fur coat hid her hands, and he could see the golden curtain of her hair part, exposing dark roots.

"Everything all right, ma'am?" he asked, amazed, trying to fathom her actions.

"Perfectly all right." She did not raise her head to him. She looked like a big polar bear hugging its raised knee. Her undone bootlaces grew longer and longer, pooling under the fur coat. Suddenly one boot was in her hand, and she put it on the floor, next to her foot in a sheer nylon stocking. She lifted her left foot and again bent to unlace the other boot.

"I was thinking about this stain in the ceiling," he said, ill at ease, trying to divert his attention from the woman who was doing her bizarre act with such determined motions. But his eyes, lured, followed the bootlaces dangling from under her coat. "Something pinching in your boots, ma'am?"

She lifted her head, her face lit by a surprised smile. "You could say something was pinching," she agreed pleasantly.

"Concerning the stain"—he grasped something familiar, trying to extricate himself from the confusion she caused him—"it can't be dampness, because in the apartment upstairs, the bathroom and the kitchen are on the other side."

"You're selling the apartment upstairs, too?" She placed the second boot next to the first.

"No . . . I just looked . . . from the outside . . . judging by . . ." With burning eyes, he followed her motions as she stood in her stocking feet, took off her coat, and laid it on the floor, its clean white lining resting on the dirty floor, which had not been cleaned for many months.

"Judging by the windows . . . Isn't it a pity to ruin your coat like that?"

"There's no choice," she said.

"I could hold it for you," he offered.

"You'll soon see that it's not so simple." She smiled, stood on the coat, bent her knees, and again standing on one foot, started taking off her stocking. He stood there, his eyes mesmerized by the thighs briefly exposed beneath her skirt when she lifted her leg to remove the stocking, which was held by a wide lace garter. The stockings rolled down her legs, and then she unzipped her skirt and let it fall at her feet on the white fur.

"Ma'am," his eyes were riveted on her short muslin slip, "are you all right?" His eyes followed the skirt that now joined the boots, followed by the delicate slip.

"We shall soon see; it depends on you," she looked at him, amused, and saw fit to increase his embarrassment by explaining, "Usually I begin to undress from the top." She watched his eyes roll in his face.

"What are you doing, ma'am?" he muttered confusedly, fearing her, yet fearing even more that the magic sight would disappear before his eyes. She asked, "Is the door locked?'

At that moment it dawned on him and he rushed to the door, his hands reaching to open his trouser belt. By the time he came back, he had managed to undo his belt—his fingers struggling with the loops and with the buckle—and she was already lying on her white fur coat, naked, her legs stretched straight forward, one foot resting on the other, her head supported on her hand, watching him undress with hurried motions. His trousers dropped to the floor revealing a small belly, surprisingly tanned legs, and dark purple shorts, the color of a velvet dress she once wore on Purim when she dressed up as a gypsy. He quickly dropped his shorts to the floor, but when he noticed her eyes following him, he thought better of it, picked them up, folded them neatly together with his trousers. When he bent down she saw a tiny, flowerlike spider tattooed on his shoulder in pink and turquoise. The sight made her laugh, a pleasant, surprised laugh, as if she were making a mental note: a man with a tattoo—now that's a first for me.

To her surprise, she felt neither embarrassment nor strangeness. She watched him as he laid his pile of clothes next to hers, and, naked, stretched by her side on the fur that her husband had given her for their tenth wedding anniversary. The fur now lay, face down on the gray pavementlike floor, in the exact spot where her parents' double bed used to stand. The touch of his body, she noted, felt familiar, and her palm stroked the inside of his arm as if she had done so many times before, and the scent of his aftershave also smelled familiar, and so was the way he slid his hand from her waist to her shoulder and bent his head in search of her mouth. She jerked her head sharply and he found himself burying his face in her neck. With his sharp merchant's sense, he grasped what it was she was trying to convey to him; so he heaved himself and took her by storm and she received him without protest.

Her eyes closed, she felt herself drawn inward, ignoring the hard floor underneath and the man above. Clear, cool water swirled around her and she traversed it in a straight line, spreading her arms, then joining her palms together, swimming forward in long, measured motions, cutting through the encompassing azure that glimmered like silken cloth. A sense of well-being engulfed her, infusing her body like a stream. And all the while—even when the blue light began to recede slowly outside the water, like a shining neon light, and she prepared to dive away from it—she remembered the man crouched on top of her, and a faint voice, like a call from afar, arose inside her: "Mommy, Mommy." Not in panic, or desperation, or supplication, or demand: "Mommy, Mommy." The voice came out of her in love, like an experienced person trying to impart important knowledge to a young and very dear one: "Mommy, Mommy, it could not be that awful with a man who truly loved you, who even in old age remembered you as he had first seen you, with the bond of war uniting you. Here I am, Mommy, with a strange man I met by chance, a man without any distinction or merit, and he is pinning my head to the exact spot where your head used to lie, my eyes facing the stains that give off a terrible, musty smell, and I wonder why you never accepted the consolation of the body, why you never taught me this great conciliatory gift, this immeasurable pleasure, and I had to learn all this by myself, as if I were a pioneer. I always remember your rasping voice: 'Chinese, I must be speaking to you in Chinese.' What were you crying about all those nights, a bitter and sullen woman, so harsh and cruel to your loved ones, so totally devoid of charity toward yourself and others?"

She opened her eyes and saw the agent's face close to hers. His eyes were closed, and he crouched above her without burdening her, supporting his weight on his elbows on either side of her body, and all the while—she suddenly noticed—whispering in her ears endearments he must have heard in movies and assumed that a woman of her sort is used to hearing at moments like this. She felt a wave of warmth toward him, for his naiveté, for the words he whispered into her neck, for the lightness of his chest against her. Grateful, she smiled, realizing how tender his actions were, how unexpected for a man whose tattooed spider was bouncing up and down in front of her as if threatening to pounce, then reconsidering and withdrawing.

Above his bouncing head she suddenly noticed the ceiling with two stains in the shape of butterflies: one, huge and gray with yellow specks on its outstretched wings, covering half the ceiling, hiding another, small and slightly lighter in color; and both butterflies were flying away from the corner toward the window, as if trying to extricate themselves from the plaster, assume bright colors, and fly away. Her eyes wide open, she followed the man's face in front of her as he groaned, shifted his body, and then relaxed, still hovering over her, supported on his elbows, opening his eyes.

"Next time we go to the penthouse," he panted in her ear. "There's a bed and a jacuzzi in the bedroom there."

Chinese, she told him softly in her heart. "Who needs a jacuzzi? Does the penthouse have butterflies on the ceiling?" she said derisively.

"Who needs butterflies when you have a penthouse?" he said seriously.

She smiled at him affectionately, with the kindness of someone to whom a secret has been revealed, and she thought: You don't even know, Mr. Eliyahu Yitzhakov, what pearls of wisdom are emerging from your mouth.

"I'm the only one who has the key to that apartment" he smiled in return. "If you wish, I could draw butterflies on the ceiling."

Without warning, tears rose in her throat and gathered at the corners of her eyes, despite herself, and she thought: You will also never know that you were the first man to see me cry naked. It is your uncanny tenderness, your warmth. Things one is not used to break one's resistance easily. She could feel the tears streaming down her face.

"Lady?" Alarmed, he lifted himself on his hands. "What's the matter? Why are you crying?"

She spread her fingers on her face, smoothing it and pushing the hair away.

"Is something wrong?" The tone was that of a person used to rendering service.

"You did very well," she heard herself giving him a grade, like a teacher to a student. Supporting herself on two straight arms, she lifted herself to a sitting position, facing him, leaning against the wall, and wiped her eyes with the back of her hand, fingers straight as if in a salute.

"Lady." His voice sounded hurt and he narrowed his eyes. "You wanted it. Don't tell me you didn't. A friend of mine was once tricked like this. A woman seduced him and then went to the police and accused him. His name was in the papers."

"Don't worry." She reached for her panties. "I won't go to the police."

His face turned red at the sight of the sudden cold, aloof expression on her face. "You dragged me here," he fumed, humiliated. "As soon as I saw you get out of your car, with your blonde hair and all your rings, I knew something was not right."

She got to her feet, her stockings in her hand, all matter-of-fact, her eyes dried. She peered at him and saw the large shoulders, contracting their muscles, extending the turquoise spider's legs. All at once she realized that he was offended because the roles had been reversed and he could not accept it. While putting on her stocking, stretching her toes all the way, she glanced at the rings on her fingers and at the white fur spread on the floor, and for the first time was gripped by genuine fear. A man of his sort, her alert sense told her, you can never tell how he may react when crossed. She smoothed the stocking and adjusted the lace garter on the top of her thigh, and then saw him approach her on his knees, naked.

"And then," he raged, "when you walked into my office and told me Ha-Mered Street, I had a feeling about you. From the beginning you wanted to drive me nuts!"

His eyes were covered with a thin film, as if hypnotized, and she glanced nervously at the door, her mind rapidly calculating: if she grabbed her blouse and skirt and dashed to the door, he would not pursue her in his state of nakedness. But he seemed to have read her mind and grabbed her arm. He glimpsed her free hand reaching for her blouse and clamped his other hand on her outstretched arm. With her hands thus imprisoned, she peered closely into his eyes, admitting to herself that she could not decipher their expression. She looked for clues in his face: its language, too, was foreign to her.

She decided to gamble, assuming that his reactions were slower than hers, and the sooner she acted, the better her chances to win this battle that was waging between them and whose rules were not known to her. She moved her arm gently, letting the pain climb from her wrist to her shoulder, and seemed to feel his grip loosen. She continued shaking her arm, until she realized that her hand was free and wondered at the ease with which she had accomplished it; she knew that now she must plan her moves wisely, so, one by one, she lifted his fingers from her other wrist. With both hands now free, she picked up her blouse, straightened, and with knees aching from the strain, stood over him and put her arms through the sleeves, fearing all the while that he might toy with her a little more, and in a minute would pounce on her and nail her down again.

But then she saw his eyes.

His eyes, she noticed, looking down on him as he stood on his knees, naked, were sad. Her fear dissipated at once. She bent down facing him, without a skirt, her blouse still unbuttoned, and cradled his face in both her hands, the way she used to treat her children when they got bruised and cried. Like them, he too let her wrap her hands around his large, stubbly cheeks, and remained thus, obedient and placid as she bent her face and kissed him on the cheek and said, "Don't be angry, I don't want you to be mad at me. I will always remember you with great affection."

He seemed confused, hovering between his anger and the realization that these were words of farewell. The hurt still lingered in his eyes, his cheeks were still flushed, but his face already registered reconciliation and wore a childish expression. "You women drive us nuts, that's all," he said, putting some distance between himself and his present predicament, as if this were not something happening between a particular man and woman, but a conspiracy of all women against all men.

She burst out laughing, with a great sense of release, buttoned up the delicate pearl buttons on her blouse, gathered up her skirt, and said, relieved, as she watched his eyelashes twitching rapidly, "You won't have any problems finding tenants; this is a very good apartment. Just make sure you paint over this ceiling—then everything will be okay."

Translated from the Hebrew by Marganit Weinberger-Rotman

Mother's Photo Album

FROM THE BAD times—Dr. Joshua Hoshen found himself thinking on the way to his car—not even a single photo remains from the bad times. It was as if they were anxious to preserve the good times, to fix them on glossy bits of paper, like a will executed in pictures. Here, this is how things ought to be. And if they turn out differently, they will be expelled from people's memories.

Before placing the photo album in the trunk, he notices, to his amazement, that in all the pictures the three of them always looked neatly dressed, their shoes shined, the necklace around his mother's neck always centered in the middle of her décolletage and her belt tight and straight. His father stood erect, two creases showing along the sleeves of his starched shirt; the child's socks were neatly folded over the tops of his shoes, and the part at the side of his hair was perfectly straight. Most often, he was seen in either his mother's or his father's arms, while later, when a little older, he stood between them, his hands in theirs, the three of them smiling broadly, as if trying to convince the photographer of their happiness.

A few minutes later, reporting for the first time to his post as physician-on-duty, he parked his car in the reserved spot, took out his case and the photo album from the trunk, and, his heart brimming with pride and trepidation, walked through the deserted hospital, clutching the album under his arm, glancing at the lighted windows of the nurses' rooms.

At the physician-on-duty's office the head nurse offered him a cup of coffee.

"So you made the rounds, did you?" She smiled. "I know from experience that on the first night of duty no doctor can fall asleep." She burst out laughing, "but the next time, you can't wake them up."

He did not laugh with her, and it seemed to him that she immediately resented him for that. "Do you want to do another round?"

"No, I want to check a couple of files."

"Right now?" Her look indicated she was a woman always suspicious of unusual behavior.

"Yes."

"You want to read medical files now?"

"Precisely."

"Be my guest," she shrugged, the astonishment in her eyes more pronounced.

Once he was behind the closed door, the medical file was in his hands within seconds. He stared at the somewhat familiar yet strange name sloppily written on it, and the name brought back the memory of his parents, anxious to preserve in celluloid the good days before they were devoured by the bad days, dutifully inviting the photographer over even when times were hard, like criminals plotting in advance an evil scheme.

He opened the photo album he had brought. The top picture on the first page showed him at the gate of the kindergarten on the first day of school, his eyes shining, his hand-stitched lunch bag neatly tied, hanging from his shoulder, his tiny fingers clutching a rolled note the teacher had sent for his mother, and a heart-shaped paper pinned to his ironed shirt exactly at the spot where the heart appeared in a diagram in the encyclopedia. In the photo in the middle of the page, taken a year later, he is already a tall boy, standing at the metal gate of the school, the straps of his schoolbag shaping grooves in his shoulders; a new and bigger lunch bag, made from the cloth of his old pants, reaches down to his thigh, and his bewildered eyes stare at the photographer focusing his lenses and at the giggling children crowding around him.

At the bottom of the page is a photo from a trip to the beach in Tel Aviv, captured minutes before the horizon darkened and a sudden shower poured down, drenching them and making his mother burst into tears. But in the picture it is still sunny, and in the background a fisherman with his line is seen against the foam-speckled sea. In the picture his father, perhaps for the last time, hoists his son on his shoulders, and his mother, after smoothing the child's hair with nimble fingers, stands motionless by, her posture suggesting that her heels are too high and her shoe-straps are too tight.

He envisioned her many years later, long after they had stopped posing for pictures, when he is a teenager: she peers at him with bleary eyes, her hair unkempt, her skin shriveled; she is lying in a disheveled bed at the far end of the ward, and a strip printed repeatedly with the logo of the Ministry of Health separates her nape from her shoulders where the stylish clasp of her necklace used to nestle.

And again, years later, the first time he stood by her bed during the doctors' rounds, with a group of students attending the head of department, his heart raging when he realized that this was the ultimate test for him, that everything he had done up to this point was leading to this moment: the head of department examines her file solemnly and says matter-of-factly, "Here we have a typical case of psychotic depression." And from within him a voice threatens to explode: "Professor, she is not a case . . . and there are several inaccuracies in her medical records. She wasn't born in 1915 but in 1924, and during the war she didn't . . ."

The voice is silenced at once. Her eyes stop wandering from face to face and focus on him, opening frightfully wide, and her mouth twitches but no sound escapes. The professor places the file on a nurse's lap, accepts another one that she hands him and leads the group to an adjacent bed. Joshua feels her eyes boring into his back, riveted on him as he moves from bed to bed with the others, and agitated, he wonders: Are the scenes all confused in her mind? Is this good for her? Will her condition deteriorate?

At the door he turns his face quickly toward the bed by the window, seeking to reassure her with his eyes, to promise her that from now on he will take care of her here. That was the reason he had applied again and again to medical school, and why he was not discouraged even when he found he was the oldest applicant. From the door he sees that she has dozed off, her mouth agape, her face to the window.

When the doctors' rounds are over, he sits in the lecture hall unable to hear a word of the professor's summary. Only one picture, in color, that was pasted by itself on an entire page of the album, rises before his eyes.

Now he turned the pages and found the picture on the next to the last page—the last picture taken. Then the letter from America had arrived and they had stopped posing and pretending in front of the camera. His parents still tried to hide the approaching storm from him; they spoke at night when they thought he was asleep, arguing in whispers, in Polish, a language that fired his imagination and sounded like the hissing of snakes. He lurked in the dark, clutching the edges of his blanket tightly, not comprehending the words, yet sensing the menace. During that period, whenever Joshua passed by his father, the latter would stretch his hand and pat his head solicitously, and Joshua thought he detected a moistness in his father's eyes. Once, he suddenly grabbed the child and clasped him tightly, sending tremors through his body like electric shocks.

But in that colored photograph—presumably taken at the time when the letter from America with the pretty stamp on it was crossing the Atlantic, lying in the ship's hold in a mail pouch—in that colored photograph pasted by itself on the album page, his mother and father stand arm in arm behind him, like a wall, their shoulders touching, and Joshua, an Arbor Day sapling in his hands, tries to stretch his arms as far as possible so that the leaves will not tickle his nostrils.

Then the letter from America arrived and Joshua stared for a long time at the pretty stamp, and his father's face darkened overnight; his mother, at the edge of their double bed, could not stop crying even in the daytime. In those days Joshua, left to his own devices for hours on end, used to pore over the pictures in the album, focusing on one of the few pictures in which they did not present a united front for the photographer's benefit: In it, his father is lying down on a patch of grass, his mother, her legs folded beneath her, is sitting next to him, a length of straw in hand, with which she mischievously tickles his chin. Nearby sits their neighbor Halina, who, on their outings, always used to bring stuffed cabbage in a dented aluminium container. In the background, swinging on a rope, is Joshua, hanging from a tree like a monkey.

A few weeks after the arrival of the letter his mother began to speak to him in Polish. At first he was alarmed. "Mommy, what are you saying?" Then he understood: she was not talking to him but to herself.

She spoke in an eerie, gushing manner, pacing about the room, standing in front of the closet emptying shelves and drawers, taking out his father's belongings and piling them up in the center of the room: trousers, handkerchiefs, ties, dressy suit, socks, felt hat; then going to the kitchen and the bathroom to bring his razors, his old pipes; gathering his belongings from all the corners of the house, adding them to the pile: his tool kit, harmonicas, newspaper clippings, books about Warsaw, string he had meticulously collected and coiled into balls and stashed in a canvas bag. Then she brought a matchbox from the kitchen, lit a match, and set fire to the mound in the center of the room. She forcefully grabbed Joshua's hand, and the two of them sat there, watching tongues of fire devour all of his father's belongings. Her eyes were also burning as she sat near the fire and watched, and he—quite fearlessly—squeezed her hand back and curiously watched a little strand of fire make its way to a shirt collar, scorching it, then the shirtsleeve, then a piece of string wound around a hammer's handle, a cuff, the cloth of his trousers. By the time the neighbors had begun shouting and stormed in, the ceiling was covered with soot and the many buckets of water that were brought in could not save a thing.

The day his mother was taken to the hospital, Halina stayed with him to help him pack his bags. With a stern face, she laid any clothes she could find in a suitcase, and he added the photo album. While they waited for the man from the Ministry, Halina did her best to soothe him: she wrote down her name and address on a crumpled envelope so he could write to her from his new home; she assured him they would find a good place for him until his mother got better and his father returned from his business in America and the three of them would live together again. In the meantime, she promised him, she would take good care of their apartment, get rid of the burned remains, hire a painter to paint the ceiling and the walls, and open the windows and shutters every other day. Joshua made an effort to listen to her, but all the while he seemed to smell the aroma of stuffed cabbage coming out of her mouth and it made him hungry, but it seemed impolite to think of food at such a time, so he summoned up all his powers and listened to her describing how well she would take care of the apartment, and especially how she would wrap up the radio so the dust would not get in and clog the delicate tubes inside the appliance.

That night Joshua was taken to a kibbutz. At the gate of the children's quarters he and the man who accompanied him were met by a heavyset caretaker who took his suitcase and put it under his bed, then introduced him to his three roommates, whose names he could not remember. All night long he tried to hold back the tears, and in the morning he asked the caretaker when his mother was coming to take him. The nanny put her hand on his neck and said that they were going to have an English lesson that day, but there was no book for him yet.

He sat quietly in the classroom, his eyes following the ponytail of the teacher as she scribbled in English on the chalkboard. After class, he went to look for the caretaker and asked when his mother was coming to collect him, and she promised to find out. In the afternoon, he took out the photo album from his suitcase, selected ten of the prettiest pictures, and hung them around his bed. Soon several kids gathered around him to watch. In the coming days, when he entered the room, there was often a kid standing there, furtively studying the pictures. One girl, who was unfazed by his sudden entry and did not even bother to apologize for standing on his pillow to get a better view, said, "When I grow up, I'll have bracelets and lots of clothes just like this one."

That week Nehama and Yigal became his adoptive parents. One afternoon Nehama brought him to their room and gave him tea and jam cookies, and Yigal looked at him and said, "The next calf born in the barn we'll call Joshua, after you. What do you say?"

Joshua reflected and then agreed. And Yigal said, "I can see you're a boy who likes to think about everything. You didn't say yes or no right away. I like that. We'll get along fine. What do you say?"

Joshua reflected and then agreed. Nehama laughed heartily and said, "You'd better check that it's a calf and not a heifer that they name Joshua. Sometimes they make mistakes out at the barn."

When Nehama saw the photographs on the wall by his bed, she was afraid that one of the kids might covet them, so she asked Joshua if he would mind taking them down. He reflected and then agreed. Together they took them down carefully and replaced them in the album, which Nehama dubbed "Mother's Album," but he rebelled. "It's also Father's and my album." Nehama stowed the album in her closet, behind the towels, and whenever he asked to see it, she took it out and let him pore over it. Together, they would sit and admire his mother's clothes and the handsome curl on his head. A new scent clung to the pages, the smell of myrtle leaves that Nehama kept between the towels. After a while it was hard for him to recapture his mother's scent, and the further it receded, the more he himself insisted on calling it "Mother's Album."

From time to time, Nehama would take him to visit his mother. They always had to check twice to make sure the right name was on the card by the patient's bed, since each time the woman seemed different. He would kiss the woman even when he could hardly recognize her, and she would give him a penetrating look, as if trying to solve a riddle. Once she peered at him for a long time, then fell to her knees and started shredding the sheet that covered her mattress. The nurse rushed in, syringe in hand, and his mother wrestled with her, her arms showing protruding veins, her entire body shaking. When the shaking subsided, the nurse helped her, now placid and limp, back to her bed, and told Nehama, who had been standing there all the while hugging Joshua, "She's been better lately. It's not a good idea to bring the child. It's not good for him either. A child his age should not see his mother in such a state."

In the bus on the way back, Nehama held his head between the palms of her hands and said, "Maybe when you grow up you'll be a doctor and help your mother."

And he answered right away, as if the matter were to be decided on the spot, "I don't want to be a doctor. I want to be a dairy farmer like Yigal."

As they were walking back from the main road he said, "I want to take your name. I don't want to go by her name anymore." Nehama, momentarily taken aback, stopped in her tracks, peered at him intently, and said, "You should remember her the way she was in the photographs."

ON HIS FIRST leave from the army, he stood at the door of her ward in his army uniform, a wrapped box of chocolates in one hand and a batch of photos in the other. The nurse eyed him suspiciously.

"She's not doing well today." She barred the entrance with her body.

"I'm her son."

"We're not aware that she has a son."

"Because I haven't been to visit her for several years. The last time I was here she didn't react well and the nurse—"

Reluctantly the nurse let him enter, and from her station watched him hand the box of chocolates to the patient, who took it but did not open it. He unwrapped the box and offered her the candy, but she kept looking at him with lifeless eyes, even when he put the pictures in front of her and asked, "Who is this? Who is this?" Only one picture made her sit upright. Her expression changed, a spark lit her eyes, her forehead smoothed, and her lips trembled, but at that moment the nurse darted from her seat and declared that the visit was over.

"Suddenly I remember a lot of things," he told Nehama that evening, when they were sitting together and she mended his uniform trousers. It was as if his mother's awakening memory rekindled his own. "I remember falling into a puddle and mud got into my eyes, and she rinsed my eyes with a lot of water and kissed them so I couldn't open them, and said something like, 'Never mind, it won't hurt you, it's the mud of the Land of Israel.' And I remember that at night, when I was frightened, I would call to her and she would come and sing to me in Polish. She said they were sad songs, but I laughed because of the language. And once she bought me ice cream and she wanted a taste, so I stretched my hand like this, and she bent down and the ice cream hit her smack on the nose, and she roared with laughter."

"And you didn't remember all this before?"

"No. I remembered only what was in the photos."

"Did she recognize anything in the photos you took to her?"

"No."

"Did you show her the photos?"

"Yes, but she didn't speak, only when I showed her the one on the beach, she got excited, but then the nurse chased me out of there."

"Of all the pictures, just the one on the beach?"

On the beach, the three of them are embracing, huddled together as if seeking shelter, their feet buried in the sand, their shoulders glistening with water. This is the only picture in the album in which his mother is seen with her hair gathered and flattened against her skull, making her cheeks look puffed. She looks very short without her high heels; the top of her head comes up only to her husband's chin, her neck is naked without the string of pearls, and her hand reaches for her throat, by force of habit, to check that the necklace is in place. His father, without his clothes, looks thinner than in the other photos, his shoulders hunched, his eyes squinting against the sun, one hand embracing his wife's shoulder. Between them a joyful Joshua, a broad smile on his face, stretches both arms to hug his parents, and his bathing trunks ride so high on his torso, its belt touches his chest.

AT THE PHYSICIAN-ON-DUTY'S OFFICE, Dr. Hoshen lifted the cardboard cover of the medical file and read the information written there in the usual order: name, place of birth, date of birth, diagnosis. The patient is a woman born in 1915 . . . suffering from prolonged psychotic depression . . . repressed trauma . . . separation anxiety. Slowly he turned the pages, corrected the erroneous year of birth, and reread the report of the doctors and the psychologist.

For a long time he read the medical record couched in dry, medical terms. History: born in Lodz, the eldest of four girls . . . Toward the end of the war, they were moved to a hiding place in a farm near Radom . . . Suspecting that one of the Christian neighbors was about to turn them in, they were forced to leave their hideaway. The farmer agreed to keep her because she was sick that day. She was sixteen years old at the time. It is not clear if sexual assault occurred, but according to a T.A.T. test, severe rape anxiety is indicated. She maintains that no one survived from her family. After the war she met a man, also from Poland; they got married and emigrated to Israel in 1951. They had one son. The disease erupted when she found out that the man had been married before the war. His wife, who had stayed with her parents in Lublin, managed to cross the eastern border and spent the war years in Russia. When asked why her husband had not told her about his first wife, the patient burst out crying. This was the only time during the examinations that she cried. After the war, the first wife emigrated to the United States, started looking for her husband, and finally located him in Israel. The husband left the patient and her son and went to the United States. The patient claims that he went because of his first wife's threats and that he promised to return right away, but he never came back and cut off contact with the patient and the son. The boy was placed in a kibbutz when the patient had to be hospitalized following an arson attempt. The patient has no relatives in the country who can verify the story, and all the details were supplied by her and by a neighbor, Halina Holz. In the first few years she was kept in the closed ward . . . Treatment: Dr. Shimshoni recommends Amobarbitalin in addition to Phenothiazine. An examination conducted by Dr. Greenspan yielded findings suggesting chronic schizophrenia, thinking disturbances, social aversion, and emotional apathy . . .

Dr. Joshua Hoshen took out a photo from the album and carefully attached it to the inner flap of the file cover. He hesitated for a moment: as a rule, patients' medical records did not feature photographs. Underneath the picture he wrote in large letters: DO NOT REMOVE.

A moment before closing the file and replacing it, he looked at the photo and felt relief, as if a tumor had been removed from his body that for years had metastasized through all his organs. This, he knew, is how she wanted to be remembered: dressed in a day suit with padded shoulders, the collar of her white silk blouse resting on the crisp lapels of her suit, a string of pearls on her chest, her head held high, her hair coiffed, her face looking fresh, a handsome man gazing fondly at her, and a child at her side, his hand in hers.

Joshua brought his eyes closer to the photo and peered at the child as if seeing him for the first time: his head, too, held high, his hair neatly combed, his legs slightly apart like his father's, planted firmly on the path, smiling effortlessly in response to the photographer's request, looking bravely at the camera, chin thrust forward provocatively, two smiling people standing firm to his left and to his right, and he, protected between them, joyously anticipating the days to come.

Translated from the Hebrew by Marganit Weinberger-Rotman

Morning in the Park
Among the Nannies

WHEN YOU SHOWED up in the playground in the public park, I recognized you at once. It had been decades since I last saw you and still—the restrained tremor behind a curtain of languor, the unmistakable gait, the feet almost dancing, the peculiarly erect head with the neck thrust forward as if you were seeking the horizon, the quick glance lashing and sailing past. You were pushing a child's stroller on the dirt path leading to the farthest bench by the water fountain when you passed me. I saw clearly the beauty that had withstood time's wrecking powers, the sky blue eyes encircled by shadowy lines, the noble forehead arching back into the roots of your hair. I couldn't take my eyes off you as you parked the stroller in the shade of a tree, walked to the sandbox, bent down, gathered a handful of sand, and raised it to your eyes to examine it.

"She's counting the microbes," the Bulgarian nanny chuckles, and the two nannies sitting with her burst out laughing. Every so often a new nanny appears in the park and becomes the butt of the Bulgarian's mordant humor, especially if she chooses the farther benches. The others watch the impending duel with glee, hoping to fill another hour with giggles. But today I don't join their hilarity. As soon as I recognize you, the scenes we witnessed together simmer inside me like poison. Few people saw those sights and lived.

For years, you know, I saw you in my dreams, always dressed in the

Chinese silk kimonos, or in those lace blouses I made for you. I saw you coming down the palace stairs with your floating gait, or standing by the window in the upper room looking at the garden, a sapphire necklace always around your neck and your hair braided on your nape like twined gold ingots nestled in a fine net. In the distance, even in my dream, the Germans laughed thickly or sang their songs, or ran up and down the black marble stairs, now and then cracking a whip with a flick of the hand. In the background, like a nightmare melody, the girls screamed and cried and wailed day and night—but not you. You maintained your dark silence.

"That's the child of the heart specialist," the Bulgarian chuckles. "They interviewed two hundred women before they picked this one. She looks more like a lady than the professor's lady."

Even in my dreams you never looked me in the eye. You looked over my head with that distant, languid gaze, but I noticed that your eyelids trembled. I would wake from those dreams as if escaping from a fire, suddenly recalling scenes much worse than the dreams: the girls bitterly crying in their first nights, very softly, almost unheard in the rustling of the beds, and sometimes a shriek, ringing in my ears for a long time, like an echo in the desert. And the next day, their eyes were worn out with weeping, shadows creeping on their faces, and in the days that followed the spark of life slowly faded from their eyes.

A few weeks later the eyes were already dead, drained of tears, the lovely bodies wilting, and then the eyes would take on a puzzled expression, refusing to understand the surrounding reality.

In the cellar where I live with my sewing machine, I would prick up my ears to hear the loud thud in the back garden, learning to distinguish it from the other sounds of the house: one of the girls had reached the end of her endurance, climbed stealthily to the rooftop or to a windowsill, and hurled herself down. I would close my eyes and recite the only verse I remember from the Kaddish prayer my father used to say on my grandmother's grave: *Yisgadal veyiskadesh shmaia rabba . . .*

Now you are vigorously shaking the grains of sand from your fingers and turning your head to the toddler strapped into the stroller.

"How fast she counted the microbes," the Bulgarian grins. "I bet she won't put her in the sand. God forbid the professor's dress should get soiled."

The day the German thrust you into my room and ordered me to find you a blue silk dressing gown, I stared at you as if hypnotized. The girls who were brought into my room were all pretty. But you—there was a fatal darkness about your beauty. Your glance flicked around the room and you did not ask anything. Did you already know what kind of place it was? Were you wary of me? You stood erect and regal when I dressed you, like a proud bride in her wedding gown.

You slap your palms together and walk resolutely to the shaded bench. Your body is still amazingly supple, your legs handsome, unblemished by the years, and your narrow waist shows clearly when you bend down to loosen the little girl's strap. I am watching you openly. Now that the initial shock is over, my eyes are as drawn to you as they were then. I see your iron hand gripping the child like a clamp, your fingers closing on the tiny fluttering hand. The sight awakens my hostility toward you and the sights that have been buried inside me for decades without respite. The time that passed hasn't softened your heart, you damned woman. The black light in your eyes shook me from the start.

Outside, the German snorted with laughter, calling to one of his friends, "I've brought you a present—a rabbi's daughter!" I looked at you and said to myself, trying to shield you from what I had seen, "Soon she will be found dead. Obviously she has no idea where she is, and when she understands she will want to die."

The little girl squirms in the prison of your arms and you shake and scold her. I was not wrong about you, as I hoped. You understood quite well when you stood in front of the mirror in my room. How did you guard your soul in that place?

One of the nannies runs around with the carousel, panting, shouting, "If you don't eat the apple right now, I'll give it to Michael. You want Michael to grow up big and strong, and you'll be little and weak? He'll never let you go on the swing; is that what you want?"

At night, you remember, the girl with the auburn braid used to sing. She had the sweet voice of a schoolgirl. When she sang, the weeping in the room would cease. One night a new girl was brought to the room. The night before, she told us, she had married her beloved. In the camp to which they had been transported from the ghetto, two kerchiefs had been tied together to form a canopy and a rabbi had performed the ceremony. The girl with the braid sang bridal songs for her: "The voice of mirth and the voice of gladness, the voice of a bride and the voice of a groom . . ." Later, at night, the two would sing Sabbath songs and hymns.

One morning the two girls were found lying hand in hand by the fountain in the garden, the blood flowing from their wrists. A few days later I asked you about them and I noticed that your fingers did not tremble as you smoothed your hair.

A child jumps from the carousel and bursts out crying when his knee hits a stone. The nanny pounces on him: "Why do you jump without looking? Don't you remember we couldn't go out for three days because last Monday you jumped and hurt yourself? It was awful at home— you behaved terribly. Now you're jumping again? You think I want to be cooped up with you again in prison?"

It was for you that the German wanted those exquisite Chinese kimonos. I wondered where they got them in such quantities. In my room you preened yourself as though you were going to a ball. You alone, of all the girls, were an enigma: girls came and went, tore out their hair, howled like wolves—you alone kept your head up. Week after week I observed you and saw no change in you, unlike the other girls— the clear skin, the rosy tinge fading into the neck, the dark halos around the limpid blue irises, the wide, rounded forehead turning to the high temples, the red lips, the proud chin, the sculptured body, rounded shoulders, slender waist, narrow feet, the waist-length hair, the supple body movements, the dancing gait.

Once I saw you being dragged from the parlor by an officer. Another time, when you left my room, I heard the laughter of the drunken men greeting you outside. And one day, when by chance I went through the hallway to wash the filth from the carpet at the foot of the stairs, I saw you on the floor—the Chinese kimono all awry, your hair wound around your face like roots, your hands tied with a rope between your knees. At night you staggered like a drunk down the stairs, your bleeding arms groping along the railing. The next morning you stood serenely, looking out the window, pieces of a broken vase at your feet, sipping soup, quietly sucking up the thick liquid, putting down the bowl, and, without looking, picking up a chunk of salami and biting into it noisily; and all the while your eyes gazed at the lilac bush and your right hand held the drapes. I picked up the pieces of the broken vase, my eyes drawn to your mutilated arm holding the drapes: fingernail marks like furrows plowed in your arm, on the back of your hand. And on your elbow, like a drawing, were three flower-shaped burns.

The girls aged overnight: their complexions became ashen, their eyelids swelled, their hair lost its sheen, their bodies lost their vitality. You alone never changed, as if accustomed to vicissitudes and knowing that nothing goes on forever. And I watched in amazement as the injuries on your arms healed and your lovely skin triumphed.

The Bulgarian nanny jumps to her feet, dashes forward, and threatens, "Yuvali, get down this minute. Don't climb up from the bottom. Can't you see there's a girl ready to slide down? Do you want such a fat girl to fall on your head? Go to the ladder and slide down after the fat girl like you did before. See how she hit the bottom—kerplunk! Lucky for you I noticed her, or you'd be on your way to the first-aid station."

The night the girl from the Lodz ghetto told us about Passover Eve you were the only one who stayed in bed. All the others gathered around the girl, who told us in whispers how she and her mother had been left alone in the cellar where they were hiding. The week before her elder brother had gone out to look for food and never came back. The younger brother was sent to look for him, and he, too, never came back. The mother picked up some bread crumbs and flattened them into squares, which she moistened with water, and before she went out of her mind and ran screaming out into the street, calling for her sons, began to lay the Seder table, putting stones on the table in place of wine bottles, plates for fish, soup, and meat, put down the squares of bread crumbs for matzo. She walked around and sang: "How is this night different from all other nights? That on all nights we eat . . ." The whole time she was telling us about the ghetto I didn't take my eyes off you. You sat with your back to us, motionless, as if you were a piece of furniture. Did you know, as I did, that the very next day the girl from Lodz would collapse and the Germans would throw her out at noon?

"Why did you hit her?" The nanny's voice rises shriller than the children's. "I saw you hitting her. Don't lie to me. Why is she crying then? Just because you don't know how to play on the monkey bars you have to come here and hit? Aren't you ashamed to play with girls anyway? Look at all the other kids playing nicely. Only you go looking for trouble. You think you're so smart picking on little girls? Where is your nanny anyway? What's she being paid for?"

Often I wondered whether you would have triumphed over the place if it weren't for the senior officer who took you under his wing and kept the others away from you. For a while we were both protected—I with my sewing skills and you ensconced in your benefactor's room.

We both regarded the others as if their fate did not touch us. Do you remember the three girls who were taken out one night for an orgy? The Germans were drunker than ever. At dawn two of them crawled back, their bodies bruised all over. The third girl had been rolled up in a carpet, her long hair hanging out of one end, dragged out into the garden, and set on fire. The drunken Germans stood and watched the hair, flaring up readily, and the smell of burnt flesh filled the rooms until the wind blew. One of the girls told us, before she was taken to the doctor and never returned, that the Germans had strangled her friend while violating her body. In the morning the other girl began to spew blood. She came to my room for shelter and showed me the fist marks on her lower abdomen.

Sometimes, when I sit here on the park bench with the nannies, listening to them bickering and chattering, watching the toddlers playing in the sandbox under the trees, I am reminded more and more of the trees at that house: the linden tree tops converging above the fountain, the thick foliage, the somber shade, the goldfish swimming among corals gleaned from the ocean depths, the dew stored in the grass, the sky on clear nights. What are they doing now, those girls who sat on the Germans' knees, who wallowed on the floors? Are they living their lives, carrying the memories from night to day, from day to night? I try to figure out how old they would be today, and the thought alarms me.

Do you remember that time, at a party, when our eyes met over the back of a girl crouching on all fours, her forehead touching the pulled-off boots and licking the bare feet of the officer who stood like an artist's model, a hand on his hips, his trousers down and his underpants sagging around the pillars of his legs? His companions laughed. One of them said, "Not many of them can brag that they've caught a German officer with his pants down." What was the girl thinking of, crouching there in the noisy room? Her mother? Her father? The boy who peeped at her from behind his prayer shawl? What were you thinking of?

A young woman is dragging a weeping girl to an adjacent bench. "Tell his nanny, dear heart. Don't cry, sweetie. There, there. I'll tell her! Your kid spat at her. Is that how you teach him? Sure you're responsible. You sit here chatting about wages and gossiping about your employers while he's spitting at other kids. Some nanny! Come to the faucet, my heart, I'll wash your dress."

You were beautiful in those days. You must have found some makeup somewhere, or else your benefactor gave you some. You put on mascara, rouged your cheeks for him, and I, who knew your features like the back of my hand, noticed a new sparkle in your eyes. You braided your hair and searched in the jewelery box in my room and took out a necklace of sapphires to put around your neck. You examined yourself in the mirror and waited for his arrival. Once, when you were in his room, the two of you came out on the little balcony. He hung his jacket around your shoulders and you talked the whole night long. I saw you from my window, talking earnestly. What did you tell him, sitting so erect, wrapped in a German officer's jacket? What did he tell you?

In the spring the garden suddenly burst into my cellar in all its glory: the spring azure of the Polish sky, the light clouds, the air laden with buds and pollen, heavy clusters of chestnut blossoms peering through curtains of leaves, young leaves thickening the treetops day by day, the gurgling of the fountain in the garden, the row of white lilac bushes along the fence like ornate gowns lined up for a fashion show. In the middle of the garden stood the palace itself, where a prince used to live before the Germans came, with huge murals, molded doors, embroidered tapestries, inlaid cupboards, lion-footed armchairs, heavy silverware, crystal chandeliers—and at rare hours, a profound silence between the walls, when the screams of the women and the stomping of jackboots on the marble stairs subsided. In that silence I could sense the staring eyes, the quivering flesh, the nameless fear. And one morning, in the sweet lilac fragrance, I lingered by the wall in one of the rooms and noticed little dabs of blood behind a chest of drawers, the dabs forming letters: Shifra daughter of Shimon. What possessed Shifra to leave her father's name in that accursed place?

"You get down this minute! We're going home now! You want to tear your pants again? Your mother won't buy you a new pair so soon. All right, just a little more, only get off those bars and come play in the sand. Better play with the girls."

On exceptionally fine summer nights the Germans would sit in the big garden, drinking beer from huge mugs, singing with their heads thrown back, sometimes amusing themselves by sitting a girl on their knees and bouncing her from lap to lap around the circle. From my low window I followed you with my eyes. Your German had seated you on a chair by his side and offered you a drink, but you declined. Gently he caressed your cheek. I was shaken. In that place the sight of endearment was intolerable. You said something to him and he immediately bent his head to you to catch it, nodding attentively. You both rose and walked down the path to the end of the garden. A few minutes later shots were heard from that corner, and the Germans jumped to their feet. The girl they had played with remained sitting like a statue. It quickly became clear that your officer was only showing off his marksmanship to you. Loud laughter rose from the edge of the garden.

You make sure the bench is meticulously clean. You pick out cigarette butts and popsicle sticks from the sand and put them in a trash can nailed to a tree trunk. Then you spread a napkin on the bench beside you and feed the child, wiping her mouth constantly, picking crumbs from her blouse—and all the while your back is straight, your thighs pressed together, like an actress in a movie.

In the days that followed you were protected, sleeping in the officer's distant, overheated room. Sometimes you stood by the window, watching the summer showers fall on the garden. Every day, by your master's orders, your food was brought to you on a tray, and you received it like the mistress of the house, sitting in an armchair and gazing at a painting over my head while I changed the sheets on your bed. Unlike the other girls, you never asked me anything. Did you not want to understand more than you had to? I knew more about the Germans than about you.

The nanny beside me pulls a crying child to her bosom. "And his father is a doctor! Can you believe it—a big doctor, with such a stupid son? Always sticks his head where he'll get hurt. Why don't you watch your head? Ask your father, he'll tell you how important it is to watch your head."

One night the house was suddenly empty and silence fell on the lawn and on the grove behind the palace. The girls, made tense by the unwonted silence, gathered like sleepwalkers in the parlor. Some lay on the sofas and on the carpets, eating candy from ornate boxes, drinking wine, whispering. One burst into tears and couldn't stop. In the morning we were woken by the stomping boots of the returning Germans, and it turned out that the officers had been summoned to a special conference. In the afternoon it was discovered that the golden-haired girl who had been brought the day before from Majdanek had taken advantage of the commotion and disappeared. They sent the dogs after her and found her hiding in the bushes, under the porch columns. We saw the dogs dragging her to the bottom of the garden.

On the morning when your officer was found dead in his bed, you were no longer in the room. The doctor was called in and suddenly there was panic in the palace—people dashing to and fro, exchanging short phrases like a secret language, passing each other on the stairs. Through the door I could see him lying in bed like a mountain, his neck red even in death. The doctor declared that his heart had given way. When the body had been removed, covered in a velvet blanket, the others pounced on you in your upper room. All that day and night the Germans kept going to your room one by one, to do to you what they had been prevented from doing while your protector was alive. In the morning I saw you staggering on the doorstep. I recognized you by the kimono.

You take no part in the general hubbub in the park. The child, too, keeps her distance from the other children; she only pushes her stroller in circles around your bench. Her pretty sandals sink into the sand. For a moment your eyes seem to focus on the baby sitting on my lap. Did you recognize me? Your hand seems to have lost control; your fingers grope along the bench, grabbing the metal edge of the board. Your body maintains its calm, your back is erect, there is only the tremor of your whitened fingers clutching the metal.

One morning the Germans were suddenly gone. They left in haste, but still took two girls with them. We got up in the morning— seven girls—to a new silence. The doctor's daughter from Lublin was the first to realize what had happened. She climbed to the fourth floor and opened all the rooms one by one, her roar growing louder the farther she went. Leaning on the top floor railing she shouted, "The swine are gone!" She shouted in Yiddish, defiantly, and a shiver went through me at the sound of those words. The girl who had been the last to arrive, her pallor glaring in the dark room, started rocking to and fro, raising her eyes to the high painted ceiling and chanting, "Blessed art thou, our God, Lord of the universe . . ." A moment later another one burst out laughing and started destroying the paintings on the wall with her bare hands.

The Bulgarian, who is as easily overcome by compassion as by cruelty, cries, "Look what a heart of gold he has! Every day he gives his chocolate milk to the cat. I tell his mother he shouldn't be so softhearted. When he grows up the girls will make his life miserable. You know what girls are like when they get hold of a nice guy—they ruin him."

We still didn't know that the Russians were already in town. We were still delirious, roaming through the rooms. You were the first to leave. You cocked the beret on your head, packed a small suitcase, broke into my room, opened the jewelery box, scooped up a fistful of jewels and put them in the bottom of the suitcase, chose two dark sweaters and a gray woolen skirt, packed them quickly, and left. At the main gate the vicious dog leapt at you, and you bent down, picked up a rock, and threw it at his head. As soon as you left, all hell broke loose, as if you had given the signal for a new life.

You gather your things, harness the child in her carriage, rise, and turn to the park gate. Once again, when you are a pace away from me, I see the icy eyes surrounded by black halos. The nannies fall silent, following you with their eyes as you pass by. For a moment I seem to feel your glance lashing at me. Have I awakened a memory in you? An echo of German voices? The touch of flesh against your flesh? The fluttering of silk against your skin? The smell of the chestnuts? Have you succeeded in forgetting? The girl who had aged in days, the one who wiped the marble tiles, who removed the soiled sheets and spread fresh ones, who sewed the glamorous dresses, ironed and stitched, and never took her eyes off you all, lovely daughters of Israel. How they gathered all that beauty and then destroyed it—were you able to forget?

Suddenly the steely eyes are on my face. And you say in a dull voice devoid of wonder, "What sandals?"

I reply, "The little girl's."

You look directly at me: "I don't know. I didn't buy her the sandals. Her mother did." And you propel the carriage onto the gravel path and walk away.

I stumble back to my seat on the bench. The Bulgarian makes room for me and peers into my face, concerned.

"What's wrong, dear heart? Come, sit down." She pats my back amiably and smiles. "How you ran after that lady! As if in her you'd found Cinderella's slipper that she lost at the palace."

And they all join in her laughter.

Translated from the Hebrew by Marganit Weinberger-Rotman

Compassion

ON HER KNEES in the darkness, groping with determined fingers through the sand and fragments of ancient flooring, Clarissa peered between the board that served as a door and the rock that formed the lintel and fixed her eyes on the two retreating men. The wintry light blurred their shapes against the mountainside as they made their way westward, each hidden in his heavy coat, careful to maintain a fixed distance between them—as if they intended to separate and go their own ways when they reached the end of the chalk path, as though they had not plotted together before taking the knife. They disappeared at the first fig tree, only to reappear near the last one, growing smaller in the pre-rain mist.

Clarissa stretched her fingers repeatedly to tug at the lock that hung on the outside and found it secured fast. Sometimes, intentionally or unintentionally, they would leave the lock loose, and she was able to go out onto the path in front of the hut, wander in the moonlight along the paved road and gather the apples that had dropped from the trees in their heavy ripeness, stand at the edge of the precipice and gaze at the village houses on the other side of the wadi.

Now the men were dwarfed by distance. Clarissa shook the door savagely, trying to widen her field of vision. Had she been free and light-footed, had she had a knife in her hand, she would have sped after them on the mountain slope to stick the knife in their backs, withdrawing it and plunging it in again and again until they sank dead at her feet.

Then she would nudge them with her feet into the abyss, not looking at their faces, knowing: Her husband. Her son Ibrahim. In the morning she would return to the spot, examine the scuffs on the path to make sure she had not dreamed, sit down cross-legged by the trees, eating apples and gazing up at the vultures circling above the wadi. Then she would slowly stand up, her time her own, follow the path with a light step, gathering sprigs of summer savory in her skirt, and return to her former home, from which she had been banished two winters before. She would throw out the young woman her husband had taken to replace her, withdraw the vow her husband had made to his old friend—that he would give him his daughter Aisha when she turned sixteen.

Aisha—like a stone fist inside Clarissa—beautiful, proud Aisha. Was she now in that place, where they had cunningly taken her, her young heart dreaming its dreams? Was she awake there in the dark, scenting the approaching hunters, like an animal? The two of them would come to her at dawn. Her father would wait in ambush outside the door, her brother would steal in and slash her throat as she slept. The cry of the jackals would rise above the scream and the rain would wash away the tracks.

Rocking on all fours, banging her head on the ground, Clarissa grieved for Aisha, her rebellious daughter, who scorned both young and old, who had since childhood amused herself with that which was forbidden. She had brought four daughters into the world, and only Aisha had triumphed over illness. Aisha had a powerful life-force, but—Clarissa felt her heart crack—her father's force was greater. Her head banged against the corner of a stone as a pang of guilt overcame her: Had I myself not rebelled, had I not refused my husband's command to go to his old uncle, perhaps my daughter would not have dared to rebel. Except that I rebelled in my old age and she—in her girlhood. And I am paying with my freedom, while she, very soon . . . We did not even say good-bye . . . She pushed back her thoughts.

Clarissa straightened her back and, still on her knees, groped her way to the mattress that served as her bed. She had last seen Aisha before the summer, when she stealthily came to her, as she had done a few times before—growing out of the heart of the dust path, her hair like ropes on her shoulders, the wind flapping her dress about her hips, her back erect, carrying a kerchief tied in a bundle with bread, cheese, olives, apples. A shout away from the entrance, Ibrahim pounced from his hiding place and drove her away, the bread and apples clutched to her bosom. Through the crack Clarissa saw her looking over her shoulder, ignoring the stick her elder brother was brandishing at her back. With failing eyes she saw her daughter disappearing, and she stood for a long time gazing at the empty path.

That night her husband came, again trying with threatening and seductive words to break her silence, to persuade her to go to the home of his father's brother. As always, when leaving, he threw a bundle with soap, a bag of rice, some flour, and several garden onions onto the floor. For a moment he stood facing her as if on the verge of striking her for her obstinacy, then reviled her and locked the door.

The next day Clarissa heard the sound of approaching footsteps and she ran to the door, hoping that her daughter had secretly returned to tell her what Ibrahim had prevented her from saying. Clarissa saw her neighbor Soubhiya on the path and her heart rejoiced, but her suspicion was immediately aroused: perhaps the woman had been sent to see if she had retracted her refusal? Since Clarissa's banishment, the two had not seen each other. Soubhiya had not come for two winters—why should she come now? She hardened her heart against the visitor, but the closer Soubhiya came, the more Clarissa remembered the hours they used to spend in the yard, amid the tumult of babies, separating lentils in flat copper bowls that rested between them on the ground; embroidering the hems of dresses and decorating bed linen; drinking tea and dropping hints about boys and men with suppressed laughter. Throughout the years that they had shared a courtyard, they had suckled each other's babies and cried over each other's pain.

As soon as Soubhiya saw the section of Clarissa's face beyond the locked board, she burst out crying, and they pushed their fingers into the narrow space, touching one another in greeting.

"How are you?" Soubhiya's voice was full of tears.

"You see with your own eyes—locked up."

"All day inside?"

"It's open at the back."

"And what's there?"

"Nothing. Rocks."

"And it is impossible to get out?"

"Impossible. Because of the mountain."

"And water?"

"There's a well at the back."

"And is there water in it?"

"A little."

"It will rain soon."

Clarissa's eyes rest on Soubhiya's fingers stroking the back of her hand.

"How is it in the village?"

"The same. Did they bring you a table?"

"No."

"And a bed?"

"Ali brought a mattress."

"A good boy, Ali."

"God bless him."

"Ibrahim won't let him visit you."

Clarissa's words came quickly, "Was it he who asked you to come?"

"My heart wanted to," Soubhiya leaned her head towards the little space between them. "I had a dream about you last night."

"What?" Clarissa was alarmed.

"That you came from the wadi to the village with sheep and goats."

Clarissa put her head near the board, hissing the words, "I am not going to his uncle's house."

"You, you have no other place."

"I'm not going to the old man's house!"

"And this is any better for you?"

There was a long moment of silence between them.

"What do they say about me in the village?"

Soubhiya turned away, looking aside in embarrassment. "They talk nonsense."

"What?"

"They say—witch. Eats spiders. Follows the moon at night."

Clarissa laughed from a throat that had long since forgotten the sound of laughter and emitted a long gurgle: "Is that what they say?"

"Yes. They say: She used to be a Jew, she used to be a Christian, and she used to be a Moslem—not one God wanted her."

Clarissa broke off her laughter all at once and Soubhiya made whispering sounds.

"Is it true you used to be a Christian?"

"No. I was just a child with the nuns."

"You never told!"

"What was there to tell?"

"When was it?"

"In Europe. In the war."

"But you were a Jew!"

"Yes."

"And a Moslem?"

"When I married."

"So what are you now?"

"Dead!" Clarissa shouted into Soubhiya's eager ear, and she withdrew her head. As soon as Soubhiya's head vanished, Clarissa was gripped by panic: the thing she most wanted to know had not yet been asked and maybe Soubhiya had already left. She shouted with all her might into the narrow opening, "Have you seen Aisha?"

"Yes." Soubhiya's voice came from close by and her face reappeared at once.

"Did she marry the old man?"

"No."

"And . . . ?"

"They say she's going to run off with the teacher."

"They'll kill her!" Clarissa was startled to hear her mouth say what her heart even feared to contemplate.

"That's what they're saying."

"Her father gives his women away like gifts. Takes what he wants." She thought of the young bride he had taken for himself from the neighboring village, and she stole a look at Soubhiya's eyes.

"Did he bring her?"

"He did." Soubhiya lowered her eyes as if the guilt were hers. "May the demons find them both in the night."

"And is she happy with him?"

Soubhiya expressed everything in her soul with one powerful gesture, her eyes burning: "She looks like a dead woman."

"He kills his women!" Clarissa, to her surprise, found within herself sorrow for the child-bride who lay in the very bed from which she had been banished, and heard Soubhiya saying, "And your daughter-in-law, Ibrahim's wife, is also sick. They still haven't brought her back from the hospital after giving birth."

The baby! Now Clarissa sat up on her mattress, alarmed, listening to the patter of the rain and recalling Soubhiya's weeping eyes. She peered through the crack and saw light outside. How could she have forgotten the baby? When her husband and her son Ibrahim came to her toward evening, they had brought two bundles. One, containing food, they had placed on the ground in front of her. They had put the other in an inner niche and her son had said, "This is my baby. Her mother is in the hospital. You'll take care of her today. Here's some food for her."

Before even seeing her, Clarissa felt abhorrence for the child lying in the niche, wrapped in rags, with bad blood flowing inside her. She looked at her from a distance, calculating how many hours the baby had lain without food—from sunset till midmorning—and was astonished that a two-month-old baby's hunger had not stirred for so many hours.

She slowly approached the wrapped bundle lying in the niche and peeped at the baby's face. She drew back immediately, shaken. The baby wasn't asleep at all! She lay with her eyes open, fixed on the bare wall, her face tinged yellow like a man in pain. Clarissa's gaze was drawn to the baby's face: the contracted eyelids, like someone flinching from a hand raised to strike, the little wrinkled forehead, the worried eyes, as though the features had already prepared themselves for hard times—as though from birth her heart knew what lay in store for it and was hastening to teach the body to guard itself.

Clarissa went over to the food bundle lying near the entrance and took out a bottle of milk. The baby turned her head sideways as though following the sounds. Her eyes opened wide and a look of fear came into them. Clarissa stood for a moment above the creature lying at her feet, clasping the end of the bottle of milk as though aiming for a throw. A voice echoed within her: There isn't even any need to throw it . . . if it just slips . . . as if by accident . . . The baby's pupils froze, staring at the shadow lurking over her. Clarissa, her hand gripping the bottle of milk until her knuckles whitened, shuddered, for the first time seeing the little foot that had freed itself from the garment and the end of the tiny transparent toe that seemed infused with a turbid color.

Clarissa crouched on the floor and tugged at the baby. She held it away from her body and put the bottle to its mouth. The baby immediately pressed against the arm that supported her, closed her eyes, sucked the nipple of the bottle into her mouth, and noisily swallowed her food. Clarissa looked at her, filling with wonder. She felt the seeping pity despite herself: all those hours the baby had lain hungry without uttering a sound. A wave of anxiety passed through her: it was a bad sign. This baby did not know how to claim what was rightfully hers.

With the baby in her arms, Clarissa rose and began to pace around, the suckling infant gradually drawn closer, gathered to her bosom. A distant nursery song beat inside her of its own accord, and with its notes came pictures of another life: a nun whose hands were always warm and the painted faces of mother and child in loving embrace; the rich, enthusiastic voice of her father as he stood beside her mother in front of the silver utensils on the set table: "Blessed art Thou O Lord our God, King of the Universe . . . Who has sanctified us with His commandments . . ." And she thought about her life—how it had rolled on, sweeping her from place to place like the currents of a river carrying foam. Maybe she should have insisted and run after her aunt and not stood paralyzed next to the nun when her aunt had turned and left swiftly through the gate of the convent. She had known, after all, that her aunt would not come back as she had promised. Perhaps, after she had learned to love the smell of incense and the prayers, she should have insisted on staying there and not gone with the young woman who came to take her to her aunt's sister on the kibbutz. And perhaps, after leaving the kibbutz, she should have made a greater effort to learn the new language, should have tried the job she had been offered. And perhaps she should not have followed the man who smiled at her in the Arab market, should not have accepted the string of amber beads he gave her, should not have gone with him to his brother's house in Hebron.

The baby stopped sucking and her face seemed to have filled out. The wrinkles had gone and plump cheeks had emerged, and she met Clarissa's gaze with her own. Clarissa stood beside the crack in the door, peering curiously at the new face that revealed itself in the strip of light that streamed inside. She extended her finger near the baby's open fist, which clamped around it like a trap awaiting its prey. Clarissa looked at the tiny fingers clasping so powerfully and was alarmed. This was very bad, she thought; such strength did not bode well. Strength that had no outlet would end in disaster. Suddenly Clarissa saw her own fingers, their tips stroking the baby's clenched fist, and heard herself confiding to her as if she were thinking aloud: about those who sometimes come into the world to a place that isn't right for them, about the soft ones who are punished for their softness and the courageous ones punished for their daring. With a full heart, Clarissa spoke to her granddaughter, mixing languages, whispering words she had not used since childhood, warning her against what awaited her: the homelessness, the helplessness, her father and her brothers and her uncles, her husband and her husband's brothers and her sister's husbands, who would close in around her, the household chores from one night to the next, the loneliness, the heart fluttering encased in the body, the man in her bed, rolling her over as he wished, coming into her as into a wound, and the fear for her daughters and their spilled blood.

Suddenly Clarissa shuddered, tensed, and hurried to the door, the baby against her heart. With one hand she pushed at the board and looked outside. On the bright path, in the dawn mist, the upper half of a man's body was rising, and she squinted her eyes: her son Ibrahim, her daughter's blood on his hands, had come to fetch his daughter. Clarissa hurriedly laid the baby on the mattress, ran and brought a basin of water, and loosened the napkin that was wound around the bottle of milk. With knowing hands, she removed the soiled diaper from her granddaughter, cleansed the little body with cold water, spread the dry square of cloth, tugged at the frayed corners, and secured them around the toes that were turning blue. She quickly straightened up and stood like a statue for a moment, her arms bound around her granddaughter and her eyes on the gate that barred the approach from the path. Then she spun around and rushed into the backyard, climbed the winding slope, and ran down the path that snaked around the hill while clutching the little body to her heart, covering it with her skirt to protect it from the wind.

She stopped beside the well. Her heart expanded. The heavens were on her side: they had filled the well almost to the brim. She freed her granddaughter from her imprisoning arms, kissed the tiny forehead and the closed eyes and the cheeks growing purple from the cold, and again clasped her to her heart, soothing her tremors. With immense tenderness she leaned over the wall of the well, laid down the bundle as though placing it into a cradle, and watched the little face sinking and disappearing without protest into the water that closed over it.

Thus she stood, her eyes captive in the depths of the well, until the sound of her name being shouted emerged from inside the hut and the waters settled and became still.

Translated from the Hebrew by Riva Rubin

The Homesick Scientist

I HAVE BEEN prey to troubling thoughts from the moment his telegram arrived two days ago. Dormant pictures are resurrected in my mind; I keep asking myself, perplexed: Why, after twenty years, is he coming to visit me now? After I received the telegram, I sat for a long time, unmoving, on the bench outside the store that also serves us as a post office, suspicion gnawing at me. Is he coming to demand something of me? Could he be after his share of my late wife's inheritance? Has he been infected by his mother's obsession with the family diamonds? During the following two nights, scenes kept passing through my mind, one crowding onto the other, depriving me of sleep. Yet, in spite of myself, with these scenes there trickled the feeling of warmth that I had reserved for him in my heart in those far-off days.

Last night I recalled how, a week before the cable arrived, I had suddenly noticed the mimosa bush blooming beside the old cow shed fence. For several years, the mimosa bush had been struck by various afflictions, and I did not send anyone to take care of it. I assumed that its roots had all shriveled within the parched, crumbling earth. But then I caught sight of the bush, and I was astounded; the blossoms were breathtakingly full-blown, the yellow cottonballs seductively emitting their familiar fragrance, fine, feathery leaves drawn out around them. I leaned against the picket fence and laughed out of joy and amazement. At that moment, I thought of my nephew as a boy—how excited he had become at the sight of blossoming mimosas, how he had studied them and taken the flowers apart to examine where the fibers came from, and how the mimosa had punished him with an eye infection; and then how he had lain in the hammock, his eyes bandaged, crying in pain and misery, and how I sitting next to him, agonized and helpless, had tried to distract him with stories from Greek mythology.

All that happened many years ago. Now I sit at the bus stop in the village square, awaiting his arrival, weary after a sleepless night, barely able to contain the turmoil in my heart. This is the third time that I have had to move my wooden folding chair into the shade, away from the road. Yehezkel, the owner of the nearby grocery store, cocks his head through the window over the outer counter.

"Well, Zerubavel, what did I tell you? Didn't I say that he meant he was leaving Haifa at ten, not arriving here at ten?"

"You were right," I reply dryly, positioning my chair in its new spot. In days gone by, when I was chairman of the Cultural Affairs Committee and he was treasurer, Yehezkel and I waged fierce battles over anything that happened to crop up: the budget for the Independence Day celebrations, the purchase of a new accordion, replacing the screen in the club. But all this was just pretext for the two of us, dating from the day I had found him lurking under my window and suspected him of trying to come on to my wife.

When the big battles were over, we continued for years—force of habit—to fan a small flame: following an argument, I quoted a verse from Ezekiel, "Have you not seen a vain vision, and have yet not spoken a lying divination," placing alongside it a loose sketch suggestive of my antagonist Yehezkel's sharp profile, and I published it on the front page of our bulletin, Valley Landscapes, of which I am editor. On his part, he never missed an opportunity to cast aspersions on me: accusing me of maliciously hindering young teachers; spreading rumors about a youth from Kfar-Avraham who imagined himself a poet and whom I encouraged, thereby luring him away from his father's home.

Nowadays our strength has dwindled. At the cemetery, my wife's grave lies next to his daughter's. Together we water the myrtle bush that grows between the two graves. Even the admonishments: "What did I tell you? Didn't I say . . ." come out of his mouth sounding conciliatory, devoid of their previous fury; I detect in them more of an attempt to engage me in conversation than provocation. Longevity can make the heart either very bitter or very soft. The two of us have softened with age.

We have been in each other's eyeshot for half an hour. I follow the shade of the deserted bus stop, and he stands at the entrance of the grocery store.

"The main thing is that he's coming," he says, and I nod in agreement.

He disappears for a moment, then comes out and places a folding chair next to me. "Want a mint?" He offers me pearly drops in a tiny tin box, leans forward to check how many candies I lift in my fingers, and asks, "How long do you think he'll stay here?"

"He didn't say."

"He'll have to stay with you today if he wants to go back on the express bus. Tomorrow the express bus stops here at eight-twenty. But if he's in a hurry, he can catch the local bus from the main road this afternoon."

As if I am unfamiliar with the local and express bus schedules. He only wants to make conversation, I explain to myself, without anger, restraining my fear. I think to myself: If he flings the word "deserter" in my face, I will get up and leave. I'll wait on the other side of the road until the bus gets here.

"So what does he mean to do here?"

"I don't think he's coming here to do anything. He's coming for a visit." I notice that I, too, construct my sentences to sound hostile, but instead they come out empty.

"For a visit?" he sniggers. "What is there for him to see here, after all the places he's seen—and abroad, too?" He looks away, then adds in the same breath, "I read about him in the paper," and his voice assumes a sudden tone of importance.

Pride wells up inside me, dispelling my misgivings. The reverence in his voice does not go unnoticed.

"He's an important man now." He waves his hand high up in the air to illustrate the word.

"Yes."

"Something international, something in the big world."

"Just so." I am pleased he is so knowledgeable. He never congratulated me in the past on my nephew's successes, as others have.

He halts momentarily, narrowing his eyes suspiciously. "I'm not talking about that poet from Kfar-Avraham. I'm talking about the son of Leah's sister."

"I am also talking about my nephew."

"He's something at the university, isn't he?'

"A scientist."

Suddenly he bursts out laughing, slapping his knee with his hand. I spear him with a loathing glare. The animosity cannot be eradicated, only temporarily lulled. "And to think that for a few years, every summer, he hung around here. A little carrot-top. He used to come here every summer, didn't he?'

I calm down. He has no intention of condemning my nephew's emigration from Israel. "For more than ten years, every summer."

"A quiet boy, a little mouse," he laughs. "Who would have thought there was such a mind there, so international. The brains of a minister."

I sink back in the creaky chair and make a mental note that the expression "little mouse" does not connote rebuke, only affection, a touch of wonderment. I am filled with pride.

"Lives in America?"

"In New York and Alaska. Conducts research."

"Well, then, you should be happy."

I make no reply. I won't tell Yehezkel about the pent-up rage toward my nephew that rises up whenever my pride in him mounts, that shouts at him from within me: "Deserter, deserter—that's what you are. How could you leave this troubled country without a second thought to go seek your glory in America?" My head inveighs against him, but my heart clings to my love for him, and with it a great capacity for forgiveness. And yet I dread our meeting. Since the day he completed his military service and went to study in America—more than twenty years ago, I reckon again in disbelief—I have not seen him. For my seventy-fifth birthday he sent me greetings, one of those ready-made American cards with a printed message for every occasion. For every award he received—I found out about most of them from his mother and I read about one in the paper—I sent him a letter of congratulation.

Now I have to confess: I don't know him. The boy who once lived in my house exists no more. The man, I calculate, must be forty. I cannot help thinking: When I was seven years older than he is now I was already a bereaved father. What shall I tell him when he arrives? What shall we talk about later? What does he want from me?

"How he used to scamper around here like a little mouse." Yehezkel's voice sounds bemused and delighted. "To the library and back, to the library and back, all the time. Whenever I saw him, he had a book in his hand. As if there weren't enough books in your house. And the way he would cling to the wretched thing! As if it had plans to run away!"

MY NEPHEW WAS ten years old when his father died. His mother, my wife's sister, concerned about his pallor and small stature, sent us a hesitant letter asking if he could come stay with us for three weeks during his summer vacation. My late wife, Leah, seemed to come to life upon reading that letter. But as far as I was concerned, an ancient resentment rose in me toward her sister who, from our first encounter, had always regarded me as a ne'er-do-well, a daydreamer. I resented the fact that she did not think I deserved a rest and wanted to burden me with looking after her son during my vacation.

After quarreling, which was not our habit, Leah and I decided to invite the boy for two weeks. "And if he starts running around and making noise here, it won't be for more than a week!" I called after her when she went to mail her reply.

That summer he stayed with us for six weeks, at my special request. And in the ensuing years, summer after summer, he would come during the second week of summer vacation and stay with us until the beginning of the final week. Leah, whose body had started sprouting malignant tumors right after our son Uri was killed in action, got a new lease on life thanks to those months of grace. For a few weeks every year our house came alive as sounds of laughter and echoes of life were heard there again. And I, who had feared a noisy, bothersome child, found myself calling him away from his reading, inviting him to follow the remote village paths, to pick prickly pears from the tall, spiky hedges on the edges of the fields, reciting the names of trees and bushes we encountered on our way, teaching him to play chess, waking him up in the middle of the night to look at the Milky Way and listen to the giant cricket that lodged itself behind the old doghouse.

Right after the Passover break I would start preparing Uri's old room for him, fearing all the while that his mother might decide not to send him to us, realizing that he was now old enough to be left alone in the house, praying that no one would offer him a summer job in town, plotting to find him a paying job with one of my neighbors.

When he was in elementary school I enriched his mind with fairy tales, parables, biographies of famous people. When he became a high school student he turned into a fascinating interlocutor, telling me about books he had read, lectures he had attended. He would bring books in his suitcase, and together we would prove geometrical theorems, read about magnetic fields and black holes, and decipher scientific articles. While our feet carried us along paths crossing cornfields and peach and pear groves all the way to the neighboring village, we would discuss phenomena that fired our imaginations, such as the Bermuda Triangle, telepathy, hypnosis, brain waves, and the spiritual lives of the patriarch Abraham and the biblical prophets.

Then, all at once, I was bereft. But until I became bereft, I did not know how happy I had been. The last summer he stayed with us, he suddenly upped and left in haste, claiming he had a headache. He expressly asked me not to see him to the bus stop, and he was angry at me for not complying with his request. His head bowed, he climbed into the bus, dismissing me with a wave of his hand.

He left a book on parapsychology under his pillow, and I read and reread it like a mourner. Then he joined the army. Once he came to visit me in uniform, setting off my heart in a terrible flutter, reminding me of my son Uri. And then he wandered across the sea, leaving a rift that could not be repaired, just as Uri had done. But unlike what happened with my son, there lingered a gnawing bewilderment.

Yehezkel's voice intrudes, "Zerubavel, I hear the bus coming!"

EVEN BEFORE THE bus comes to a stop I recognize him through the window—a stalwart man, dressed in a light jacket, a hat on his head like a disguise—and my heart stops. As if I had been expecting the slight boy hopping off the bus steps, dropping his little suitcase to the ground, and running toward me with outstretched arms, and here instead is a strange man in strange clothes, searching for me with his eyes. Part of me wants to turn my back on him and run for my life; part of me is irresistibly drawn to the man alighting with mea-sured steps, shading his eyes with one hand and putting the other in his jacket pocket.

"Uncle Zerubavel, how wonderful to see you!" He puts his suit-case down and stretches both hands out to me. I don't remember giv-ing him my hand and I don't understand how all at once we are locked in an embrace, my head brushing his neck. I am embarrassed by the physical contact. It's been years since anyone hugged me like this. I has-ten to disengage myself from him. And at the same time I feel a sigh of relief rising inside me: he speaks Hebrew like a native! I allow myself a chuckle. On the way to the bus stop I had been suddenly perturbed by a question: How will I talk to him if he has forgotten his Hebrew? But his diction is good and his voice sounds deep and rich. I remem-ber that when his friends' voices changed at puberty, his voice remained thin and high as a girl's, and his mother agonized and sought advice from doctors. The new voice surprises me. For a moment I find myself peering into his eyes to make sure he is the right man. A second before he pulls out his sunglasses and puts them on, I notice his dreamy, rust-colored eyes, looking as if he had just awak-ened from sleep. In the old days, when he ran to embrace me, he used to lift his eyes to the tops of the cypress trees behind the station, as if to assess how much they had grown since he had last seen them. Now, too, his eyes rest briefly on the treetops and his face contorts at the glare of the sun.

"Did you have a good trip?" My voice sounds high. For years now I have not been straining my voice when talking with people.

"It's a little hot," he smiles, and shifts inside his jacket. I am slightly irritated by the note of complaint that I seem to detect.

"My eyes aren't accustomed to this light no more."

My irritation grows. My ears hear the grammatical error but I restrain myself from correcting it. I notice the creased palm that he raises to shade his face and a sudden sadness grips me, though it does not quell my anger—as if at that very moment, right in front of my eyes, the child has turned into an old man.

"Is everything all right?" He peers at me. My hand is still trapped in his.

"Yes," I hasten to announce, and I remark to myself: He is as sensitive as he used to be; he can still discern the hidden fluctuations. I add, "It's been so many years."

"Twenty-one years."

For a moment we stand facing each other, at our feet an elegant brown suitcase fastened with white buckles. This is the awkward moment I have dreaded. What do I say to the stranger?

"So your trip was okay?"

"Yes, perfectly okay. I intentionally didn't rent a car. I'm a little afraid of driving here." He is still smiling. "But mainly I wanted to make the trip by bus, like I used to."

"And was it the same?" There is genuine curiosity in my voice.

"No." His eyes rest again on the cypress trees. "Experiments can be repeated only in a lab." He suddenly turns and scrutinizes me. "Is something wrong?"

"You have changed a lot," I blurt out.

"Same goes for you," he replies immediately, not looking at me, his hand on my shoulder.

My heart feels a tug. The tone of his voice is almost that of a grown-up speaking to a child. Lately my ear has become particularly attuned to this note in people's voices. Only yesterday I heard it from the nurse at the clinic when she explained to me, slowly and clearly, how to treat a rash that had suddenly sprouted on both my elbows. Suddenly I glimpse Yehezkel's face peering at us from the window of the grocery store.

A great weariness descends upon me. It is the vexation and the excitement, I reason with myself. The man who looks like a tourist and I take the main road toward my house. His suitcase bumps now against his leg, now against mine. He looks at me curiously, in silent joy. I keep my eyes on the road before us.

"I wasn't sure if there was a sidewalk by the station, and all the way here I tried to remember." The smile never leaves his face. "I really racked my brains."

I steel myself against him, work myself up, suppress that part of me that wants to accept him, to respond to his bright face; just arrived and already he is condescending!

"I'm so glad there is no sidewalk and everything stayed the same. I was afraid I'd get here and wouldn't be able to recognize the place—it would all be high-rises, streets, and shops."

He means no offense at all, but I am not readily reconciled to him; my ire flares quickly and does not easily subside. I stare disapprovingly at his blue moccasins sinking into the soft dirt.

"Have you two made up yet?"

"Who's that?'

"You and Yehezkel."

"You recognized Yehezkel?" I stop in my tracks, sensing my eyebrows rise involuntarily.

"From the bus I saw you sitting together, and then he went in."

"Why . . . what do you remember?" I resume walking.

"When the two of you got together, I was always afraid a war would break out."

"You were afraid?"

"That's what I remember."

"Well, you needn't worry. We are too old now. Making up is a priv- ilege of the old and the weak."

He nods, pensively.

"Well, were you afraid? I'm not surprised. You were a weak boy." I get a strange satisfaction from teasing him.

He continues to nod. "I'm glad I was."

"Why?"

"If I hadn't been a weak boy, my mom would never have sent me here."

We walk a few paces together. He manages to break through my wall of anger, and I can feel my resentment subsiding, making way for affection, in spite of myself. Yet I still cling to my anger. I am now angry at myself, at the confusion that has overtaken me. I stare at his dusty moccasins. Suddenly they stop.

"This is where it happened." He sets the suitcase down.

Without lifting my head, I know: the gate to Malkiel's house. Here, when he entered the yard to gather some pine cones, the trained German shepherd attacked him and bit him ferociously. When I was summoned to the clinic and saw his injuries—his bloody face and legs, the exposed shinbone with the torn flesh and skin—I wept like a child. I could not calm down until the dog was shot, and for months I kept send- ing letters to the Ministry of Health to report the case. For many years afterward, Malkiel and I did not exchange a word.

"I screamed to high heaven." His voice is low, his gaze fixed on the spot where it happened. "I thought I was going to die."

I remember how he looked at me then, when I cried—he himself crying and begging me to stop. What would I not give to expunge that moment from both our memories.

"Does he still live here?"

"Malkiel? No. He died about seven or eight years ago. His grandson lives here now."

"His grandson?" He scans his memory.

"You may not remember him. He was just a baby then. Now he is very active in the village council."

He still stares at the same spot. His eyes blink behind the glasses. "For many years I had nightmares about the incident. Even today I sometimes . . . There are lots of pine cones there, no?" He speaks softly.

I start to walk, but he cannot remove his eyes from the plot of earth all covered in dry pine needles. Did he come back to see this place? To rid himself of the terror that preys on his dreams?

"I'm so glad I came," he says when he catches up with me, and I am not sure what I am feeling right now.

When we reach the house I realize how tired I am. I no longer function well after a sleepless night: my legs buckle under me; dark circles dance in front of my eyes. I leave my guest a few steps behind me, and he walks slowly, as in a dream, gazing wonderingly at the trees, at the fence, then bends down and scoops gravel in his hand. He has already conquered my heart. I hasten inside and collapse into a chair in the kitchen. I inhale long and loud, force myself to drink a glass of water. Lately my body has been defeating me. "The spirit," I found written in an old poem of mine, "will triumph in the last frontier." I was young and foolish then. Now I know better: the body will triumph. I close my eyes to blot out the flickering circles.

When I reopen them, I see him seated next to me. Now that he has taken off his hat and sunglasses and a broad smile illuminates his face, I immediately recognize the features of the child who so many years earlier used to sit here with me in the kitchen, on these very chairs.

"You shouldn't be angry with me," he says.

"I am not angry," I lie without hesitation.

"I couldn't come before." His eyes linger on his fingers.

"Why?" The question erupts within me, but aloud I say, "I see," thinking, "I don't see anything."

"I thought about this place all the time . . . It's just that I couldn't come."

"I see."

"How I loved sitting here," he whispers.

A warmth toward him emanates from me. Hesitantly, my fingers make their way to his arm, which rests on the oilcloth with its pattern of intertwined sunflower stems. It has been a long time since I felt such warmth coursing through my body, and I have forgotten how pleasing the sensation is. A thought hits me like a revelation: We tend to forget things we do not feel. To what extent is memory dependent on or independent of reality?

"I loved your visits with us, this is no secret—so did Leah, very much."

"I was very sorry to hear about Leah . . ."

"Yes, I got your cable. I responded, too, if I'm not mistaken . . . I thank you again."

"And since then you're alone here?"

I spread my arms on the oilcloth. "The books keep me company. I read, I read a lot. Fortunately, my eyes are still good. Lately I have been studying a very interesting philosopher. Henri Bergson. A Frenchman, you must have heard of him. He says very clever things. In my opinion he is even more interesting than Kant. He talks about time and space, but his approach is totally different from Kant's . . ."

I stop in mid-sentence, surprised to realize how I got carried away, then add, "Would you like some juice?"

"You know . . ." he looks at the printed sunflowers, "lately I have been thinking a lot about this place . . . about Uri, all of a sudden."

"Uri, my son?" I straighten up in my chair. We were always careful to steer clear of this subject.

"Yes, I don't know why . . . I started dreaming about him."

"But you hardly knew him. You were just a kid when he . . . was killed."

"I was eight."

"Eight? Do you remember him?"

"Vaguely. He came to our house a few times, and then my mother would take me to their bed and let him sleep in my room. He impressed me tremendously with his uniform, and later, when I stayed in his room, with all the airplanes . . . Recently, all of a sudden, I started dreaming about him."

I look at him and a new perplexity rises in me: Did he come back because of his dreams? Does he mean, in some devious way, to usurp Uri's place?

"Do you still work? Do you teach?"

"No, not anymore. For years I served as regional superintendent, and eight years ago I retired." My mouth speaks but my mind keeps surmising: Is it connected to the will? Is he making small talk before he pops the question about the diamonds?

"Do you still write poetry?" he asks suddenly.

I silently shake my head, afraid that any sound would betray more than I care to reveal.

"No?" he asks amazed. "I remember you always writing, with papers strewn on your desk . . . So you stopped writing altogether?"

"It's been several years now." My voice is strained.

"Why?"

"Because I was not a good poet." There was a time when this sentence would have broken my heart. Today my heart is inured. I now speak about my poetry as a pious man accepts a fatal disease. "God mocks us, you know. Sometimes a talent is coupled with the wrong temperament. Sometimes a person is born with artistic temperament but with no talent. Me, I lack both talent and temperament. I wrote a few good lines, a couple of good poems—but great poetry? No. I forced myself to stop."

"I'm very sorry," he whispers. I look into his eyes, and it seems that indeed he knows how great the loss is.

I smile at him softly, one of those rueful smiles that conveys more sorrow than tears. "Once I thought that you, too, would become a poet."

"Did you really?"

"Yes, you were such a dreamer, a child with unusual sensitivities. You expressed beautiful ideas, and your outlook had a special quality, beyond your age . . . Come to think of it, a poet and a scientist aren't so far apart as it might seem."

"And that other poet, Arie—?"

"Arie Artzi?"

"Artzi, yes. Are you in touch with him?"

"Yes," I straighten up in my chair. "He has had great success. Phenomenal success."

"Does he come to visit you?"

I smile. They say time heals all wounds. But sometimes the passing days sharpen the memory, bring to surface things not recognized before. I remember one summer my student came to visit me, dressed in an army uniform. We sat on the porch and talked about his studies at Beersheba University and about his writing. And all the while, from the corner of my eye, I watched my little nephew furiously hurling rocks at the eucalyptus tree. For a long time after my student had departed the child remained sullen and hurt.

"He's very busy. A published poet. He lives in Jerusalem now."

"So he doesn't come at all?" he asks in an accusatory tone, the child in him trying to settle old accounts.

"He was here six months ago. His mother passed away. Passed away is not the right wording—she committed suicide. His parents lived in the neighboring village, you know. A very sad story. She was a very unusual woman. Educated, refined. I knew her many years ago, when she used to come to parent-teacher conferences. He was my student, you know. Six months ago this tragic event occurred. He came to see me before going back to Jerusalem."

"Committed suicide," he says, reproving.

"A very unusual woman."

"And apart from that, he doesn't come?"

He wants to hear me say something that perhaps lingers in my heart. Have the two of them met? In recent years my student has been going abroad quite often.

"This is the way of the world. People leave and go their own way. I am proud of him, and I am proud of you. He succeeded in his own field and you are famous throughout the world. We read about the big award you received."

"Did you?"

"Sure. Not every day do people here happen to know a Nobel Prize nominee."

"I wasn't nominated."

"But you were nominated to be nominated. And the other award, whose name escapes me, also very distinguished—that one you got. There was a big to-do here when it was reported in the paper."

"Really?"

"Yes, certainly. People remembered you. They recognized your picture, even your name."

Fire flickers in his eyes. "People talked?"

"They talked, of course they talked. After all, everybody here knew you."

"But how did they all find out?"

"You think because we live far from New York, nothing reaches us? We get the papers, thank God. It appeared in several newspapers and it was on television, too. You were seen very clearly, and then our TV correspondent there interviewed you, didn't he? You see, I'm up to date."

His face looks a little tense. "Who talked about me?"

"Many people did. I don't remember every single one of them, but many came to congratulate me. You want to know who came? Hang on a minute and I'll tell you: Zalman, Chayim, Shosh from the Union —there was great excitement."

"Did girls come?"

I look at him, perplexed. "Girls? What girls?"

"Local girls, neighbors . . ."

"Well, a few girls came, Shosh from the Union." I strain my memory. "I think Chayim's wife came too."

"But of the younger ones, the girls I used to know?"

"The young girls you used to know?" I look at him astonished. "Who were the girls you used to know? I don't remember."

Embarrassed, he breaks into a lengthy laugh, as if reminded of an amusing incident, waves his hand as if to pooh-pooh the whole thing, and says, still laughing, "Maybe now I'll have some juice." And I feel a whip of jealousy: Did things happen to him that I was not aware of? Was I not privy to all his experiences?

He helps me prepare a light lunch. He is a little self-absorbed, his eyes shining strangely. He chops vegetables for salad, slices bread, and, after the meal, washes the dishes, rinses fruit, and places it in a bowl on the table on the porch, the way he used to in his youth. We sit silently on the porch for a long time. He is wearing white tennis shorts that he put on just before lunch; his legs are very pale. He stares pensively at the old bindweed that for many years twined around the cypress trunk halfway up its length and now looks like a swordless sheath. I sit next to him, watching him watch the cypress, noticing his bemused eyes, the lines of bewilderment drawn on his face. Slowly, searchingly, he moves his eyes over the garden trees and the vegetable patch, lingering on the bed closest to the tool shed: this used to be his garden bed where he planted carrots, lettuce, and radishes, and every morning ran barefoot in his pajamas to check if the seeds had sprouted and the leaves had thickened. His face looks flushed, and suddenly it hits me—he's yearning.

It is this yearning, I reason, that brought him back from across the ocean. What is he longing for? The sounds of the village? The new freedom he first experienced here? I hesitate for a moment, delaying the thought. Me? Is it me he is missing?

"Once we held a contest: who'll spot more birds on the roof of the rabbit hutch."

"Did we really?" I am worried; my memory is deteriorating apace.

"You always cheated me," he says softly.

"I cheated you?" I am alarmed.

"You always said a lower number than mine."

I calm down, although I do not remember that, either.

"You were so nice to me." His voice sounds a little cracked.

"I loved you very much." My voice cracks too. "I cherished you as my son. You know, this morning at the bus station, I remembered how I used to get ready for summer as early as Passover, preparing your room, writing to your mother to make sure she would not send you somewhere else."

His eyes are still fixed on the cypress, but the tense expression on his face tells me his heart is responsive to me. "It was the happiest time of my life."

"But . . ." I am alarmed by the responsibility his admission places upon me. "Aren't you happy there, with your work, with fame?"

"Fame . . ." The corners of his mouth stretch downward. "Fame does not bring happiness. The work is interesting, that's true. But happiness—nothing brings me as much happiness as what I had here."

If that's the case, I ask him in my heart, why haven't you come here for twenty years? Why did you never mention it in any of the few letters you wrote me? Why did you send a commercial card, as if you could not be bothered? Why did you allow yourself to walk out of my life, as if you meant to punish me?

In a broken voice I presume to ask, "Your mother said you had a wife . . ."

"I have no wife."

A question gnaws at me, but I dare not ask.

"It is not like you and Aunt Leah. I always think about you when I read or when someone talks about 'true love.' I live with a woman, but she's not my wife." His voice sounds normal, matter-of-fact, not hesitant. "She's a Norwegian scientist. As a matter of fact, I don't actually live with her. We live in separate apartments and see each other when we feel like it."

"And at work, what is it you do?"

He holds his breath. "I don't want to talk about it. Please, don't ask me."

I am taken aback, disappointed. "I am very interested in knowing. Especially what exactly you got the award for. I hoped you would write to me about it. Then I asked your mother, but she could not explain. I am very interested."

"I'm sorry." A harsh line forms on his face and his hands are raised in a gesture of refusal. "All this is far away now. I don't want to think about it here. Perhaps some other time. You understand . . ."

"I would very much like to hear." It is hard for me to give up.

"Some other time."

"Just tell me one thing: What is your area of research?"

His hands drop to the table.

"I won't ask you again. Just tell me your area of expertise."

"The left lobe of the brain," he gives in.

"The brain!" I blurt out. "It must be very interesting . . ."

"Yes, very interesting—but it cannot replace life."

Lonely, I sum up to myself. This is the sadness of a lonely man. I should have recognized it right away. Then I apologize to myself; we are slow to recognize in others things that we would rather not see in ourselves. An old sensation grips me—a heaviness of heart and a suffocating distress that burdened me in the past, then sank deep within me and became part of my being, mingled with my blood until I could no longer identify it.

A little while later, when I drift into an afternoon nap, I think to myself: To hell with the homesick scientist. Who needs his visit now?

WHEN I WAKE up from my slumber, dazed, closer to daydreaming than wakefulness, I remember the glint in his eye when he asked if any girls had inquired about him, and, ill at ease, recall the strained laugh he emitted. Then my shocked, palpitating heart realizes: He has come to look for Ya'ara.

Ya'ara, who used to be my student. Elazar's slutty daughter. One night, I remember, he came home very late, after midnight, and told me he had walked her home after a youth group meeting at the club. Another time I thought I saw them running in the dark, giggling, in the grove behind Lippa's house. Was the excitement that gripped him all through his last summer here, the short summer he spent in my house, from the day after his last matriculation exam until a couple of weeks before his induction into the army—was that excitement occasioned by Elazar's daughter? And how did this slip my mind? Why did I not remember it when he asked specifically about girls he used to know in the village?

Gingerly, I open a door to things that have been locked inside me for many years, and sights assail me like a windstorm, then retreat and fall into place like mislaid objects: Ya'ara, then a high school junior, smiling elusively, staring me in the eye tauntingly. I see her gleaming eyes as she sits facing me in the classroom, the impudence she displays again and again when she approaches me after examinations, demanding me to change her grades, the giggles she sends in my direction when she stands with her girlfriends and I pass by.

"Why did Moses cast a rod before Pharaoh?"

I stop in my tracks. "I beg your pardon?"

"It's a riddle, sir: Why did Moses cast a rod before Pharaoh?"

I wrinkle my brow. "Moses . . . why did he cast . . ."

"Because he wanted to give it some action," Merav bursts out, and Ya'ara, upset, throws her schoolbag at her. She had meant to mock me, to gloat at my embarrassment as I try to quote from the Bible.

"You wouldn't have gotten it, would you?" she taunts. "So you get an F, sir. This student needs to improve performance."

I smile faintly, pretending to take part in their game, whose rules I hadn't set.

"Besides, Merav got it wrong. It should be: 'Because he wanted to see it perform.'"

I am beginning to have the uneasy feeling that somehow I have become her debtor. I cannot figure out how I came to be indebted to her, but from her behavior toward me and from my own feeble reaction it is becoming clear to me that it is indeed the case. In the days that follow, I dread meeting her, and I give her a wide berth whenever I spot her. For long hours I deliberate whether I should have a talk with her parents, then realize I do not have anything specific to bring up against her. Everything between us is oblique, subtly intimated by the signals she transmits that I do not know how to decipher. Once, she leans over her desk, her breasts pressed on both sides of her cleavage, as if on a platter, the opening of the blouse spread to the right and left, and I can discern the young tanned flesh, the lace edging of her brassiere, and the delicate gold chain she is wearing, which shifts and shimmers at the base of her neck. I also notice the glint in her eyes, the hint of a secretive smile.

In the recess following that class, my breath is short. I sit in the teacher's lounge, my forehead perspiring, and pant like an exhausted athlete. The deputy principal walks by and stops to scold me: "Don't say that I didn't offer to move your classes to the first floor." My colleague, the Talmud teacher smiles: "A couple more years to retirement. What can one do?"

In the afternoon I still cannot find peace of mind. Leah fusses over me incessantly, talking about annual checkups, high blood pressure, a urine analysis where the results got lost and she said we should have them repeated. Her fussing tires me. I wish to retire to my room. At the door, just before I close it, I see the hurt in her eyes.

At night I have a dream and wake up perspiring and tense. In the dream, Ya'ara is lying on the ground behind the tool shed, on a pile of hay, leaning on one elbow, an amused grin hovering upon her face; she is dressed in an English schoolgirl uniform—like the one on the cover of a brochure issued by the British Ministry of Education, which I found in the teachers' lounge. I yearn to touch her hair, to loosen the severe knot on her uniform tie.

Several times that summer, when I come across Ya'ara on the village paths or in the club, she sends me a knowing smile, as if the two of us are privy to a common secret. Physically developed and more mature than her girlfriends, she looks me straight in the eye, and I find myself ill at ease, as if she could read my thoughts.

On the first day of her senior year, my student Ya'ara sits facing me, her eyes darting back and forth, slung sideways over the arm of her chair in a languid, lurking position. I stumble over my words several times. I cannot help noticing that through the entire lesson her eyes are fixed on my crotch. When I turn around to write something on the blackboard, imperceptibly, as if by chance, my hand checks the buttons but finds nothing wrong. When I turn back to the class, her face is shining. In the months that follow, when it is my turn to supervise the students at recess, I find her occasionally within the range of my vision; she glances to see if I have noticed her, walking arm in arm with one of the boys from her class or rubbing up against a soldier, an alumnus who has come to visit the school. And once I find her almost at my feet, tussling with a younger boy while trying to extricate a picture of a popular singer from his trouser pocket.

It is my custom every year, when I return term papers after the Chanukah break, to confer with each of my students after hours. Together we go over the comments I have written in the margins. Ya'ara's work is very deficient.

"You'll have to try harder during the year."

"Why is that, sir?" I ignore the term "sir," which is not used in my class.

"Because at this rate you won't be ready for the matriculation examination."

She sniggers aloud.

"I don't see what's so funny." I raise my voice. My irritation with her has been building up inside me for some time.

"You think I need a matriculation certificate, sir?"

"What do you mean, 'need'? Don't you want to take the exam?"

"Don't you think I'm mature enough already, sir?"

I am shaken. It is the first time I hear her speak explicitly. I notice how she straightens up, her breasts heaving under her blouse. I feel ashamed for her parents. Her father, one of the founders of our settlement, is an honorable, austere man and her mother is a modest, industrious woman. How could they have given birth to such a shameless creature?

At night I have a dream, like a frozen frame in a movie that comes to life of its own volition: Ya'ara is lying on a straw pallet, the English uniform she is wearing crumpled, the tie undone; she is embraced by some man's arms and her laughter pierces my ears: "He wanted to see his rod perform."

I wake up with a start and decide that tomorrow I will ask her father to come and see me.

The next day her father sits in my living room, his eyes like a beaten dog's, a sob straining from his throat: since we have known each other for a long time and there are no secrets in the village, he will not hide the truth from me. It has been almost a year now that his daughter Ya'ara has been causing them grief. She does not study at all, but that isn't his main worry. His fears are for his wife. Her health is in danger because of the girl; they never stop fighting, and on Saturdays the house in pandemonium. The words that come out of the girl's mouth I would not believe it if he repeated them. He had already warned his daughter several times that her behavior would send her mother to an early grave—in just those words. Ya'ara behaves as if she is not accountable to anyone, as if she has not seen or learned anything in her parents' home. She does whatever she pleases. Last Tuesday she did not come home at all. He sat up all night waiting for her. In the morning he lied to his wife, telling her the girl had left early. The next day she showed up at sundown.

"And where had she been the whole night?" I ask in alarm.

"At some friend's house."

"Which one?"

"One of her girlfriends. She has plenty."

"And you didn't try to find out?"

"I asked her but she wouldn't answer me."

"What do you mean, 'wouldn't answer'?" I demand reproachfully.

"Why," he replies, "what difference does it make which girl-friend?"

There was no point asking him for a conference. I cannot tell him what I wanted to say. He is blind to what is happening to her. He does not see that his little girl has turned into a woman. When he left, I told Leah, "Sometimes we don't see things that take place under our noses."

But I did not miss the wistful look she gave me.

I WAKE UP, get out of bed, rinse my face, and go out to the porch. He is sitting there in Leah's old deck chair, his eyes staring at the eucalyptus. In days gone by the tree's lower cradle of branches was his hiding place. Squeezed between three branches, on an old doormat he had placed there, his chin resting on his knees, he would hide in his corner for long hours, dreaming undisturbed. Once a branch snapped under him, and he fell to the ground and sprained his wrist. His mother punished both of us and the next summer refused to send him to us for first two weeks of the summer holiday. In the third week I went to their house in Tel Aviv and brought him back with me.

"Didn't you sleep at all?"

"I just rested in this chair—Leah's chair."

So, he remembered the chair with the wobbly leg.

"I can no longer just rest. I now need to take an afternoon nap. This must be old age. I'll make you coffee. Do you remember . . ."

"How you wouldn't let me drink coffee before I turned thirteen?"

"Yes."

"I remember a lot of things—and I'm reminded of more and more all the time. I found a book on parapsychology that I gave you once."

Gave me! Has he forgotten the way he bolted from here that summer as if fleeing a fire, leaving the book under his pillow?

I pour coffee and nibble on some chocolate squares I have found, wondering how they have escaped tasting stale. I explain to myself: He has read my thoughts. Next, he is standing behind me, arranging the cups on a tray, just as he used to.

"How old are you?" he asks unaffectedly, carrying the tray outside.

"Seventy-nine come winter."

"So you're older than my mother!"

"Of course!"

"You look younger than she does."

"Must be the country air," I chuckle, suddenly thinking of Ya'ara.

He gulps the coffee down, then asks about television programs scheduled for that evening, hardly listening to my answer. I seem to sense some restlessness in him, and wonder if it is not the restlessness inside myself.

"Shall we go for a little walk?" I offer hesitantly.

His eyes beam at me. "Really?"

"Well, why not? Do you think I'm too old?"

"I thought . . ." he pauses, his eyes still shining. "You've already walked all the way to the station today . . ."

I LET HIM choose the path, like a rider who drops the reins, trusting the horse to lead. He goes south, turning right at the crossroad. At the third house his steps slow down, his hands sink deep in his pockets, his eyes are drawn to the window. I peer at him from the corner of my eye. I feel compassion for him and at the same time I wonder at myself: How could I miss it? All the signs were plain to see, in the right order, and yet I did not read them properly. So it was Ya'ara who had laughed that snorting, contemptuous laugh that I heard from behind the myrtle hedge, followed by the scrambling of light feet. The next morning at breakfast I saw the boy's pale face, and soon after he left on the eight-twenty bus despite Leah's urgent pleading. I also remember—without apparent connection—how he refused to take a sandwich she had hurriedly prepared for the road. Had Ya'ara seduced him that night, the last one he spent with me? Had she trifled with him, taunted and humiliated him, laughed in his face, driving him away?

"This is Ya'ara's house." I utter what we both know, leaving an opening for pent-up things.

"What . . . what ever happened to her?" he asks hoarsely.

I smile at his excitement, at myself, at the memory of a girl who at the time could have been my grandchild, yet kindled in me, at the age when the body should start dying down, an intense, short-lived fire. Old age, contrary to what young people tend to think, brings no rest to either body or soul, only growing distress over things that might have been but now will never occur. And eighty years is not such a long time, as young people think. It was only yesterday that everything happened, and it passed so quickly, as if somebody were in a hurry and spurred time on.

"What ever happens to flowers that bloom too early."

"What happens to them?" He sounds alarmed.

"They wilt too early."

"What do you mean?"

"I mean that at nineteen she already had a baby, at twenty-one she was divorced, and at thirty or thereabouts she was divorced a second time, and now she's about to become a grandmother."

Suddenly he rushes ahead, starts to walk, turning his back on the house. The expression on his face is the one I used to see when he was a child, during his first couple of summers with us, which I never saw again once he grew up—the drooping corners of his mouth, the quivering upper lip, the chin contorting in an attempt to restrain himself. Again, in amazement, I search for an explanation: he is disappointed. Did he expect her to wait for him all these years? Did he expect to see her come out of her father's house wearing the cotton dress with the wide belt that she used to wear? Does a man who leaves a place believe that time will stand still there until his return?

"So she doesn't live here anymore." He is talking to himself.

"She lives in Afula."

"She doesn't come here anymore?"

I am not sure why I withheld the information from him until now. Reluctantly, feeling defeated, I tell him, "She comes here every day."

"Every day?" He stops in his tracks; the edges of his lips straighten.

"She works in the grocery store."

"Every day?"

"Yes. In Yehezkel's store."

"The one in the town center, by the station?"

"Yes."

He resumes his walking, with me at his side. He stops by a hedge of castor oil plant, puts out his hand, and crushes a fruit, spilling the seeds, runs his fingers over the hard shell, and makes some remark about the medicinal properties and industrial uses of castor oil. Suddenly, he bursts out laughing and the castor oil seeds shake in his hand.

"What's so funny?"

"When I arrived this morning, was she in the shop?"

"Yes."

"Did you see her?"

"When I got there I saw her, yes. I took a chair from the shop." I stop, remembering, and smack my thigh ruefully. "I forgot to bring it back."

His eyes look dreamy. He does not listen to me. I feel I must hasten to draw him away from his thoughts, as if to save him from danger.

"Do you still play chess?" I ask with great eagerness.

AT NIGHT, WHEN we sit in the living room and I am about to check-mate him, he suddenly remarks, "Her daughter must be the same age she was then."

He is trying to fan the flame of memory, I reflect sympathetically, to set the clock back twenty years, to resume where he left off. I forego the move that would grant me victory, and start collecting the chessmen.

"Her daughter doesn't look at all like her. She is dark, like her father. They say she herself is in the family way. I haven't seen her in years."

He watches as my fingers scoop two knights off the board, but does not offer to help.

"I was in love with her," he blurts out with obvious difficulty, his tongue licking his lips, as if the words had scorched them.

I move my hand toward the queen, saying to myself, "So was I," but I say aloud, "You were too young for her," adding silently, "and I was too old."

He follows silently as my hands fold the chessboard, then he whispers, "It's very rare for people to meet at the right moment for both of them."

I look up, amused by the connection. "This is right up your alley—a question of probability."

I am not sure he hears me. He seems to be listening to voices inside himself.

"I want you to know," he says, his voice strained, "I didn't come just to hear about her."

"Of course not," I smile, thinking about the diamond heirloom and about the bitter fights between his mother and my wife, who were suspicious of each other until Leah's dying day.

"I also came to see you. I really wanted to see you." He watches me shake my head. "Don't you believe me when I say I came to see you?"

His face contorts, and the eight-year-old's features are again discernible. Suddenly he gets up, his hand gripping his thigh, murmurs an apology, and goes out into the garden.

FOR SOME REASON I am suddenly reminded of the Bedouins. At the time I was greatly agitated by the incident. Yet, amazingly, until this moment it had been completely erased from my memory. How could I forget that unassailable proof of his love for me? It happened when he was in the eighth grade, on the day of the annual school outing. After a row with his mother, he took a sleeping bag and provisions for two days, and instead of going to school he hitchhiked north, toward Haifa. At noon, a pickup truck dropped him off at the entrance to a village neighboring mine. He waited a while for a car traveling east, then got impatient and decided to cross the fields and walk to my house. When he started climbing a hill, he was stung by a scorpion. In the evening a Bedouin knocked on my door and with downcast eyes, politely but adamantly refusing to enter the house, stood erect on the threshold, black as the columns of the porch. Softly he told me how he had found an unconscious boy near the orchard where he worked. He just happened to be passing by when he noticed him. The boy kept mumbling my name and the name of my village. Five minutes later we were on our way together with Laizer, a ranger at the nature center who was also an army medic, equipped with his gun and first-aid kit. The Bedouin walked in front of me, treading softly as if walking on carpets. At the Bedouin encampment, I saw the boy and my heart broke: he was pale and feverish, his face shiny with perspiration, and he tossed and turned in his bed like a woman in labor, his eyes staring at the Bedouin who bent over him, at the girls huddled in the doorway, at the silent, ancient woman crouched at the edge of the tent brewing fragrant leaves. As in a dream I recall how Laizer's hands made a cut in the boy's thigh as one would carve beef, and how I put my hands around his panting mouth, saying, "Everything will be all right, I'm here now."

A MOMENT AFTER he went into the garden, while my mind is still on the Bedouin tent, he returns, his face looking scrubbed, and he sits at my side. "The bindweed is creeping on the electric wire."

"Pardon?" I still see the open gash in his thigh, bleeding on the curly sheepskin.

"The bindweed has climbed high."

"Ah . . . yes."

"It touches the electric wire."

"That high?"

"You must take care of it. It's dangerous."

"True, it hasn't been trimmed in a long time." I have no desire to discuss the bindweed. I try to change the subject. "When you went out just now . . ."

"Yes?"

"When you were outside, I thought: How come you have only good memories of this place? After all, you underwent so many misfortunes here: a dog bit you, you fell out of a tree and cracked your arm, that eye infection, and you almost died at the Bedouin camp . . ."

He nods, as if remembering the incident. "Still and all," he does not allow me to distract him from what is on his mind. "Your tool shed is almost empty."

"I beg your pardon?"

"I noticed that the tool shed is empty."

"Yes, whenever someone comes to borrow a tool, especially the young ones, I tell them right away not to bother to return it. There's no need for me to take care of things anymore."

He raises his eyes, and I notice signs of fear in them. I feel compelled to explain: "That way it will be easier to say good-bye."

His eyes sink within the crow's feet that surround them like lines of makeup.

"When I was a child I thought you were the wisest man in the world. I still think you're a very wise man."

A kind of bitterness fills me. "If this is the case, I'm not so happy about it."

"Why?"

"Because I pay dearly for it and receive very little in return."

He ponders this for a moment, his face still wearing a tearful expression. Then he stirs and rises to his feet.

"I'm returning to Tel Aviv tomorrow."

"You are?" When he was young I was the one to decide when he should leave. For a moment I rebel.

"Yes, I have a meeting in Jerusalem the day after tomorrow. But first, if possible, I would like to see her . . . You said she comes to work every morning?"

I laugh, feeling sudden relief, like someone who is unaware of his shackles until he is set free. "This sounds like one of those TV dramas. An incredible coincidence: at twenty minutes past eight, the express bus leaves here, and she starts work at the shop at eight. She arrives on the very same bus."

At breakfast the next day I can tell he is agitated by the way his fingers shake when he uses a knife.

"Take some chocolate." I offer him the plate with the chocolate squares.

He takes a piece, looks at me and smiles, then puts it in his mouth. "If I eat a lot of chocolate, I'll end up falling in love."

"What do you mean?" I ask, surprised.

"It contains a substance that makes the brain fall in love."

"Chocolate does?" I ask.

"Phenylamine," he pronounces the word effortlessly.

"Is that so?"

He laughs and I join him, and for a moment we laugh together, each for his own reason.

"Tell me something," I say with some hesitation, not looking at him. "I know you don't want me to ask you, but please, since we already brought up the subject, I have a question about the brain that's been bothering me. Lately, you see, I tend to forget things. I make silly and not so silly mistakes. This week, for example, I interchanged 'e' and 'i' in 'receive' . . ."

I look at him cautiously, but he smiles. "Happens to me all the time."

"It never happened to me until a year or two ago." I do not smile with him. "I made the same mistake three times until I noticed that it looked funny. Doesn't this indicate some abnormal brain activity?"

His smile disappears. "At your age . . ." I hear my doctor's voice in his voice. "At your age, it's natural. You have a very lucid mind for your age."

"What makes you say that?"

A thin smile creeps onto his lips. "The look you gave me yesterday when I mentioned Ya'ara."

I think my face is turning red, another sensation I haven't felt in years.

"I also want to ask you something." He bites his lips. "You're under no obligation to answer if you think the question is too personal."

"What, what is the question?"

"You really don't have to—"

"What? Ask!"

"Your life . . ." He stops, and my heart stops with him. "Does your life seem long to you?"

I reply right away, so he won't detect my agitation. Why did he choose to pose this question? One does not ask such a question, with such feeling, without a reason. Is he about to die? Has he been told that he has a terminal disease and that his days are numbered? Is this his reason for coming here?

"Like a twinkling of an eye," I answer, but it is to myself I am speaking. "A twinkling of an eye. It was only yesterday that my mother brought me to Hadassah's play school, and when she came to collect me, it was raining for the first time that year, and we ran through the fields getting thoroughly soaked." I stare at his wide-open eyes as into a mirror. "No, it was the day before yesterday, because it was yesterday that Uri was born."

There is no mirth in his eyes. I become serious too. "I'll tell you something. You asked a serious question, so I'll answer you seriously. Sometimes I stop and say to myself, "Eighty years—you've been living for eighty years. So many days and so many Saturdays and so many winters. Sixty-year-olds regard you as Methuselah, as good as dead; twenty-year-olds think you are a ghost. But let me tell you—life passes too quickly. Adam made a mistake when he ate the apple in the Garden of Eden. One hundred and twenty years are nothing—unless you're physically or mentally sick." Are you sick? I cry to him soundlessly.

"So it is short?" He echoes my words, reassuring, concern in his eyes.

"A twinkle. And here you yourself are already halfway there. Let me give you some free advice: Don't waste your time on nostalgia."

A light comes on deep in his eyes, and I rejoice. It was, indeed, his longing that brought him over the oceans to the Valley of Jezreel. Am I right, then? Does it mean that he is not sick?

He straightens in his chair. "I told you yesterday, you're a very wise man. Your insight into life . . ."

I guffaw. A bitter note of maliciousness rises unrestrainably within me. "I told you yesterday and I'll tell you again: I make all the mistakes that fools make, so what good is my wisdom to me?"

"Your insight." His soft voice conveys his good will.

"It doesn't make anyone happy."

"Happiness is not what counts."

"So what counts?" I laugh, surprised at the turn the conversation has taken and curious what his answer will be.

"Insight," he replies.

I shake my head. "Well, perhaps the scientist and the poet are not so similar after all. See, I learned something, too."

I SEE THEM through the new, polished glass door, as if in a film. Ya'ara is looking good today, I remark to myself, relieved. Her hair is nicely combed, as if she had been forewarned to take special care with it. Her face still looks fresh, not as I sometimes see her in the afternoon when her hair is disheveled, tied back with a rubber band, her skin oily and her features weary. I am glad to see that she is at her best, a little closer to the memory he has been carrying all these years like a photo. Perhaps in his eyes the intervening time has only served to enhance the golden hair and the provocative blue eyes that flutter with deliberate languor. I see his back through the door, sense his excitement; he shifts his weight from leg to leg and spreads his hands on the counter. After the initial shock of recognition, she is the first to recover. Like a hostess welcoming an unexpected guest, she quickly takes off her blue shopkeeper's apron. Their animated conversation lasts longer than I realize. She shakes her head, which once had curly tresses bouncing around it, but now only the head motion remains, looking rather pathetic from a distance. Her body movements, I note, have reverted to those she practiced in her youth: the swinging shoulder, the protruding chest, the hand resting on her hip; but the youthful grace is gone, and all I see is a fat lady heaving her plump limbs.

SUDDENLY, WITHOUT ANY apparent connection, a distant picture, amazingly lucid, comes to my mind: It is the end of his first summer in the village and, at his request, we are going to bid farewell to the wheatfield abutting the prickly pear hedges. We have seen that field several times before, but today it assumes a whole new guise because of the gusts of wind sweeping through it. We are standing hand in hand, our backs to the wind. The stalks of grain sway back and forth, and strips of gold interlace with strips of silver. To our right, a row of trees marks the edge of the field, and facing it, as far as the eye can see, the stalks sway madly, as if some subterranean giant had pounded the roots, sending tremendous shock waves through the field. Suddenly the wind changes, whipping our hair up on our heads like savages, whacking the wheat as if chastizing a riotous mob, blurring the color lines, mingling gold and silver. I am filled with joy, feeling the warm hand in my palm infusing me with the child's excitement as I undergo the experience with him, as it were, for the first time. I take in the entire scene as if I am standing on Mount Gilboa: a man and a boy facing a frenzied wheat field that contorts like some colossal, brilliant beast. That night I wrote in my notebook:

> To stop precious moments of fleeting Time—
> And emboss them in gold.

AT EIGHT-FIFTEEN HE glances at his watch and hurries out, his face agitated. His eyes look frantic, behind the sunglasses.

"Was it a good meeting?" To avoid embarrassing him I avert my eyes. We both focus on the end of the path that leads from the cypress-lined boulevard to the main square, where the bus is waiting.

"A very beautiful woman," he whispers.

I stare at him, amazed.

"As if time had stood still!" He is obviously moved.

As if time had stood still and he is once again eighteen, his voice tremulous, as if the vocal chords have just thickened. But it is not the fragrance of eucalyptus trees that has awakened the sleepy boy in him, nor the sights and smells of the village—only a fat woman who gracelessly attempts to imitate the gestures of the girl she once was. The bus revs its engine, and the two of us are hastily jolted from our reveries.

"I want to tell you something." He bends down, picks up his suitcase, shifts it from hand to hand, not noticing that it bumps my knee. "I was afraid the village would look small to me—but it doesn't."

When I see places that I knew in my childhood, they seem frightfully small to me. What seemed a wide open space to the child is now a backyard of three paces' length. But here this is not the case, and the rules are different: this is the pain of a man who has wandered afar and never learnt to relinquish his yearnings. Those who have never dared to wander afar will not understand such anguish.

"Well," I prepare myself for his departure, using humor to conceal my trepidation, "we'll see you again in twenty years, just in time for my hundredth birthday?"

He laughs uninhibitedly. "You haven't had a chance to tell me about Bergson. At any rate, two years or twenty years, what's the difference? Here time stands still anyway."

A few minutes later Yehezkel and I stand watching the departing bus, our arms at our sides, our faces toward the sun. Yehezkel prattles excitedly.

"Yesterday I told Haya he had arrived. We talked about him a little and remembered how he used to sit in our house, silent as a post. Then all of a sudden he'd jump up and start running around the guava trees in the back, then come back inside. We thought he wasn't quite normal. And suddenly—a genius. What do we know?"

"We know nothing, Yehezkel."

"And a handsome man besides," Yehezkel says cheerfully. "Time's on his side, as they say."

I make no reply. He swallows audibly and asks a question that I know has been gnawing at him since yesterday. "So what was he looking for here?"

"He was homesick," I reply. I reply to myself.

Yehezkel jerks his head. "Homesick? What can one possibly miss here?" There is more sadness than argumentativeness in his voice. "A few poplars, a few eucalyptuses, a bus stop—that's all there is here! And I forgot to mention, a road without sidewalks."

You don't understand, Yehezkel, I tell him in my heart. What we really long for is our own reflection, engraved in other people as in passing scenery. I sense a poetic verse forming in my mind. But even if it is a felicitous phrase, I shall make no effort to remember it, as I did in the past. A single suitable line does not a poem make.

Watching the distant bus, I sense a strange yearning rising in me. I try to figure it out and reason thus: I am experiencing a yearning for something I have never really known, for another place, a place where the air has a different tint than the country air I have known all my life. I am yearning for my own image as reflected in the man now going away.

When the bus is out of sight I stir myself, like a man forced to extricate himself from a fascinating dream. I turn to Yehezkel and say in the tone he is accustomed to hearing, "As for the road you mentioned before, Malkiel's grandson, Reuven, is taking the matter in hand. In six months—so he said—in about six months, they'll start paving the sidewalk."

Translated from the Hebrew by Marganit Weinberger-Rotman